PETER CROMARTY

DEATH or GRIEVOUS BODILY HARM

Death or Grievous Bodily Harm
© Peter Cromarty 2022

All rights reserved. No part of this publication may be reproduced, stored in a retrieval system, or transmitted in any form or by any means, electronic, mechanical, photocopying, recording or otherwise, without the prior written permission of the author.

ISBN: 978-1-922854-44-5 (Paperback)
        978-1-922854-45-2 (eBook)

A catalogue record for this book is available from the National Library of Australia

Editors: Chloe Cran
Cover Design: Ocean Reeve Publishing
Design and Typeset: Ocean Reeve Publishing
Printed in Australia by Ocean Reeve Publishing

Published by Peter Cromarty and Ocean Reeve Publishing
www.oceanreevepublishing.com

Contents

Dedication v
Acknowledgements vii

Chapter 1 1
Chapter 2 9
Chapter 3 23
Chapter 4 27
Chapter 5 39
Chapter 6 49
Chapter 7 55
Chapter 8 69
Chapter 9 75
Chapter 10 83
Chapter 11 87
Chapter 12 91
Chapter 13 95
Chapter 14 99
Chapter 15 109
Chapter 16 113
Chapter 17 117
Chapter 18 119
Chapter 19 127
Chapter 20 133

Chapter 21	139
Chapter 22	145
Chapter 23	147
Chapter 24	157
Chapter 25	159
Chapter 26	165
Chapter 27	173
Chapter 28	177
Chapter 29	181
Chapter 30	187
Chapter 31	193
Chapter 32	199
Chapter 33	203
Chapter 34	213
Chapter 35	221
Chapter 36	231
Chapter 37	239
Chapter 38	251
Epilogue	253
About the Author	257

Dedication

To Kate,
I've never been happier.

Acknowledgements

A big thank you to Ciara, Jon, and Gerard, who spent time and effort giving me comments on draft versions of this book.

I am particularly indebted to Mel, who made many useful suggestions, and to Terry and Rhiannon, who gave me voluminous corrections and suggestions.

Cliff at the Long Yard Larder, thanks for the biscuits for Remmie and the suggestions about computer security.

A significant thank you to Sally Odgers at Affordable Manuscript Assessments for her editing of the manuscript and valuable comments.

To Mark Rilatt - many thanks for the use of the image of the C17 on the front cover.

Kate—I couldn't have done it without your patient support and encouragement. Thank you.

I am deeply indebted to Ocean Reeve and the team at Ocean Reeve Publishing for their invaluable contributions, which have improved the manuscript immeasurably.

Chapter 1

I looked down at the person on the ground at my feet and thought, *Damn. I wish I'd done that first-aid course Hannah kept reminding me to do.* Unfortunately, I never had the time or inclination. You know how it is; there are so many more important things for a retired bloke like me to do. What is it they say? 'Don't put off until tomorrow what you can put off until the day after.' Something like that.

It was obvious that the man on the ground had been badly bashed because I could see blood oozing out of wounds on his hand and head. He didn't appear to be breathing. His face was a terrible mess—there were bumps and dents, his nose was smashed, some of his teeth had obviously been knocked out, blood was running from the corner of his mouth, and there were open wounds and nasty red welts that would become painful bruises. His eye was puffing up and swelling closed as I looked at it. Even his mother wouldn't have recognised him.

I had been walking back to my car in the car park of the local grocery; it had been a very brief visit, just for some fruit. I like to go to the shop more frequently than most people so that stuff at home is always fresh. It also gives me an opportunity to stop at a café in Dayboro or Samford on the way home for a cuppa and a read of the papers. Luckily, I had gone to the passenger door to load my shopping. I say 'luckily' because if I had gone to the driver's side, I probably wouldn't have seen the fellow on the ground and could easily have added to his wounds by driving over his arm, which was lying sprawled under the rear wheel of my car.

I dropped my shopping bags and bent to see if I could help him. He seemed in a very bad way. Certainly, he was beyond the first aid I gave to my kids—wash it, put a plaster on it, and push them out to play with, 'You'll be right, mate. Off you go!'

I thought about ringing for an ambulance and pulled out my phone, but I immediately remembered the battery had gone flat on the way to the shops. Because I hadn't followed my wife Hannah's very sound advice and been on that first aid course, all I knew was what I'd seen on TV.

I picked up the bloke's wrist and found a weak, really fast pulse. I have to say I was shocked—not shocked that he had a pulse, although that was a surprise, considering the mess he was in, but shocked to find someone beaten-up, lying next to my car. It's not something you expect to find anywhere—a bloke with horrific wounds—and certainly not next to your car in the car park of your local shops. I thought, *I'd better get some more help or I'm just gonna stand here and watch this chap die.*

He tried to say something. I held his bloody hand and said, 'You're going to be okay, mate. I'll get the ambos. What's your name?'

He murmured, 'Trent,' followed a second or two later by, 'Boot.'

At least that's what it sounded like, but it made no sense to me. I looked at his feet again, and it struck me as odd that he wasn't wearing anything on his feet: no thongs, no shoes, and certainly no boots. Just stripy, brightly coloured socks. Looking around, I noticed his shoes lying discarded nearby. Maybe his second name was Boot. Before I could ask him to repeat it, he passed out.

At that moment, another shopper walked past, so I waved and called to him, 'Quick, phone for an ambulance!'

He stopped his trolley-load of groceries and edged warily forward, craning around me to see what was on the ground. I think he must have seen more than he probably wanted, because he turned very pale. He hurriedly pulled out his phone from his pocket and dialled. Fortunately, the emergency services answered straight away, which seemed to take his mind off what he had seen.

My less-than-extensive medical training from TV and movies had taught me not to move the victim in case his neck was damaged. Therefore, I stood up and looked around over the cars to see if there was anybody who might know CPR in case he needed it. I said to the shopper on the phone, 'Do you know how to do CPR?'

'What's CPR?' he asked.

Yeah, good question, I thought. 'I don't know,' I called. 'Cardiac Something Resuscitation?'

He shook his head. Nobody else to be seen—typical. I kneeled down to listen to the man's breathing and tried his pulse again. His pulse was still fluttering lightly. Then it felt as though his pulse stopped, but perhaps I had my fingers in the wrong place. I leaned down and put my ear near his mouth—I couldn't hear him breathing. I waited two or three seconds, hoping it would restart. It didn't.

I decided it was better to move him than to let him die, and I rolled him on his back to start CPR compressions—or, at least, what I thought were CPR compressions from my TV training. As he flopped over on his back, I noticed a wooden handle projecting out from under him. *That looks uncomfortable,* I thought. I pulled on it, and out came a rather expensive-looking ball-peen hammer—the sort with a hickory shaft and a traditional steel head with one side for driving nails and a ball on the other for working sheet metal. Well, it would have been nice had it not been covered in Trent's blood and gore. A useful tool for driving nails, working metal, and beating somebody to a pulp.

I set it aside and put my two hands together, palm down on his sternum, and started compressions, just as I had seen in the emergency rooms on TV.

The shopper came off the phone and said the ambulance was on its way. I told him to run back into the supermarket and ask them to put out a PA announcement for a doctor or nurse or someone who knows first aid.

After a couple of minutes, I paused and felt for a pulse on his wrist. Nothing. I tried his neck, next to his windpipe. No good, couldn't feel anything there either. In the distance, I heard a siren, then the sound of many feet running in my general direction. 'Over here!' I shouted.

A woman called, 'I'm a doctor; what happened?' as she turned sideways to squeeze between the door mirrors of the cars. She kneeled next to Trent and picked up his wrist to feel for a pulse.

'I don't know what happened. He was like this when I found him.'

Rocking back on my knees, I gave her room, and she adjusted his head to lift his chin to make sure the airway was in a good position. She bent low over him to check for breath sounds while feeling for a pulse in his neck.

'I was trying to give him CPR, but I don't really know how.'

The doctor said, 'He's in cardiac arrest. Now, watch how I do this, then you can do it,' and she started fast, vigorous compressions. They were so hard I thought she might break his ribs, and I said so.

She replied, 'Better we break his ribs if it means his heart starts. You take over again. I want to see what other damage he has apart from his face.'

I leaned forward and took over.

'Let me know when you're getting tired, and we'll find someone else to take a turn,' she said.

By then, a small crowd had gathered among the cars. Between compressions, I asked the shopper with the phone who had rung for the ambulance if he had also called for the police. Apparently not. I heard someone talking on the phone to the police.

In between compressions, the doc undid Trent's shirt and felt around his chest and tummy, then down his legs. 'I think he has several fractures, but I'm not sure. He's been badly beaten or maybe hit by a car or run over.'

'Don't you have a bag of medical gear in your car?' I asked.

'No, those days are gone. Anyway, I'm a consultant oncologist—you know, cancer doctor. This man may need a CT scan if he survives, but I don't carry one around in my car.'

The doc told me to pause for a few seconds as she took his pulse. 'Keep going!' she said. 'There's still no pulse.'

She organised a volunteer from the crowd to take over from me, as I was tiring.

As I backed out of the way towards the crowd, I saw the ambulance, all lights flashing, arrive at the car park and pick its way slowly around the aisles over the speed bumps. It pulled up next to my car, and the paramedics ran to us. It was getting pretty busy in the gap between the cars now with the doc, Trent, various customers, and staff. We all stood back from Trent as a paramedic took over performing CPR.

The doc explained to them briefly what little we had been able to do for Trent. I told them his name was Trent. We all stood, heads bowed, watching. I was fascinated by watching the professionals at work. I hoped my dithering earlier would not have put poor Trent beyond even their help.

The male paramedic paused his compressions to cut open the bloody shirt, exposing the man's chest. He listened briefly with a stethoscope and then looked up at the other paramedic, Sandra, according to the name tag on her uniform, and shook his head. She pulled out two plastic packets from a backpack on the ground next to her. From one, she ripped a swab, and from the other, a preloaded syringe. Having swabbed an area of Trent's upper arm, she stabbed the syringe into his muscle and delivered the contents by pushing the plunger. Adrenaline, I guessed.

Sandra turned back to her bag and pulled the business ends of a defibrillator to the man. She placed the two sticky pads on the man's chest, turned to the machine, and pressed a button. In an automated voice with an American accent, the machine said, *'Evaluating heart rhythm.'*

Sandra spoke loudly to us all. 'Right, everyone, stand back!'

Shortly afterwards, the machine said, *'Stand by, delivering shock. Everyone clear, do not touch patient, delivering shock.'*

There was a short warbling sound followed by a click, and Trent jerked slightly as the electrical pulse passed through him. Then the machine said, *'Shock delivered. Provide chest compressions and rescue breaths.'*

'Right, Norm, back onto CPR please, straight away!'

The teamwork was pretty frantic but controlled. There was complete silence among the onlookers, who watched with rapt attention. Sandra put on her stethoscope, and Norm paused momentarily while she listened for a pulse. It was her turn to shake her head, and Norm continued pounding Trent's chest. Sandra picked another syringe out of her bag and jabbed it into Trent's upper arm. Contents delivered, she pressed a button on the defibrillator, and it again went through its process to shock Trent's heart into action.

Sandra listened again and said, 'Okay, we've got a pulse.'

She lifted Trent's right arm and examined the inside of the forearm and the back of the hand. She frowned, put it down, then did the same with his left arm. She tore open a small packet and wiped a small swab of disinfectant over Trent's left forearm. From another packet, into the same area she had just cleaned, she inserted a needle. Obviously not satisfied, she put a small plaster over the hole she had just made, pressing her finger on it for a few seconds, and tried the same process again, slightly higher up Trent's arm. 'I can't get a cannula in, Norm. I'll go with the IO.'

Sandra dug around in her backpack and pulled out a pair of scissors, a preloaded syringe, and what looked like a small cordless drill. Working quickly but surely, she cut up the leg of Trent's jeans from hem to above the knee, swabbed an area just below his knee, and injected the contents of the syringe—an anaesthetic, I guessed. Next, she attached a spike to the tip of the drill and, with the drill making a slight buzzing sound, drilled into his shin just below his knee. I flinched inwardly. To my slight surprise, there was very little blood.

She detached the drill from the bit, leaving it in the bone, withdrew the bit by sliding it out from within a tubular shaft, and stabilised the tube that remained in his bone with a pre-cut self-adhesive dressing. Sandra connected a plastic tube.

'Okay, Norm. IO is in. I'll give him the adrenaline.'

She pulled two more packets from her backpack. One looked like water, which she flushed through the tube into his knee. The other was presumably the preloaded syringe with adrenaline, which she delivered immediately after the flush.

Chapter 2

Working as an undercover police officer could be considered a 'high risk, high reward' occupation. It means living in perpetual anxiety for one's own safety and the safety of colleagues and loved ones. The life is a constant lie; one is constantly acting out the role, and there is little, if any, respite from the risk of having one's cover blown and suffering retribution.

Working undercover in a drugs operation can be very high risk, especially if the operation is well-established, well-run by the standards of a professionally run business, managed by ruthless and violent people, and astronomically profitable. Such operations attract people who often have little regard for human life. The risks to an undercover police officer trying to gain acceptance in such an operation are, therefore, significant. However, an undercover police officer bringing down such an operation and getting the operators incarcerated for considerable portions of their lives is a very high reward.

This combination of adrenaline-filled work and the enormous emotional high when the drug dealer is brought down produces a lifestyle that can become addictive. Once one has succeeded in bringing down one dealer, there is a fierce, visceral desire to do it again. And again.

Michael McInerny, who came to Australia from Ireland as a boy, was one such undercover police officer. When he first joined the force, he was known to his colleagues and friends as Mick, but he was also known as 'The Three Irishmen' because his name sounded like three blokes—Mick, Mac, and Ernie. Mick was drawn to undercover police work because he was attracted to the theatre of it. He had always liked pretending to be celebrities, mimicking their voices for his mates, reciting whole sections of movies and stand-up comedy routines off the internet, playing the fool. 'Death Star Canteen' and 'Cake or death' by Eddie Izzard were particular favourites of his.

However, once he went into the shady world of the undercover police officer among the miscreants running the drugs operation in much of Brisbane and the Gold Coast, it wasn't a case of 'Cake or death' but one of 'Be totally convincing or death'. He had to change his name, his whole identity, and he became known as Trent Kipek. The gang he was infiltrating had been using him for increasingly important jobs in their operation for about three months and, to them, Trent was quick, efficient, and ruthless. He fitted in well.

Over those months, Trent inveigled himself with the boss, Alan Smith, to the point where he'd been given the task of dealing with many of the logistics of the operation. He had recently been given access to a laptop computer in the boss's office. He had learned his way around the email, messaging, contacts, and calendar apps because he needed to organise scheduling and the staffing of collections and shipments of base chemicals and finished product. He worked with all the usual processes of a logistics business.

During this work, he had discovered that Smith backed up the contacts list on his phone to the internal hard drive of his laptop. Trent reckoned there was enough information in the contacts for his police colleagues to identify the main operators in the drugs system from end to end, fill in any blanks, and shut down the whole operation. The entries in the contacts list weren't completely obvious—they weren't straightforward, like *'Rashid Azadi: Dhow captain, Main Street, Bandar Abbas. No drug smuggling job too small!'* But there were many names and nicknames with phone numbers or email addresses. With some judicious, sensitive, and smart investigative work, the critical path could be traced and stopped. It might require some delicate negotiation and cooperation with foreign police forces, but that wasn't his problem.

He could easily identify contacts who were in Afghanistan and Iran. Some produced raw materials; others produced the finished product. The drugs were moved from the chemical labs in villages in the region through to small fishing ports on the Iranian coast. Then they came by dhow to the UAE. From the dhow port in Dubai Creek or other landing places in Sharjah, Ras al Khaimah, or Khasab, the drugs were transported to Al Minhad Air Base near Dubai. There, the consignments were split into smaller packages to be hidden in avionics and electrical spaces or other nooks and crannies in the C17 Globemaster military transports used by the Royal Australian Air Force—abbreviated to RAAF but pronounced 'Raff'. The C17s were huge freighters supporting the Australian effort in the region, which had been ongoing for many years—the longest war Australia had ever fought. The names and numbers of the distributors in Australia were all there, mainly members of the Cannibals bikie gang. There were also the details of the banks where the cash was stored in offshore accounts in the Isle of Man, Luxembourg, Switzerland, and the British Virgin Islands. To close this lot down was Trent's goal.

For that, Trent needed the contacts list.

He had been pondering how to get a copy without Smith knowing and giving it to his handler in the police force. The problem was that Smith was very cautious where technology was concerned. He was keen on strong security for his phone and his laptop. That went for both the devices themselves and the data on their respective memories. Trent had heard Smith consulting his techno-specialist, who was on the payroll to keep Smith's correspondence and phone calls safely encrypted. Technology changed so fast, and Smith knew so little about it, that he felt it was a cost of doing business to employ someone at above-premium rates to keep his equipment and software at the cutting edge.

Every month, Smith sat at the desk, and the techno-specialist stepped him through the process to back up his phone and his laptop.

Unfortunately for Trent, Smith's techie was an older bloke and liked old-school security: physical security. You can't beat having your backup in a different physical location to the device you've backed up. Having your backup device locked up securely in an old-fashioned safe for which only Smith knew the combination was much better than the cloud, where any fifteen-year-old hacker or police IT specialist could look at it.

Therefore, the only place Trent had any access to the contacts list was on Smith's laptop. He had considered uploading the list to an account he had set up in the cloud, but there was a problem with that, which wasn't the vulnerability of his cloud account being hacked. He couldn't have cared less about that. Trent's problem was the upload speeds that were so slow it would take too long to get the data to his account. Too big a risk.

He had tried downloading his own contacts list from his computer to a USB memory stick at home to see how long it took, just as a guide. Less than ten seconds. The memory stick was obviously the way to go. All he needed was an opportunity, a few seconds alone with Smith's computer. He had been waiting weeks for Smith to drop his guard.

Smith was still wary of leaving Trent on his own. He hadn't risen to this position of power and wealth by trusting people unless they were staunchly loyal and earned his trust. Trent wasn't there yet, so he was never left on his own with the laptop and was only given access for limited periods for specific jobs—organising deliveries of base chemicals, distribution of finished product, and so on. A bit like the Australian Taxation Office, the mail didn't go out under the name of some middle-ranking factotum; Smith liked the mail to go out under the name of the boss. His name. Admittedly, he used an alias, but the recipients knew it was him. He felt it was important to project an image of power. Smith liked being in charge, and he loved power.

Trent was constantly alert for an opportunity to copy the contacts list. Even when Smith was on the phone, Trent was aware that Smith was, if not watching, at least conscious of what he was doing.

However, today, Smith wanted a cup of tea and asked him if he wanted one as well.

'Yeah,' Trent replied. 'I'll get them.'

'Yeah-nah, mate, you stay there, and I'll get them. How many sugars you want?'

'None, thanks. Just milk.'

Smith got out of the chair and walked into the kitchen. Trent could hear him filling the kettle and getting the mugs out. This was the opportunity Trent had been waiting for so patiently. He dug in his pocket for the memory stick and, with hands trembling, plugged it into a spare port on the USB hub connected to the laptop. He called up the contacts list and highlighted the whole lot. Then he right-clicked on the mouse and told the laptop to export the whole lot to the stick. Done. He ejected the stick as Smith came out of the kitchen. Trent closed the contacts list, but the stick was still in the hub. He prayed that Smith wouldn't notice it as he leaned over to put the mug of tea on the drinks coaster next to the laptop.

'You all right?' said Smith.

'Yep, lovely. Thanks, Alan.'

In the few seconds it took for Smith to turn and walk back to his armchair, Trent pulled the stick out of the hub and put it in his pocket. Trent heard some footsteps approaching down the carpeted hallway from the door to the garage, and he cursed himself, knowing he had probably been spotted hurriedly pulling the stick from the laptop. He also realised he may have looked pretty suspicious in the process, even though he had tried to keep it looking normal and casual. The room was air-conditioned, but Trent was sweating and frightened.

He turned slowly, picked up his tea, and looked up. 'G'day, mate!'

Another of Smith's thugs, apparently one of the Cannibals' bikies, was standing next to him, with a slight frown furrowing his brow. His hair was clipped short, almost shaven apart from a long, plaited thread hanging down from a patch on the back of his head. He had a large, grey beard the size of a dinner plate. He was dressed in a T-shirt with greasy sump-oil stains down the front, worn-out jeans with more oil streaks where he had wiped his hands, and boots with scuffed toes. His mum would have been proud.

'Is that your Harley outside?' Trent tried to keep it light.

'Yeah.'

'Nice bike.'

'It's a 1978. Got an 88 cubic inch FXS Shovelhead with Super E carbs. I rebuilt the transmission and had the whole thing powder-coated. It's better now than when it came out of the factory—they were garbage in those days. People called Harley Davidsons 'Hogly Fergusons' because they were like tractors. Not this one. Way better than the British shit like Commandos and Bonnevilles.'

Trent replied, 'Really? That's so cool!' He had no clue what the thug had just said; he knew nothing about motorcycles.

The thug went on. 'I'm here to work on the one in the garage—belongs to the boss.'

'Nice.' Trent turned to Smith, keen to change the subject and get out of the office to unload the stick somewhere safe. 'I've finished ordering that lithium and phosphorous for the ice. Think I'll go to the shops and pick up some stuff for lunch.'

'Okay,' replied Smith.

Trent pushed his chair back and casually stretched his back. He couldn't wait to get out of there. His instinct was to run, but his brain still held enough self-control to make his exit look relaxed, as if he had all the time in the world. He wasn't sure what the bikie had seen or whether he would say anything. He walked through the house, passed the boss's Harley Davidson with ape-hanger handlebars, and went out to his car.

***

The bikie turned to watch as Trent walked out, still with the quizzical expression on his face. 'Boss?'

'Yeah, mate,' replied Smith.

'That bloke just pulled something out of that computer and stuck it in his pocket.'

Smith looked up and paused for a second.

'Get after him on your bike and let me know where he goes. Make sure he knows you're following him.'

Smith rang his computer tech and told him to pull the keylogger records and call back with whatever Trent had been doing in the last half-hour.

After a few minutes, his tech rang back and told him, *'So, he's been on your email account, wrote and sent some emails to some people in Australia and one in the UAE. Do you want the addresses?'*

'Not now.'

'Then he exported some contacts in the form of vCards to what looks like an external hard drive or memory stick. I don't know how many contacts you have, but he downloaded, er, let me see, 287.'

'What the fuck is a vCard?'

'Yeah, sorry, it's the file that contains all the information about one contact. So, name, address, email address, phone numbers, date of birth, stuff like that.'

'Shit!' Smith sat still and considered this for a moment.

'Anything else, boss?'

'Nah, mate. Thanks.' And Smith rang off. The significance of what he had just heard wasn't lost on him. If that stick found its way to the police, he and his operation were finished.

Smith rang his number two, a smart, vicious young man named Jiwani.

'Yes, boss,' answered Jiwani after one ring.

'Trouble. Trent has stolen all the names on the contacts list from my computer and downloaded it to one of those USB thumb-drive-memory-stick things. I've got Rick, the old guy who does my bike maintenance, following him. Trent said he was going to the shops. He's probably there by now, if he really did go there. Get going down there with a couple of the blokes and see if you can cut him off before he gives the stick to the cops. Ring Rick for an update. Wait a minute, Rick's calling.' Smith put the call to Jiwani on hold and answered Rick, 'Yeah, Rick.'

'Boss, he's just arrived at the supermarket at Woolooma.'

'Did he see you?'

'Couldn't miss me! I was right on his tail most of the way.'

'Good. Okay, wait for Jiwani and the boys. If Trent comes out before they arrive, keep following him and let me know.' He rang off and reconnected with Jiwani.

'Trent's gone into the Woolooma supermarket. Brief two or three lads, whoever you can get hold of, and let them do the work. You stay clear. I don't want you spotted.'

'Okay, boss. Glebbo and Cyril are with me now. I'll send them.'

***

Trent was really concerned. Rick was obviously sharper than he looked and must have told Smith that he had seen something, although he may not have known exactly what. Trent guessed Smith had sent Rick to tail him in case he tried to dump the stick. Trent reckoned he could lose Rick if he could get back to his car before reinforcements arrived. However, he thought he had better come out of the shops with some shopping just in case his cover wasn't completely blown. He picked up a couple of sandwiches and a drink near the checkouts, took a new plastic carrier bag off the rack, and paid for them all.

He walked as nonchalantly as he could, as though he didn't have a care in the world, just enjoying the sun, back to his car.

On his left, at the far end of the row where his car was parked, he spotted Glebbo hanging around. He turned left into the row towards his car. As he looked over to his right, he saw Cyril with Jiwani and the bikie thug who had followed him. *Okay,* he thought, *they're trying to surround me.* As he approached his car, a bloke in a Jaguar SUV reverse-parked into the space right next to his car. Glebbo, Jiwani, and Cyril started moving through the cars towards him. He wasn't going to get away without some sort of distraction. He moved between the Jaguar and his car to the rear passenger door and put his shopping on the back seat.

The bloke who got out of the Jag was pretty lean and fit-looking, probably in his fifties or early sixties, grey hair, shorts, runners, and a black T-shirt with *'Ban Cluster Bombs'* on the front. He came around to the back of his Jag as its tailgate opened automatically.

'G'day,' he said to Trent as he picked out some reusable shopping bags.

'Howyagoin',' Trent replied. 'Hey, you wouldn't happen to have a screwdriver in your car, would you? I sometimes have difficulty with the door-catch closing this door.'

'Yeah, no worries, just a sec.' The grey-haired bloke lifted the boot floor covering the spare wheel to retrieve his tools, which were rolled up in a plastic sleeve. Trent moved to the Jag's boot and held the boot floor panel up for the bloke so he could retrieve his tools. Trent casually scanned the car park—Glebbo, Jiwani, the bikie, and Cyril were standing a few cars away, trying to look like innocent members of the public going about their normal shopping.

The man unrolled the sleeve. 'Here you go,' he said, holding two different-sized screwdrivers. 'What seems to be the problem? Can I help?'

The grey-haired bloke moved to the door that was still standing open. As he did so, Trent pulled the stick out of his pocket and placed it in the corner of the boot in the Jag while the guy was studying the door latch on Trent's car. Trent made a mental note of the Jag's rego so he could trace him later. The grey-haired bloke gently shut the car door, which closed easily with a click. He turned back and laughed. 'Well, I don't know what I did, but that seems to have fixed it!'

'Oh, great. Thanks very much. It is an intermittent thing. Sorry to have wasted your time. Er, what's your name?'

'Yeah, no dramas. I'm Toby.'

'Thanks again, Toby. I'm Trent.' They shook hands.

As it was apparent to Jiwani and the other three that the grey-haired bloke was about to leave, they started moving briskly towards where Trent was standing.

'Yep, no worries,' replied Toby as he turned back to his car boot, slid the screwdrivers back in their slots in the bag, rolled it up, and put it under the floor panel by the spare tyre. He seemed not to spot the stick still lying in the corner. He pushed the button in the tailgate, and it gently closed.

'See you later!' he called as he set off towards the supermarket, pressing the locking button on his remote as he went.

Jiwani and the bikie held back as Glebbo and Cyril approached Trent, one from the front and one from the rear, before he had a chance to get into his car.

***

Glebbo was a cheerful, jovial, slightly overweight man with a squarish head and hooded eyes. He stood by the car's door mirror, ready to stop Trent from opening the door. 'So, Trent, howyagoin'?'

'Yeah, good thanks, Glebbo. I saw you hanging back when I was talking to that bloke. What's up?' Trent was still trying to brazen it out.

'You've been a naughty boy, Trent. You've taken something from Alan that wasn't yours, and Alan wants it back.'

'Don't know what you mean, mate. What does Alan think I've taken?'

'Some stuff off his computer. He wants it back.' Glebbo glanced around the car park. He didn't expect Trent to own up immediately, but if they had to resort to some persuasive techniques, he didn't want witnesses. Fortunately, at that moment, the car park was clear of nearby shoppers.

Glebbo noticed Trent's furtive glance around the car park. He could see the fear come into Trent's eyes as he realised he was about to cop a flogging.

'Well, look, mate, I don't have anything of Alan's, so I'll get back to the house. I've still got work to do.' Trent put his hand on the car door and had got the door open a fraction when his right shoulder was smashed by Cyril hitting it from behind with a hammer. Glebbo saw the blow coming over Trent's shoulder and slammed the door closed. As Trent turned to his right and started to drop, Glebbo stepped in and hit him in the face. Trent went over backwards, and Glebbo landed on top of him, sitting on his chest, pinning his arms.

'Give me the hammer,' he said to Cyril. 'Trent, I shall say this only once. Where did you put the stick?'

'Mate, honestly, I don't know what you—' that was as far as he got before Glebbo started beating him around the head and face.

After a few seconds of fierce, powerful, relentless hammer blows, Cyril grabbed Glebbo's hand and said, 'Stop, you'll kill him! We need to keep him alive until we've found the stick. Check and see if it's in his pocket.'

Glebbo rolled to the side on his knees and started searching Trent's pockets. No luck. He examined Trent up and down, wondering if there was somewhere else he could have hidden it on his body. Glebbo pulled Trent's shoes off and looked inside them. He squeezed along Trent's legs and arms, under his armpits and groin. Not there.

'Check in the car!' he snapped at Cyril. Glebbo stood up and looked around, watching for shoppers.

Then he watched as Cyril opened the driver's door and sat in the seat. Cyril scanned the interior of the car; looking in the door pockets, along the dashboard, the centre console, he lifted the armrest lid and dug about in the detritus inside—coins, receipts, KitKat wrappers. He leaned over to open the glove box in front of the passenger seat and pulled out all the bags, more KitKat wrappers, the owner's manual, and other bits and pieces. Not there. Cyril got out and lifted the mat in the footwell. Nope.

Cyril went around to the other side and checked the front door pocket and floor mat. Then the back door pockets both sides and the seats. Under the front seats. No. 'Pop the boot!' he said. Glebbo stepped forward and pulled the little lever by the driver's seat. Cyril gave the boot a cursory glance—it was obvious nothing was in it—it was clean. He lifted the boot floor, checking around and under the spare tyre—again, clean. No stick. He walked around the car, checking on top of the tyres in the dark of the wheel arches. No. Back at the boot, he bent down and looked into the end of the exhaust pipe. Nope. Glebbo watched Cyril stand upright, and they stared at the boot for a few seconds while they pondered where else it might be. They knew Trent hadn't had time to open the bonnet and hide it in the engine compartment.

'Glebbo, he must have passed it to that old bloke in the black T-shirt he was talking to.'

'Okay, let's back off and wait for him to come back,' replied Glebbo.

They scurried away from the car between the parked vehicles to a stanchion holding up the car shades and tried to look as though they were waiting for someone. Well, they were.

Cyril asked, 'What are we going to do if he doesn't hand over the stick straight away?'

'We'll take him somewhere quiet—back to our place—and I'll get him to tell us where it is.'

Glebbo took the opportunity to ring Smith and update him on the situation. Smith made it clear to Glebbo the likely consequences of not recovering the stick. Intimidation and the threat of physical violence were management techniques that Smith sometimes used on his junior staff just because they seemed to work so well.

Before he rang off, Smith added, 'And I also don't want the dickhead who's got himself involved living through it to tell the tale! Clear, Glebbo?'

'Clear as, boss.'

It was only a couple of minutes before Glebbo nudged Cyril. 'Here he comes.'

'Yeah, okay, you bring the car, and I'll grab him,' said Cyril.

Chapter 3

I've been retired for a while. I did forty-five years in the workforce. I started off as an air traffic controller for many years in the UK, followed by a short spell as a commercial pilot and flight instructor in Texas—a common way to build flying hours and experience. I couldn't make enough money at it to survive, so I went back to Air Traffic Control (ATC) for many more years, this time in Bahrain. Then I returned to the UK, where I became an ATC safety regulator. Competence checking, approving equipment, writing regulations—all safety-related stuff. I worked my way up the management ladder, gradually managing greater and greater numbers of staff, until I was invited to do a similar job in Canberra, Australia. I've been in Australia fifteen years.

There was a short period in the 90s when I found it all a bit of a slog but, by and large, I've enjoyed every minute of my working life; it's been challenging and interesting. I thought I'd work until I dropped; I loved it. However, the last eighteen months at work had been a bad period, always flat out like a lizard drinking. Budget cuts, stress, more responsibilities, fewer staff members, stress. Senators going for me at Budget Estimates hearings in Parliament House. No strategic direction from the board. No support or communication from the CEO. Did I mention stress? Yeah, that'd be right. Suck it up, princess.

I rocked up to work one day, as usual, and by three that arvo, I was finished. I was made redundant, along with most of the other executives, during a roll-over of all the senior personnel.

'No reflection on your work, which was impeccable, and I'd be happy to be a referee for you,' I was told by the CEO, who couldn't look me in the eye as he delivered the news.

There was going to be a reorg, and I would be over-qualified for the post I had been doing apparently 'impeccably' for the last nine years.

Oh, yes, I thought long and hard about whether to retire. I gave the concept the proper deliberation. I think it took me just over twelve seconds to conclude that retirement would be just fine, thank you very much.

Working one day and, completely unprepared, retired the next. Like a lot of retired people, I struggled somewhat to get to grips with the concept of 'retirement' as it applied to me. It took me two or three years and a few conversations with my general practitioner and a psychologist to get used to the thought that this was what retirement was like. I wondered if I was the only person ever to be told by their doctor to play more golf.

People are recognised for what they do. I certainly identified myself by what I did, and when I wasn't that, what *was* I? When I was working and people asked me what I did, I would tell them, and conversation would ensue. Now, when I meet someone new and I tell them, 'I'm retired,' they either say, 'So, what did you do before you retired?' or they just nod and go quiet. Society doesn't value its retirees. People don't ask you what you do now you've retired because they know: you do nothing all day except read, watch daytime TV, walk the dog, and take naps. I wish.

As it happens, I am happier now than I've ever been. I'm used to being retired, and loving it! A post-graduate degree in English Literature has been keeping my mind busy, I volunteer with a teenage mentoring program, and I'm learning woodworking. Keeping fit is important to me, and I run a few kilometres three times a week. Also, as a compliant patient, I do as my doctor prescribed and play golf occasionally.

You know what they say: 'A bad day on the golf course is better than a good day at work.' Well, it's true.

My wife, Hannah, and I live with our adult boys, Ollie and Will, in what's called a semi-rural area just outside Brisbane. Hannah and I found one another later in life. We'd both been married before—I was divorced, and Hannah's husband had died of cancer. We both wanted kids, and she was quite a few years younger than me. It didn't work for us immediately, and as I was getting on in years, we did the tests and went down the IVF path. Twin boys!

We all live in a 100-year-old Queenslander house near the crest of a hill, ten acres of horse paddocks, Hannah's three horses, and the family dog. So that all means work. And lots of it. Grass cutting, fixing and painting fences, hedge and tree trimming, weed spraying, general repairs, house painting, maintenance, and so on. Of course, there may be some reading, dog walking, and nap taking in there as well, but they are rarities. I'm as busy as. Never any daytime TV—I'd have to be seriously bored for that!

Hannah still works, so every evening, I fetch the horses into their yards and feed them. The way I look at it, I could let her do her own chores, but then we would have less time together doing what we want to do. I also do all the domestic stuff: cooking, cleaning, laundry, and, of course, grocery shopping. And it was the shopping that I was doing when I, literally, stumbled upon Trent.

Chapter 4

I stood watching the ambos do their stuff on Trent with the assured, brisk confidence that comes with plenty of training and lots of practice. I felt a slight tap on my arm, and a man standing next to me dressed in jeans, a polo shirt, and a hi-vis yellow jacket like tradesmen wear nodded to my left and said, 'Can you just step that way, sir, for a moment, please?'

I must have looked a little puzzled and hesitant, so he tried again, 'Only a moment of your time, sir, please. I would just like to have a quick word with you, if I may? Can we just step away from the crowd over there?'

I couldn't think what he might want, and I wanted to stay to watch what happened to Trent.

I hesitated and said, 'I really want to see if that chap is okay. Can this wait a few minutes?'

He pulled his jacket open very slightly, just enough that I could see a pistol in a holster on his belt. My face must have been a picture of surprise and horror, so he leaned towards me and hissed, 'No. Please don't say anything or make a fuss. Go that way between the cars.'

He nodded away from the crowd surrounding Trent. I glanced around to see if anyone else had heard or seen what had just happened.

He said, 'Don't do anything stupid, mate. Just go that way quietly.'

On reflection, I suppose I should have just said 'No' and moved to the middle of the crowd. How many times have I thought of the sharp and witty riposte when it was too late? Anyway, I was so stunned, I meekly succumbed, turned, and picked my way between the cars to the next aisle, where a Holden Commodore was waiting with its engine running and a man sitting in the driver's seat.

The man in the hi-vis jacket said, 'Get in the car and don't make a fuss.'

That was the second time he had used that word—he obviously didn't like fuss. He could see my reluctance and confusion, and I said, 'Can I just put my shopping in my car first?'

I tried to think of anything that might break this process to the car.

'No,' he said firmly, 'don't be a dickhead! Now keep quiet and get in the car … now!'

I was getting really frightened, but I was in denial. *This can't be happening to me.* My mind couldn't come to grips with the idea that I was being abducted in broad daylight at the local shops. He pulled open the rear door, and as I moved to get in the car, I looked around to see if there was anybody watching. They were all concentrating on Trent. Hi-Vis Jacket shoved me into the car and told me to get across to the other side. I shuffled across to sit behind the front passenger seat, and he dropped into the seat next to me, behind the driver, and slammed the door. The driver stuck the transmission in gear and set off. We were still picking our way through the cars and shoppers as a marked police car arrived with lights and sirens going full blast.

I watched the two in the car with me, and they kept their faces firmly forward as the police car drove past. That was when I realised I was in deep trouble. I didn't know what trouble or how deep, but I knew something was very seriously, as they say, 'up'.

Hi-Vis Jacket sat in the back with me. His gun and his eyes were both pointing steadily at me. I had never had much to do with guns and certainly had never been threatened with one. A bit like my medical training, my knowledge of guns came from TV and books. I could tell the difference between a revolver and an automatic, but that was pretty much the extent of it. This one wasn't a revolver, so it must have been an automatic. It was charcoal grey and looked the business.

Although we were travelling quite slowly towards the exit of the car park, I didn't feel that I could shout or jump out of the car or do any of the things that zipped through my mind in those few seconds without the strong possibility of retribution. I didn't know how serious these characters were, but they looked it. And if they had had anything to do with the mess that bloke on the ground's face was in, they were deadly serious.

He handed me a cable tie and told me to put it around my wrists. So I looped the cable tie over one wrist, put the other wrist through the loop, and he leaned over and sharply pulled it tight. The only small win I had was to keep my wrists as far apart as I dared so there was some slack left in the cable tie. Not much, but at least it would allow me some blood flow and maybe some movement.

It was really weird. In those moments, as we picked our way out of the car park, I could see people going about their daily lives, completely oblivious to what had happened to poor Trent and what was going on inside the car. My mind was slightly numb from the shock of what was happening to me—I must have been in denial. On one level, I was taking it all in—the cool, clear weather, the cars, the people going to and from the shops. On another level, my mind was racing to work out what was happening to me and what I had done to make these two thugs want to hold me at gunpoint. I couldn't believe it.

'What's going on?' I asked. 'Who are you? What do you want?'

'Shut the fuck up,' said Hi-Vis Jacket calmly and quietly.

We drove out onto the main road and in the direction away from my home. The thug next to me put a towel over my head so I couldn't see where I was being taken. That absolutely petrified me. My heart pounded, and my leg and stomach muscles were knotted tight. We drove on. Pretty soon, I lost track of where we were—too many lefts and rights to remember. All I could tell was that we were in Brisbane somewhere.

After what I guessed was a quarter of an hour, we pulled sharply to the right and stopped. A few seconds later, we pulled slowly forward, and when we stopped, I heard the clanking of what sounded like a garage door closing behind us. The driver got out of the car, came around to open my door, and took the towel off my head.

I looked around—yep, a double-sized garage. We were parked slightly to the right, so there was more room on my side to get out than on the driver's side.

'Get out,' said Hi-Vis Jacket with his pistol waving in the direction of the stairs at the back of the garage.

The Driver went up the stairs and through the door at the top first, I followed, and Hi-Vis Jacket brought up the rear. We were in a kitchen with dining and lounge areas off to the right. The Driver pulled a chair away from the dining table and indicated for me to sit, which I was happy to do. I wanted to be as cooperative as I could be—to build up any kind of good favour I could because I was afraid that pretty soon they were going to want something from me, and I was pretty sure that, whatever it was, I wouldn't have it. I was also pretty sure that was likely to make them unhappy, and I didn't want a couple armed thugs at all unhappy with me. That could be very bad.

'The bloke in the car park gave you something,' said Hi-Vis Jacket, still with his gun pointing at me. 'We want it.'

'I don't know what you're talking about. He didn't give me anything.'

'You will give us whatever he gave you, or I will hurt you,' he said so matter-of-factly, so menacingly, that I completely believed him.

I thought, *Perhaps if I give them a bit more detail, they will see that I'm not the person they want.*

'Listen, I got out of my car, and he was there by the rear of his car next to mine. As I went to get my shopping bags out of the boot, I said 'G'day' to him. He said that he had had a problem with his car door and did I have any tools. I got a screwdriver out of the back of my car and had a look at the door, which seemed to work fine. I put the screwdriver back in my car. He thanked me, and we went our separate ways. The next time I saw him, he was on the ground, having been beaten to a pulp. By you, I presume!'

Hi-Vis Jacket turned to his mate, the Driver, and said, 'Maybe, it's still in Trent's car?'

'We checked his car; it wasn't there,' he replied. 'This bloke must have it.'

I quickly jumped into the conversation. 'Look, I don't know what you're talking about. I haven't got whatever it is you want. Just let me go!'

I was getting even more anxious and frightened. They had beaten Trent, probably to death, in full view of any passers-by. They were making no effort to hide their faces, so they knew I could identify them if I lived through this. I reckoned I would finish up like Trent if I couldn't give them whatever they were looking for.

'Stand up,' said the Driver. I stood. He then punched me in the stomach.

I hadn't had that happen to me since I was about thirteen at school. I doubled up in pain, winded, unable to breathe properly, and I dropped to my knees. On all fours, I leaned forward, putting my forehead on the back of my hands. After a few moments, I got my breathing to return to normal.

The Driver quietly and evenly said, 'Give us whatever he gave you.'

Wheezing breathlessly, I said between gasps, 'I don't know what you want!'

He kicked me in the side. It hurt so badly, I thought he may have broken some ribs. I crashed over onto my left side, gasping, groaning, and rolling around on the floor.

The Driver waited patiently. It seemed he was in no rush and wanted me to understand that this beating hadn't ended yet. He put his mouth near my ear and whispered, 'That bloke in the car park gave you something. You will give it to me, or you will die wishing you had.'

They both stood back and waited for me to recover. I was regaining my composure and could think about things other than just my stomach and my ribs. He made a very convincing argument, but I still could not think of what he wanted.

Between gasps, I pleaded, 'Mate, look, please, I don't know what you are talking about. If I had something from that bloke, why would I *not* give it to you? It makes no sense. If he gave me something, I would just give it to you. He means nothing to me, and whatever you think he gave me would mean nothing to me either. So I would just hand it over if I had it. But I don't—'

He kicked me again. Same side, same ribs, same result. But worse. I was shocked by the stabbing pain. I could hardly breathe. Gasping and groaning, I felt faint, even though I was lying down. I desperately wanted lungfuls of air, but breathing sent a sharp pain down my side. For many seconds, I could think of nothing but the searing pain in my side.

He waited patiently. 'Get up,' he said.

I was in no state to do anything but lie on the floor.

He and Hi-Vis Jacket got me under my armpits and lifted me onto the dining chair, where I leaned forward and clutched my right forearm into my right side tentatively, feeling around the ribs and shocking myself at the stabbing pain from a gentle squeeze with my arm. *I'm not going to do that again,* I thought.

After two or three minutes, when the Driver could see I was recovering some semblance of composure, he crouched down in front of me. In a conversational, cheery tone, he said, 'Here's what is going to happen next. You are going to tell us where the item is that the other bloke gave you, or my colleague here'—he nodded towards Hi-Vis Jacket—'will cut off your little fingers on both hands. After that, he will cut off your thumbs—they can be quite tricky because we know from experience that the joints are quite tough to get through. Sometimes people pass out when this happens. So, after that, as we need you awake and talking, we will give you a little time to think about your situation, and then, if you don't tell us what we want to know, he will kill you. Either way, this will all be over very soon. You will either have told us what we want to know … or you will be dead. Now, does that sound like a plan?'

He got up and walked behind me. His arm swiftly came around my neck and pulled me tightly into the chair. I was in no state to resist because my ribs hurt like hell.

Hi-Vis Jacket said, 'Look, Glebbo, do I have to? I suppose I can shoot him, but cut his fingers off? Nah, mate. Can't you do it?'

'No, you've got to. If you want to be in with Smith, you have to be able to do stuff like this. Now, get a knife! Over there, in that knife block.'

Hi-Vis Jacket walked across the kitchen to the benchtop, where there was an angular lump of laminated timber with slots in it from which several knife handles were protruding. He selected a mid-sized knife from the block and walked back, examining it, gently running his thumb across the blade to test the sharpness.

'Not very sharp, but sharp enough,' he conceded. 'If I press hard enough, it should do the trick.'

'Good, well, get on with it, you pussy.'

Standing on my right, with his left hand, Hi-Vis Jacket grabbed my hands, which were still cable-tied together, and dragged them onto the dining table. I pulled as hard as I could, but as I clenched my stomach muscles to pull, a searing pain jabbed me in my side, and I had to give way to him. He forced my left hand down, the back of my hand to the table, and quickly jabbed the point of the knife between my little finger and ring finger.

The Driver, the one Hi-Vis called Glebbo, asked quietly in my ear, 'What did the guy at the shops give you? Where have you put it?'

'I don't—'

Glebbo nodded to Hi-Vis Jacket who, in one motion, levered the blade down and cut my little finger off at about the second joint from the tip. I shouted long and loud—the tears of pain rolled out of my eyes as I squeezed them shut. I needed to breathe, but every time I went to suck in air, my ribs screamed with pain from the kicks.

It was painful but, strangely, not as painful as I had feared. I sucked great gulps of air and, in comparison, the stabbing pain in my ribs hurt more than the finger. Maybe that was to do with the adrenaline. However, it shocked me to see my finger lying on the table and blood welling inexorably out of the stump on my left hand. I continued to shout; the blood pumped in my ears, and they rang with dizziness.

Glebbo the Driver withdrew his arm from around my neck, and I leaned forward onto the table. I gasped and groaned, shook my head from side to side, closed my eyes, and rocked back and forth on the chair, grunting in agony. My hands dropped into my lap, and I tried to ease the pain and stem the bleeding by pushing the stump into my midriff. I lolled forward and rested my forehead on the tabletop.

Through the ringing in my ears, I heard Glebbo the Driver say, 'What did the other bloke give you?'

I was now very desperate. I had come to the realisation, even during the beating, that I was about to die. These two had beaten Trent to death, possibly in front of onlookers, witnesses. They had been prepared to take the risk of being seen and recognised, and they'd gone through with it. Using their own names in front of me showed they were confident of not being caught. One of them was even wearing a hi-vis jacket, for goodness' sake! What sort of thug does that? If they were prepared to kill him in public, they wouldn't let me go alive. Even if I could tell them what they wanted to know, I realised that inevitably, sooner or later, probably sooner, they would kill me.

Hi-Vis Jacket wandered into an adjoining toilet. He closed the door, and I heard him slide the lock. Strange how the mind works; even in my hazy state, I wondered why he'd locked the door—there were only the three of us, and he had a gun! I wasn't going to be banging on the door and asking him to hurry up!

A phone rang. Glebbo the Driver pulled out a phone from his pocket, pressed the answer button, and said, 'Yeah.'

I could tell from his body language that this was his boss—he straightened his back and became quite deferential. He turned, glanced at me, and then, completely engrossed in what he was hearing, he walked into another room—a bedroom, I guessed. He was so deep in quiet conversation he seemed not to realise he'd left me without my armed guard.

I could hardly believe it! As soon as he turned away from me, I started trying to get my hands free—I could nearly get one hand out of the loop around my wrists, but not quite. I hunted around quickly for the knife—it was on the far end of the table. There were more in the knife block on the bench. The bench was nearer. I got up, hobbled to the knife block, gasping quietly, hoping my trainers wouldn't squeak on the timber flooring, and pulled out a short-bladed paring knife with my right hand so that the blade was lying along the back of my left forearm. I tried to get the point between the cable tie and my wrist, but I couldn't manipulate the knife to get enough leverage on the point or the sharp side of the blade to cut the plastic.

I decided to try escaping first. I heard the toilet flush. I ran on the balls of my feet through the door to the garage and down the stairs. At the bottom of the stairs and to my left was a door. I tried the handle, but it was locked and had no key in the lock. I spotted the release for the roller door, which was a pull-cord hanging from a motor unit on the ceiling, but before I could get to it, Hi-Vis Jacket came through the door from the house—he had the gun in his hand, pointing at me, and from the top of the stairs he said, 'Stand still!'

I stood still.

He came down the stairs, taking them carefully and watching me. 'Come back over here.'

I kept the knife hidden as best I could behind my forearm. I walked towards him, watching for an opportunity.

My nerves were shredded; I shook with fear, anger, and adrenaline. My finger was bleeding steadily. I was thankful the cable tie was not so tight that it cut off the blood to my hands—they felt fine but for the lack of independent movement and, of course, the missing finger. I felt light-headed but alert. Time slowed down. I was completely aware. The basic instinct in the deep, primitive part of my brain had taken over. Of the fight-or-flight instinct, the flight part had been taken from me. So be it. I was ready to fight.

As I walked past, I lunged at him. I stabbed the knife into the soft part of his gut between his ribs and hips. It penetrated easily up to the hilt. Warm, sticky blood spurted out over my hands. He dropped the gun, and his hands flew to his side. Looking down in horror at the handle protruding from his side, he wrapped his hands slowly around it. As he slid the bloody blade out of his side and let it fall, he grunted repeatedly, short and sharp. He put the palm of his hand over the wound to staunch the blood, which was pumping out down his side, bright red against the fluoro yellow of his jacket, and down his right leg.

As Hi-Vis Jacket sank to his knees, I picked up his gun, aimed it at the door at the top of the stairs, and slowly climbed each step with my eyes fixed on the door jamb where Glebbo the Driver would appear.

My hands were shaking and so slippery with blood that I feared I wouldn't be able to hold the gun steady.

I heard Glebbo the Driver calling gently in an urgent stage-whisper, 'Cyril!'

Then he appeared at the door with his gun pointing in the general direction of the garage floor. I pointed my gun up at him and shouted, 'Stop! Don't move!'

But before I had finished, he swung his gun towards me and fired twice. Fortunately, his arm swinging across the target, me, meant that it was quite a difficult shot for him. He fired the first shot a fraction of a second too soon, and the bullet flew past me into the wall at the bottom of the stairs. The second shot went past me into the wall by my right ear. In that second's heightened awareness, having never fired anything but air rifles, I aimed for the biggest target: his body. In my favour, I was already stationary and had the gun braced as best I could with both hands cable-tied together. I pulled the trigger. Almost simultaneously, he fired at me again, just as my bullet hit him above his right knee and spun him to his right, causing his shot to veer off to my left. The leg was not the result I wanted, but it would do to slow him down and, I hoped, give him second thoughts about coming down the stairs for me.

He slumped to the floor, sitting at the top stairs.

The noise from my gun was incredible! It was much louder than I had expected and way louder than the gun that Glebbo the Driver had fired at me, which sounded more like an air gun. It made my ears ring, but the kick of the gun was not as great as they make out in the films. Although my hands shook with fear and tension from the wound to my finger, they were both still tied together, so there was enough stability. What I had heard and felt barely registered when he slowly raised his gun to fire again. The pain from his leg must have been getting to his aim because he was way off the mark, and his shot went down into the garage somewhere. I fired again a split second later, still aiming for his body. My mind was working so fast, everything felt like slow motion—I thought I could almost see the bullet fly to him and hit him in his left arm.

He seemed to be really struggling with the pain from two bullet wounds, and his right hand, still holding the gun, was down at his side. I took the opportunity to climb the few remaining stairs as quickly as I could, which wasn't that quick. My ribs objected, and I heard myself grunting at every step. He was trying to raise his gun once more as I reached the top step and, with all my might, I kicked his arm between the wrist and elbow, and the gun flew across the kitchen, sliding to rest against a kitchen cabinet.

Chapter 5

I grew faint. I didn't like killing anything—wasps, spiders, even a brown snake near the house on one occasion. Okay, I may have made an exception for mosquitoes—I really react badly to mossie bites. And ants in the house. But I tried to avoid killing other animals if I could.

The beating I had taken and the thought that I may have killed these men had made me feel nauseated. My stomach clenched, and the vomit climbed into my throat. Keeping quite still, I swallowed hard, as though just concentrating on not vomiting would command my stomach not to chuck up.

I turned briefly to look at Hi-Vis Jacket on the garage floor. He was holding his side but wasn't moving, and his blood had formed a small pool on the concrete like a small oil slick slowly expanding on the sea.

Glebbo the Driver was sitting, leaning against the door jamb, clutching his leg. 'Get me a tourniquet, mate!' he pleaded.

'Use your belt!' I snarled back at him. I didn't feel much like helping him after he cut my finger off. Speaking of which, I wandered around the kitchen, opening drawers and cupboards, hoping to find something to use as a tourniquet myself on the little stump of my finger. I looked in some drawers and found one with rolls of cling wrap, aluminium foil, greaseproof paper, and some zip-top bags. Scattered in another, I found lots of rubber bands. I put the gun in my right hand on the worktop and picked out a couple of elastic bands, but I couldn't reach my finger because of the cable tie.

I picked up the knife that Glebbo the Driver used on me, but my hands were too weak and shaky to cut the cable tie around my wrist. I considered giving the knife to Glebbo the Driver to cut the tie but decided it might be wiser not to give him a weapon. I put it down and picked up the gun in my right hand. I checked on him as I went down to the garage again. He seemed okay, all things considered. He had managed to get his belt on his leg as a tourniquet, and his arm didn't look too bad to me. But what do I know?

In the garage, I checked on Hi-Vis Jacket. He was still lying on his side, seemingly unconscious, actually breathing steadily, although he was still bleeding. The flow wasn't as bad as it had been.

I looked around the garage for a toolbox and found a pair of pliers. Gingerly, I picked them up in my left hand and plodded back up the stairs to Glebbo the Driver.

'Cut the cable tie,' I demanded.

He seemed reluctant to help.

'Do you want some medical assistance, arsehole? If so, cut the tie!'

I gave him the pliers, and he cut the tie. I took the pliers back and put them on the worktop.

From a drawer, I selected a couple of rubber bands and treble-wrapped them around my finger to stem the bleeding. Then I selected a small zip-closure plastic bag and emptied some ice cubes from a tray in the freezer into it. The blood from my severed finger end turned the water slightly red as I pushed it down into the bag among the ice cubes. Zipping the bag closed, I put it in the fridge.

I picked Glebbo the Driver's gun up off the floor, placed it on the worktop, and then pulled my phone out of my pocket to ring for the police and an ambulance. Nothing happened when I flipped open the leather cover and tried to unlock it with my thumb. There was too much blood on my thumb for the fingerprint identification system to work. Then I remembered the battery was dead anyway—it seemed like years ago I was in the car park at the shops. During my search of the kitchen, I noticed a phone charger, so I plugged in my phone. It made the small, familiar chime, and I left the phone on the worktop near the guns.

I was angry at them for making me try to kill them to escape. I was literally sick with shock and adrenaline. Now the urgency of the situation had passed, my legs began to feel weak and my ears rang; I suddenly felt dizzy and sweaty but clammily cold at the same time. I stumbled quickly to the toilet and vomited into the bowl. I groaned and felt as if I was going to faint. The ringing in my ears got louder, and I could almost feel the blood draining from my head. I kneeled down and dropped my head to the floor next to the bowl. The tiles felt beautifully cool on my forehead. I stayed like that for a few moments until my ears stopped ringing, and I felt the blood flowing back to my head and my temperature returning to something more normal.

I couldn't believe what I had just done. I relived it in my mind and wondered if there was anything I could have done differently that would have allowed me to escape without the stabbing and shooting. As the adrenaline cleared from my bloodstream, a huge sadness and depression gradually swept over me. After the 'high' comes the 'low'.

I sat on the tiled floor of the toilet, leaning my back against the wall between the toilet bowl and the basin. I knew I should get on the phone and help them, but I was finding it hard to get myself moving.

I tried to think, but I couldn't drag my thoughts away from the horror of what they, and I, had just done. I looked at my finger again. After a while, I'm not sure how long, I thought, *Well, someone must have heard the gunfire, so the police will be here any minute, and they'll call the ambos. I can hand it all over to them.*

I started to feel a bit better. Well, less like fainting and vomiting. I struggled up and looked in the mirror above the wash-hand basin. The old guy I saw looked all of his sixty-eight years: grey—and that wasn't just the hair. I rinsed my hands and very gently allowed the cold water to run over my little finger stump. The bowl streamed with reddened water—bloody hell, it stung! I splashed water on my face with my good hand and rinsed my mouth because it tasted as if the acid in my vomit was eating away my teeth. I dried my hands gently on the towel next to the basin and then rubbed the towel over my teeth to try to remove the acid taste. As I left the toilet, I spotted a roll of kitchen paper towel and gently dabbed at the wound on my finger end to dry it off. The elastic bands seemed to do the job of stemming the bleeding. I wrapped one paper towel around the end of my finger.

I was so convinced that someone in the neighbourhood would have heard the gunfight that it didn't occur to me to ring for the police. So, descending the stairs again, I patted Hi-Vis Jacket's pockets to see if he had a wallet or something that might indicate who he was and what he was looking for. From his rear right trouser pocket, I pulled out his wallet.

Seventy-five dollars in cash. Should I take it? I decided not to. Why stoop to their level? At the front, inside a clear plastic window, was a Queensland driver's licence. I pulled it out to read the address on the back. I didn't know the road or the suburb—not surprising, as I haven't lived in Queensland all that long. Then I looked through the cards inside: credit cards, Medicare card, and an airline frequent flyer card—all in the name of Cooper, first name Cyril. I recognised the Queensland Seniors Card—I have one just like it. Then the bomb dropped—from a leather pocket, I pulled out a card on which was written, *'Queensland Police: With Honour We Serve'*. Below that was *'Cooper, Cyril: Senior Sergeant'*. Bloody hell! I didn't know what to think. I was really confused. Maybe this was a wallet stolen from Senior Sergeant Cyril Cooper. I pulled out the driver's licence again and compared the photo to the bloke oozing blood on the floor in front of me. Licence photos are never a very good likeness, but it certainly looked like him. But police? What the—?

I climbed the stairs again and went to the front window to have a look out. A normal, leafy Brisbane suburb. Hilly, with the road lined with 'Queenslanders'—a traditionally styled timber house built on stumps, some with living areas or garages added underneath later where the stumps are. Like this one, I guessed. No sign of the police. No sign of anybody.

I walked over to Glebbo the Driver. 'Give me your wallet.'

'Fuck off.'

'Oh, mate, you are soooo in no position to be awkward with me,' I said. 'Let me see if I remember what you said to me … Here's what is going to happen next: you are going to give me your wallet, or I am going to stand on the bullet hole in your leg until you wish you had given it to me immediately.'

'Okay, wait.' He pulled his wallet out of his rear hip pocket and handed it to me.

The first thing I looked for was a police identification card. No police identification card, but something nearly as interesting. A Royal Australian Air Force identity card. Name: Gleb Orlov, middle name Grigoryevich. Flight sergeant. Russian-looking name, but he sounded as though he was an Aussie born and bred. Same address as the other thug. It was a pretty fancy card with a magnetic strip on the back, an embedded chip like a credit card, and a wi-fi symbol on the front—maybe they use it to buy stuff on the base. I kept looking, finding credit cards, an airline card, and a lot of cash—I didn't count it, but there were several hundred dollars. And an organ donor card. A thug with a social conscience? I said to him, 'Organ donor card? Seriously? Do you want to make a donation of your little finger to me, you dickhead?'

I showed him the address on his driver's licence. 'Is this where we are now?'

He nodded.

'Where are you based with the RAAF?'

'Fuck off.'

I walked towards him, and he tried to scuttle backwards away from me, but he was in too much pain to out-pace me. I rested my foot on his leg. He looked defiantly at me. I pressed gently. He groaned. 'Okay, okay! Amberley!'

I gave his leg one more tweak for good measure. He didn't like that, but it made me feel a bit better. Pocketing his driving licence, RAAF identification card, and four hundred dollars, I tossed the wallet back at him and said, 'I'm taking the cash for my hospital bills for when they re-attach my finger. If they can. Okay with you?' I rested my foot lightly on his wounded leg. He nodded vigorously. Were my moral standards slipping? Yes, but I was angry and in a lot of pain.

Still no sound of police sirens. I picked up the gun Glebbo the Driver had used to try to shoot me. It was a weird-looking thing. Both the guns had 'Glock 17' engraved on their barrels, but Glebbo the Driver's had what I guessed was a silencer on the muzzle. It also had what looked like a torch mounted under the barrel called Streamlight TLR-1 HL. I located the button that made the LED light go on and off.

He said, 'Hey, mate, stop waving that thing around! It's pointing at me, and it isn't safe. You obviously don't know anything about guns, do you?'

'No. Never held a handgun in my life 'til just now.'

'Those Glocks don't have a switch you can just flick to make them safe. It's loaded and cocked. You pull the trigger, it'll go off. Don't point it at me! You couldn't hit me when you were aiming at me. I don't want you killing me by accident!'

'Yeah, good point,' I admitted rather dourly.

I picked up the gun with the silencer, and he said, 'Pop the magazine and then rack the slide.'

'What? Why? Pop what and rack what?'

'To make it safe. Don't point it at me!'

'If I point it at you while I'm doing this, it gives me some confidence you will tell me the correct process. So you had better be clear, hadn't you?'

I swung the barrel around to point at him. He swallowed hard and said, 'Okay. You put it in your pocket now, you could blow your balls off.

It's a semi-automatic. You pull the trigger; it reloads automatically and cocks, ready to fire again. You keep pulling the trigger, it keeps firing.'

'Well, okay, so how do I uncock it?'

'Take your finger out of the trigger guard. Pop the magazine out by pushing that little button on the grip.'

I pressed the button, and the magazine ejected from the butt of the handle. There were three spaces vacant of a possible seventeen—he had fired four shots at me, so he must have had one bullet loaded in the chamber or breech or whatever it was called. I hefted it in my hand—not as well-balanced as the one I had fired, presumably because of the additional weight of the silencer and the light. Maybe that was why he had missed me.

He continued, 'Please! Keep your finger off the trigger! Now pull the slide back on the top of the barrel, and the live round in the chamber will be ejected.'

I did as he directed, and the bullet made a short arc onto the floor. Having picked up the bullet, I slid it back into the top of the magazine and rammed the magazine home in the butt of the handle.

'Okay, the gun won't fire until you rack the slide again. That's as safe as I can make it if you want the magazine in the gun.'

I went through the same process with the other gun, the one I had fired, and there were sixteen bullets in the magazine.

I picked up Glebbo the Driver's phone and started tapping it to see if I could make a call for the ambos. I was pretty sure I could make emergency calls without unlocking it. While I was looking at the phone considering this, it vibrated and lit up with an incoming call. In my surprise, I nearly dropped it. The display showed a name—Alan. What should I do? Ignore it? Answer it? I decided to answer it.

'Yeah, mate,' I said quietly, trying to make my voice nondescript.

'Glebbo, howyagoin' mate? Have you got the memory stick or whatever and killed that muppet?'

I couldn't think of what I might say that would be short and sharp enough that he wouldn't recognise I wasn't Glebbo. If I wasn't really quick, he would know anyway. As my mind went through the options in a split second, I realised I had probably given the game away already, whatever I said. I tried to assimilate what he meant by a memory stick—was that what Trent was meant to have given me?

So I said, 'Glebbo's not feeling very well.'

There was a brief pause. Smith replied, *'Oh, yeah? Well, I'm not surprised. He was a dickhead. I suppose that other dickhead is dead, too? Did you kill them both, or did they shoot one another? They're stupid enough! A pair of sergeants? Pair of idiots, more like!'*

'Who are you?'

'My name's Alan. You've done well to deal with those two. Very resourceful. You wanna job? I need resourceful people.'

He sounded very calm.

'No, what I need is for you and your thugs to leave me alone!'

'Yeah-nah, sorry, that's not gonna happen, mate. I want something you've got. Just a minute ...'

He obviously turned his head away from the phone and put his hand over the microphone to talk to someone else. It was rather muffled, but I could make out what he said.

'Get over to Glebbo's. He's there, and he may have killed Glebbo and Cyril, so be careful. I'll ring you in a minute.'

Then he turned his attention back to me. *'I'll tell you what; I'll pay you for whatever the bloke at the shops gave you. Then I will leave you totally alone. How much do you want?'*

'How much are you willing to pay?'

I thought if I could get a price, it would give me some idea of what I was dealing with. But straight after that, I realised he could say anything. Millions, even. He wasn't going to pay. Whatever it was, it was worth killing for. It was worth killing *me* for. I rang off before he answered.

A few seconds later, Smith rang again. I ignored it. I said to Orlov, 'What's the PIN to unlock your phone?'

'I don't use the PIN—it recognises my face.'

'Well, I want to use your phone, and I want to use the PIN.'

'I don't remember.'

I walked towards him and raised my foot towards his bloody leg.

'Try G-L-E-B,' he said. '4532.'

Good. It unlocked.

Having preferred to wait quietly for the police before so I could gather my thoughts, I now wanted them to be here before Smith's boys turned up. Much as I wanted the police to arrive, if nobody had heard the gunshots and called the police, they weren't coming.

Chapter 6

It occurred to me that even if the police did turn up first, they might be crooked and working with Smith like Cyril Hi-Vis Jacket and Glebbo. I would be in deep trouble again, and outnumbered again. I decided I couldn't ring the police. I needed time to think about the ramifications of what had happened and where the police and the RAAF might fit in, but there was no time now for that sort of cogitation. My brain was at capacity just trying to stay alive, and I needed to get away from the immediate threat and pressure to give myself a chance to calm down and think. And I wanted to get my finger fixed. It bloody hurt.

After a few more seconds of disbelief, confusion, and indecision, I decided to get out, but I also thought that being armed would be wise, just in case Smith's boys turned up in the next few seconds.

I put Glebbo's phone down on the counter and looked at the gun, turning it over in my hands, then tucked it into the top of my shorts. I unplugged my phone and put it in my right shorts pocket. My spectacles were still in my left pocket. I stuffed Glebbo's phone into my right pocket beside mine and held the gun with the silencer in my left hand. I collected my finger from the fridge, then ran down the stairs to the garage as fast as I could, my sore ribs making me grunt with each step.

I looked in the car for the remote door opener for the garage, spotted it on the centre console, opened the door, and sat in the driver's seat. I picked up the remote and pushed the 'open' button—the door started to creak and clank open. Keys. Where were the keys?

I hunted around the steering column on the centre console, inside the armrest. No keys. By now, the garage door was fully open, and Cyril was, fortunately for me, lying between the car and the stairs, mostly hidden from the road. I groaned my way back up the stairs to Glebbo and told him to give me the car keys, which he did with a little persuasion from my foot on his leg. I hobbled down the stairs again.

Into the car, gun and finger on the seat beside me and keys into the ignition, I cranked the starter. The moment the engine started, I rammed the automatic transmission into reverse and tried to turn around to look out of the back window. My ribs stabbed me, so I had to turn slowly, tensing my muscles, sensing how far I could go before it hurt too much. I gave the accelerator a good squirt to get the car moving out of the garage. A little red hatchback squealed to a stop across the end of the drive. The driveway was double-car width, so I swung the wheel and swerved around the hatchback. Its two front doors popped open as I passed. Two blokes rolled out, both holding handguns, and they both fired at me.

I swerved past them into the road and kept reversing as fast as I could in the direction they were facing when they arrived. The car swung from left to right and back as I swerved down the road between the parked cars. The unintended swerving served to put off their aim, and I didn't think they had yet got a round successfully through the windscreen. Though I hadn't looked to check—my eyes were firmly out of the rear window. They were running as they fired, which, the films led me to believe, is very unlikely to produce a hit.

I steered around a gentle bend in the road, hoping soon to be out of direct sight, only to be met with a small turning circle and the end of the road. Bugger.

I braked hard and the wheels locked, producing a short screech from the tyres. I slammed the transmission into *drive* and nailed the accelerator to the floor. I was much better at driving fast forwards! The car rocked back on its suspension, and the wheels squealed and juddered as it accelerated hard. As I went around the short bend, I could see one of Smith's thugs was getting into the driver's seat of the car, and the other was right in the middle of the gap between the hatchback and the offside curb, bracing himself in a shooter's stance just like on TV. He was right where I wanted to go. I weaved the car slightly left and right and kept my head down nearly to the rim of the steering wheel, but I kept going for the gap. By then, I was going as fast as I dared. The bloke in the road fired two or three more shots, but then he got the point—I wasn't going to stop for him. He was a fraction too late jumping aside behind the hatchback, and my car's headlight caught his leg as he dived to his right. There was a *thump* on the front left side of the car—reminded me of that kangaroo I hit a few years ago.

I checked the mirror to see whether he was going to get a few more shots off at me, but he was rolling around on the ground in obvious agony, clutching his lower leg. The other thug was turning the hatchback around and would soon be after me. I had no clue where I was, so I just drove as fast as I dared along the streets somewhere in the suburbs of Brisbane.

At the end of the street, I ground to a halt with the tyres chirping in complaint and looked both ways for traffic. What to do? I decided left and cranked the wheel over and floored the pedal again. After a slight fish-tail, I got the car fully under control and checked the rear-view mirror. No hatchback yet. Another turn. Left again, then a right turn. A short run brought me to a major road. There was a gap in the traffic from my right, so I pulled out across the road, barging into the steady stream of vehicles coming from my left to a chorus of horns blaring. If he still wanted to follow, he would have to wait for a gap, which would give me a few more seconds' lead.

Now I was in traffic, I had to cruise along at the same speed as everyone else. I recognised where I was—not somewhere I had been frequently, but I had a broad idea of this part of Brisbane. My mind was racing with adrenaline, but I was driving on autopilot.

The first thing I wanted to do was find somewhere off the road, where I couldn't be spotted easily, to stop and take stock. Just to sit and think and relax with the immediate pressure off.

There it was. Just ahead, I spotted a small car park in front of some offices. It had exits to the main road and a side street that gave me escape options if any of Smith's pals turned up. I pulled in and parked in a spot between two cars with quick access to both exits. I applied the handbrake and took the car out of gear but left the engine running. I put my head back on the headrest and closed my eyes.

I started a huge sigh, but as I began drawing breath, my ribs stabbed me. This was the first time I had had the chance to feel the extent of the damage—with the back of the fingers of my right hand, I gently explored the bruising to my right ribs. Whether there were any cracked, I didn't know. Probably. Suffice it to say, they were very sore. I unwrapped the kitchen paper towel that had, remarkably, stayed on the end of my little finger. I undid the elastic bands and watched to see if the stump bled. It did. I triple-wrapped the bands back on. 'Sore' didn't begin to describe it.

What now? Police? What would they do? They would take me into custody, where I would then be at the mercy of Smith's crooked cop friends. Have you ever heard of someone dying by 'suicide' in police custody? Yes. And it might take months to sort through this mess before they let me out. My fingerprints were all over the ball-peen hammer that was used to beat that poor Trent in the shops' car park. And there was a trail of blood and prints of mine at the house where Glebbo and Cyril were still lying. And, in Cyril's case, possibly dying. Police? No, not yet.

Did I know someone I could have called to help? I knew a few people in the Brisbane area, but not anybody I would want to get involved in this bloody mayhem. That wouldn't be very friendly!

Go to hospital? Or my local general practitioner. Too many questions at the GP, and it was quite a long drive out there from where I was parked. The GP might have sent me to hospital anyway. More time wasted.

A woman in a BMW SUV pulled in and parked. She was wearing a smart business suit, high heels, and a frown as she strode towards me, waving her finger at me. It really wasn't my day, I thought tiredly. I pushed the button to wind the window down halfway.

She said, 'I'm afraid you can't park here! This is a private car park, and you haven't got a permit displayed!'

'Do you know what this is?' I said to her, pointing at the blood on my shirt.

'Looks like blood,' she said with distaste clear on her face.

'Yes, it is.'

With my right hand, I picked up the bag of slushy, pink ice with my finger buried in it and held up my left hand next to it so she could see the bloody stump. 'It came from the bloke I just stabbed after he cut my finger off. I won't be long. Now, please, leave me alone.'

Her face paled. She turned on her heel and hurried away.

I decided to go to hospital. I switched on my phone, opened the maps app, entered 'accident and emergency hospitals near me', and accepted its directions. I put the Commodore in gear, took off the handbrake, and drove out of the car park into the traffic.

Chapter 7

I parked in the doctors' car park near the entrance to the Emergency Department. After the mayhem I had left behind me and the multiple serious charges that potentially awaited me, a parking ticket was the least of my worries.

With one of the guns in the glove box and the other with the phone under the seat because it was too big to hide elsewhere, I locked the Commodore with the remote as I set off towards the hospital entrance.

Inside the main entrance were several desks with glass windows to the ceiling. One was marked 'Visitors', two were marked 'Reception', and the last two were labelled 'Nurse'. I went to the desk marked 'Reception', showed the nurse dressed in blue hospital scrubs my bandaged hand, and held up the plastic bag with my finger and ice in it. I'll give the nurse his due; he was completely unfazed and asked me to come around the side, through the door into his triage area, and sit in front of him. He put a rubberised clip over my right index finger to check the oxygenation in my blood, asked me a few questions, and looked at my Medicare card and private health card to complete his admin, which he noted on the computer in front of him.

He took me through to a much larger room with the staff's desks in the centre rectangle and beds all the way around the walls, some with heavy paper curtains around them, others open, others with sliding doors to seal them off. The room was very brightly lit, with freshly painted white walls to keep up the light levels, yellow paint picking out the door frames and skirting areas, and railings to protect corners from scratches by passing beds. There was equipment everywhere, either in use or awaiting the call to action: computers on trolleys, steel tables on wheels, wheelie bins, folding slip-hazard signs, walker frames, wheelchairs, and a display showing an x-ray of someone's broken leg—also on wheels.

The nurse took me into a cubicle with a variety of tubes sprouting from the wall over the bed, latex glove dispensers (three sizes), sanitiser dispensers, sharps bins, a lamp on an articulated arm protruding from the ceiling. He asked me to sit on the bed and asked another nurse to come over.

This nurse, a cheerful, motherly lady in her fifties dressed in blue scrubs, took my hand gently and unwrapped the blood-soggy paper towel, examining the stump without taking off the elastic bands. She asked me to explain what had happened as she held up the bag so she could examine the finger through the clear plastic.

'I cut it off with a circular saw,' I lied.

'Right,' she said. 'I'll get a doctor to have a look. Get you sorted straight away, darl!'

She went to the central area of desks and countertops at chest height and spoke to a young lady dressed in green hospital scrubs sitting at one of the desks. Beyond them, near the far corner, a couple of uniformed police officers were lounging together, chatting. The doctor held up her hand, concentrating on what she was writing on a clipboard. After a moment, she looked up, and I could see the nurse talking to her, indicating in my direction. She got up and walked over to me.

'Hello, my name is Amena. What's yours?'

'Hello, Amena. I'm Toby.'

'What happened, Toby?'

'I had an accident with a circular saw and cut my finger off.'

I had considered whether to tell the truth but decided against it—I still didn't know who I could trust in the police. They would be bound to report an incident where one person cuts the finger off another.

'Cutting a piece of timber,' I explained. 'My hand was underneath, supporting the piece in the direction I was cutting.'

I put my hand out, palm up to demonstrate. 'My hand was under the wood, so I couldn't see where it was. I was in a bit of a hurry to finish the job and was cutting quickly. The saw had taken my finger off before I realised. So, I wrapped the elastic bands 'round the stump as a tourniquet and put the finger in a bag of ice, here.'

I gave her the bag. While I talked, she examined the wound and unwrapped the elastic bands. It immediately oozed blood. She put the bands back on.

'Okay,' she said. 'Mmmm, it is a bit of a mess, isn't it? We need to clean it up, get some x-rays, and have a surgeon look at it to decide if it can be reattached. Can we give you some painkillers, as your finger is likely to be really sore when the adrenaline and excitement wear off?'

'Yes, it throbs and aches, and my whole hand is generally sore, but it is bearable.'

'Out of ten, how bad would you say it is?'

'Four or five?'

'Okay, well, I could give you some anaesthetic or painkillers, but the surgeon may want to do that himself. Can you bear it a little longer?'

'Yep.'

'Okay, press the call button there if you need some relief from the pain. How much blood do you think you lost?'

'Not much. I got the tourniquet on within five minutes or so.'

'How did you get here? You didn't drive yourself, did you?'

'Yes, I did,' I admitted sheepishly.

'Mmmm, okay.' She seemed unimpressed. 'Well, you had better find someone to drive you home—you will probably receive painkillers and maybe a local anaesthetic. First, we'll get it cleaned. Someone'll be along to do that soon.'

She picked up the plastic bag with my finger in it, sloshing around in a mainly watery solution of pink ice.

'I'll get this onto some fresh ice and into the fridge,' she said as she left to walk to some room out of my line of sight.

'And I may have cracked some ribs.'

'What?'

'Well, when I cut my finger off, I was so shocked and surprised and in pain that I dropped the saw and jumped sideways, fell onto a saw-horse beside me, which caught me in the ribs.'

Were they really going to believe this rubbish?

Amena looked sceptical but said nothing except, 'Okay, show me.'

I rolled up my shirt and, surprisingly, there was little sign of the two kicks—just a little redness. She felt around the area.

I grunted a couple of times when she pressed around the bottom of my ribs, where it really hurt.

'Yeah, maybe. We'll get you a CT scan and a chest x-ray. Make sure there is no other organ damage. You'll need to get out of your shirt, but you can keep your pants on. Put that gown on.'

Amena motioned towards a garment lying at the end of the bed. 'Take your shoes off and lie on the bed. I'll be back in a moment.' She left the cubicle only to return shortly afterwards, pushing two trolleys: one box-shaped, the other with a computer on the top. She started the formal 'history', asking me my name, age, allergies, operations, when did I last eat, that sort of thing, which she entered into the computer on wheels. Having sanitised the top of the box on the other trolley, she pulled a dressing pack out and placed it where she had just cleaned. A cannula was inserted into my arm at the elbow, and this was connected to a drip, which she told me was a saline solution, hanging from a wheeled frame next to me. She took my temperature, heart rate, and blood pressure, and got me settled, sitting upright on the bed. She rolled the table over next to me. Having sanitised her hands and put on sterile gloves, and with an assuredness that must have come from years of experience, she deftly picked out what she needed from the wide variety of bags and packets in the box, tore them open, and started cleaning my wound.

Two doctors arrived wearing green scrubs—I understood the colour coding of scrubs by now. The elder and leader of the two was Wu, according to his name badge. The other was in a wheelchair and was named Chau. Amena moved aside and said she would come back in a few minutes to finish the clean-out. Wu picked up the clipboard and, reading from it, said, 'Hello, Mr Richmond. May I call you Toby?'

'Certainly, doctor.'

'You can call me Wu. I'm a surgeon. This is Chau. He is in his first year out of medical school and doing a rotation with us. Would you mind if he takes the lead?'

'Not at all—we all have to learn. Hello, Chau.'

Chau replied, 'Hello, Toby. Please tell us what happened.'

So I went through the story again while they took it in turns to look at my hand.

'Where is rest of finger?' he asked as he studied the stump.

'I don't know. One of your colleagues took it away.'

'Okay, we find it.'

'Yes, I hope so. I was rather attached to it.'

'Oh, yes, very good. That was like the joke.' He forced a chuckle. After a while, he leaned back in his chair and said to Wu, 'Before make decision, I like to see a finger.'

'Yes, good. Let's go and take a look.'

'Before you go, is it urgent to do the re-attachment? I mean, I heard it was important that the severed finger had to be reattached as soon as possible. Is that true?'

'Yes, that is so. And we will be as expeditious as possible,' Chau replied. And off they went.

After a few minutes, they returned and Chau said, 'Toby, I'm sorry to say it is likely we cannot re-attach the amputated finger. Probably it is with no blood supply from your body for too long time and may be beyond time when your finger we can save it. Also, nerve endings and blood vessels damage is quite severe. However, before we take final decision, we want some x-rays, and then we come back and talk again. Okay?'

'Okay, thank you.'

As they turned to leave the cubicle, a person was wheeled past on a gurney. The head was heavily strapped and bandaged. The clothes looked familiar under a loose blanket. Pipe coming out of his knee. No shoes. Stripy, brightly coloured socks. How great is that! Sandra and Norm got Trent safely to the Emergency Room! I wondered why it had taken them so long to get him here. Maybe they had struggled to keep his condition stabilised after I was abducted.

I got off my bed, pulled my drip on its wheeled frame, and walked to the end of my bed, from where I could see around the room. The gurney was rolled into the next cubicle to mine. A short, squat lady in purple scrubs passed me, and I asked her, 'Is that man from the car park at the shops?'

'Yes, he is. He's been bashed. It's been like the OK Corral out there today. We've got three more over the other side.' She pointed. 'One's been run over, another's been stabbed, and the third one shot! Apparently, a police officer was killed, too, in a shoot-out. I ask you, what's happening to the world?'

With that, she went happily on her way.

Fuck me gently, I thought. *That's not so good. Opposite, I've got Glebbo, Cyril, and the bloke in the street I hit with the car, and two policemen. And next to me, the battered Trent. With the exception of Trent, they all want to get hold of me, and I still don't know why! Well, I know why the police want me—they probably take a dim view of me putting those three bastards in hospital no matter how much they deserved it. And when they take the fingerprints off that hammer, they'll think I did Trent as well!*

Although I was concerned that they were in the same room as me, I was relieved that I hadn't killed any of them. Certainly, Cyril hadn't looked that crash-hot when I had last seen him.

I pulled the curtains almost closed so that I was standing just inside the cubicle but able to look out through the gap. After a while, I got bored and sat on the bed.

The curtains opened again, and a wardsman (purple scrubs) came in, pushing a wheelchair.

'Hello, I've come to take you to X-ray,' he said. 'Can you hop in here?'

'Too easy.'

I sat in the chair, and he detached the drip machine from the stand and hooked it to an apparatus fixed to the wheelchair. I had a quick panic in case he wheeled me past the three thugs and two cops, but no, we went the other way.

While being wheeled to Radiology, I thought about what I should say to Trent if I got the chance to talk to him.

Several corridors later, we arrived at the Radiology Department, where a very efficient older lady asked my wardsman to wait outside. She rolled me to a table and arranged my hand in the position she wanted with, nearby, a small metal tag with the letter 'L' cut out to indicate 'Left'.

Ducking around behind a lead shield to take the image, she called, 'Keep very still!' over her shoulder.

She returned to adjust the position of my hand and took another. Back to me, and she had me stand sideways against a square board with concentric squares drawn on it.

'Put your hands on that rail,' she instructed. Then she took another with me standing with my hands on my hips and my shoulders against the board.

A few seconds later, she stuck her head out from behind the shield. 'Okay, they're all fine; you can go to the CT scanner next door now.'

I struggled to wheel myself to the door and pulled the handle. The wardsman pushed the door wide, slipped behind the chair, and pushed me through the door to the next room. A large machine that looked like a bed lying through a huge metal doughnut sat in the middle of the room. The same lady bounced in.

'Okay, lie on the bed, please.'

I did as I was bidden.

'I'm going to take a scan of your chest now if that's okay. Please take down your pants if they have any metal on them.'

The belt clasp was metal, so I undid it and pushed my pants to my knees. She raised my arms so they were up past my ears. I gasped as she lifted them.

'Sorry,' she said cheerily. 'Okay, I'm going to do one run, and before the second run, I'll push some dye into your arm to help with the image. You'll feel a warm sensation circulate around your body, and it may make you feel as if you've wet yourself. You won't have, I hope!' She laughed.

After the doughnut had moved up and down twice over me and I had the warm feeling suffusing my body, she unhooked the tube to my cannula and called the wardsman to take me away back to the Emergency Department.

As we passed Trent, I looked in and saw, to my surprise, that he was sitting in a slightly raised position, awake! Admittedly, the top part of him looked like an Egyptian mummy with bandages around his head, and he had tubes and wires coming from all over his torso, but I could see his eyes were open.

After the wardsman left me in my cubicle, I removed the automated blood pressure cuff, took the blood oxygenation device off my index finger, got off the bed, and dragged the drip trolley with me. I looked around the room and could see nobody nearby who might want to arrest or kill me, so I walked into the next cubicle to talk to Trent.

I drew his curtains closed behind me. 'Hello, mate. Howyagoin'?' I asked.

'Been better.'

'I'm Toby; do you remember me?'

'Yes, I do. You saved my life.'

'Not really me. It was the doctor who came by and the paramedics. Anyway, why did those blokes bash you—are they friends of yours or something?'

He lowered his voice, so I moved closer so I could hear. He said, 'I'm an undercover police officer. You'll have to take my word for that. I'm known as Trent Kipek—not my real name, for obvious reasons. Anyway, I'm very grateful. Why are you in here?'

'Some of your buddies wanted something they thought you had given me, and they tortured me to try to make me tell them what and where it was.'

I held up my hand as evidence.

'They tortured you? Fuckin'ell, they're bad bastards! What did they do?' He closed his eyes and went quiet for a few seconds.

I paused because I could see he was struggling to stay awake.

'Sorry,' he said. 'I'm drugged up to the eyeballs with the real good stuff.'

'Nice! What is it?'

'Dunno. But it's making me very drowsy.' He paused.

I replied to his question. 'They cut my finger off'—I held up my hand—'and kicked me in the ribs.'

'Like I said, "bad bastards". The cops down south managed to stop one bikie gang killing the entire family of some bloke who owed them money. Seriously ruthless. Do you mind if I just check something with you? I can't be too careful.'

'Sure.'

'What's the rego of your car?'

I told him.

'Okay, thanks. Look, I'm afraid I have dropped you in seriously dangerous shit. Let me give you a bit of background just so you know what we're up against. What *you're* up against.

'We've been working for years on what we call TSOC—transnational, serious, and organised crime. It covers human trafficking, child exploitation, drugs, guns, cyber-crime, money laundering, police corruption—costs the country a fortune every year. It's internationally organised, well-financed and managed, but the effects are felt here. Even down to small details like having post office workers on their payroll to get packages around the AusPost security systems. They recruit like a business to get the best people; they train for the work—'

'Yeah, the one called Glebbo was doing some on-the-job training with the other guy, Cyril, teaching him how to cut my finger off!'

'Oh, yeah, they're the ones who bashed me. But they're all the same. They just don't care about the horrific effects their drug trade is having in our community. One bikie gang down south was making $21 million per month. Per month! Do you know how much a kilo of cocaine costs to buy in Colombia? No, of course you don't. It costs $2,300. And that kilogram of cocaine sells on the streets of Brisbane for between $220,000 and $450,000. Since the year 2000, the number of deaths due to methamphetamines has quadrupled, and in Queensland, 39% of cases where children are taken into care involve methamphetamines. Sorry. I don't mean to rant, but these people have got to be stopped!

'And that brings me to you. I put a USB memory stick in the boot of your car. In the right-hand corner. It has some critical and very incriminating information on it about a local villain, a really nasty bastard named Alan Smith. The papers would call him "a drug lord".'

As he spoke, a penny inside my head dropped. So that's what he was trying to tell me when he was lying next to my car and said 'boot'. It was nothing to do with his footwear; he was talking about the back of my car!

He kept going. 'I was trying to get it to my contact in the police—my handler. He's the only person I trust because some of my colleagues on the force are bent, and I don't know who or how many. The information on that stick is sufficient to bring down the whole fucking operation. I'm so sorry, but I was stuck. They had me cornered, and I had to dump the stick before they got to me. Luckily for me, you turned up in the nick of time; otherwise, I'd certainly be dead. Unluckily for you, I have dropped you in the middle of my fuck-up.'

He continued, 'So where does Smith fit in? He is only small-time compared to those people I talked about before. Smith continues to work for RAAF while he tries to build his empire. I suppose he thinks that if he has a job in the air force, he has some sort of "plausible deniability" about the drugs operation.

'He still operates much of his business "old school"—no phones for important deals, so he can't be traced. He conducts his meetings on the beach—they all wear just their budgie smugglers, as though they're going for a swim. It means he and his contacts can see that nobody is wearing a wire or carrying a weapon. But—and it's a big but—he *is* bringing in significant quantities of drugs, so I'm going to have his balls! Every one of these callous bastards that I *can* put away, I *will* put away!'

'What's the information that is so damning?' I asked.

'Probably better I don't tell you—for my own protection as much as yours. It's a bit of a "need to know" situation. All you need to know is that he and his mates, who include the Cannibals bikie gang, are ruthless, violent criminals completely devoid of guilt for the crimes they perpetrate. Sorry, probably a bit melodramatic, but true, nonetheless. Just be *very* careful.' He paused, collecting his thoughts. 'Anyway, I presume they didn't let you go, so how did you escape?'

'They asked me about the stick. Of course, at that time, I didn't know what they were talking about, so that's all I could tell them. There were two of them, Gleb Orlov and Cyril Cooper. They cut my finger off and were going to kill me, but they dropped their guard, and I was able to stab one and shoot the other. They're not dead. In fact, they are both over there on the other side of the room under police guard!'

'What?! Fuck's sake, they're here?'

'Yep, just over there.' I pointed at the curtains. 'Along with the guy I hit in the car as I escaped. One of the staff here told me a police officer was killed, too, in a "shoot-out", as she called it. So you may want to ask the management here to move you to another ward, or even another hospital.'

'Holy crap, what a mess! I'm so sorry. Did she say who the officer was?'

'No, she didn't say. Well, look, you better tell me what you want me to do with this stick.'

'Have you got a cloud account where you can store stuff?'

'Yes.'

'Okay, save it to the cloud. Then contact my handler; his name is Erik Eriksson—not his real name, obviously. Have you got a pen and paper?'

'No, but I have my phone here, if the battery lasts ... it's nearly flat.'

Trent gave me the mobile phone number and email address, and I keyed them into the notes app on my phone, which also stores its data in the cloud. I can retrieve the data from my laptop or iPad if anything happened to my phone. *Can't be too careful.*

'Don't use the email unless you absolutely have to. You never know who is looking at it. When you have made contact, and you are sure it's him, email or text him the link to your cloud account.'

'How can I be sure it's him?' I asked.

'He has two children—ask him who the godparents are. The elder child is called Amy, and one of her godparents is my ex-wife, Sylvie. Tell him you've spoken to me and use the phrase "Mick sends his love to Amy". That's our code for "you can trust me".'

'Mick sends his love to Amy,' I repeated. 'Okay. Look, I better get back. I want my finger fixed.'

'Yeah, and I'm struggling to stay awake with these drugs.'

The curtain opened, and Chau rolled himself in. 'I heard your voice. You shouldn't be here, really, and you shouldn't close curtains—staff can't monitor patients,' he chided.

'Sorry, I know this chap. Coincidence. I'll come now,' I said.

I pulled my drip after Chau. 'See you later, Trent. Get well soon!'

'Thanks, mate. A check of your car rego will give me your contact details—as soon as I get out of here, I'll be in touch. I'm really sorry to drop you in the shit like this—couldn't do this without you.' And with that, he closed his eyes and went to sleep.

Back in my cubicle, Wu was already waiting. Wu said, 'Toby, you could say there's bad news and not-so-bad news. The bad news is, I'm afraid, the damage to the tissue, nerve endings, and blood vessels, as well as the devascularisation caused by the ice, means that your finger is beyond repair. We will take you into a theatre and give the stump a proper clean and just stitch it for now. This will all be done under a local anaesthetic. However, you'll have to arrange through your own doctor to have it properly finished off at some time in the near future, probably with a small graft. We'll give you some painkillers to take with you. You'll have to go to your own doctor to get the bandages changed, and he or she can check the wound is healing nicely. As for your ribs, that's the not-so-bad news—you have small cracks in two ribs, no other organ damage. There is nothing we can do in the way of strapping, but the painkillers for your finger will help with the soreness in your ribs. Do you want painkillers now?'

I nodded.

'Okay, I'll organise that. Do you have any questions?' he asked.

'Yes. When are you likely to get me into theatre?'

'I reckon we could do this in an hour or so.' He turned to look at Chau, who nodded. 'It won't take long. I have a spare slot then, in my diary.'

'Okay, thanks, doctors.'

As Wu and Chau left, they pushed the cubicle curtains wide open.

I waited until they had gone and shuffled over to close them again. I stayed hidden in my cubicle so Glebbo and his boys wouldn't see me. I didn't check what state they were in—considerable pain, I hoped. I heard the wardsmen taking Trent next door somewhere—maybe for an operation or scans. I was sore, but it was tolerable. I had time to relax, now that the pressure was off, and review all that had happened to me.

I lay on the bed and pulled a blanket over me. I thought about my wife, Hannah. She would still be at work, and I needed to ring her. Time was going by, and I wanted to tell her about the mayhem of the day. I wanted to explain what had happened face to face. However, I knew as soon as I rang her, she would come straight to the hospital, and I didn't want her here if Glebbo and Co found out I was here and were well enough to do something themselves or call for backup. I realised the hospital staff might not let me go without someone to drive me, so I thought I would leave it until I came out of theatre—there should still be time before she left work for home.

The nurse came in to give me some mild painkillers.

I said to her, 'Do you have a phone charger that'll fit this that I could borrow for a little while? My phone battery is almost completely flat.'

'Yes, it's my own, so please remember to give it back before you leave. I'll just get it.'

I plugged the phone into the cable and the charger into the socket.

I started considering the options for what I should do once I got out of the hospital. I didn't get far with my planning, as the painkillers, warmth, and comparative safety of the environment did their work, and I fell asleep.

I woke after a couple of hours when a nurse arrived to tell me I was going to theatre. I was feeling much better—rested, refreshed, relaxed. The relaxed part only lasted a few seconds before I remembered what faced me over the next few hours and days. Still, the sleep would have helped.

Chapter 8

The rest of the afternoon went as Chau had described. They took me to theatre, did their medical stuff, and took me back to my cubicle.

Chau came by to check on me. He explained the painkillers they were going to give me to take with me. Not long after that, a nurse came in to take out the cannula, gave me the packet of painkillers with the explanation again, and asked me who was going to collect me because she recommended not to drive for twenty-four hours after my anaesthetic. I assured her I would be fine as my wife was going to drive me home, without mentioning that I intended to drive the Commodore. She told me I could go. So, I unplugged the charger and took it back to the central area and gave it to the nurse who had lent it to me.

I dialled Hannah, told her I was in hospital and had had an accident with a saw but was fine. I was very circumspect about what I told her because the cubicle had only paper curtain walls. She wanted more details immediately, but I repeated that I was fine and would tell her everything when she arrived. She would leave work immediately and come to the hospital. There was only one road in and out of the hospital complex, so I decided to walk down to meet her as she arrived. That way, there would be less chance of Smith's thugs seeing her and the car.

I walked to the multi-storey car park and positioned myself to wait where I could see her dual-cab ute drive in. I walked up the open staircase as she progressed around the floors until she found a space, and I walked down the car park to her. I was approaching the car as she got out. She ran around the car to me and gave me a big hug. I groaned with pain, and she jumped back, apologising.

'I thought you said it was just your finger. What's happened? Are you all right, Toby?' she asked.

'Let's get in the car, and I'll tell you.'

She was absolutely stunned when I recounted the story of my experiences that day. Of course, I got into mild trouble for not ringing sooner. I explained that I was concerned in case Smith and Glebbo's reinforcements turned up, but she was having none of it.

It was important that none of Smith's thugs picked up that she was with me, but I needed her to know before we left the car park what was going on and the danger in which I had put us both. Also important to me was to hang on to the two guns and phone that I had taken from Glebbo and Cyril, which were still in the Commodore.

I asked her to drive home and said I would follow her in the old white Commodore.

'No,' she said. 'You're not driving anywhere with your hand like that.'

'Okay, but I want the guns out of that car in case we need them.'

'Why do you think we'll need them?' she asked, rather horrified.

'Because these people are very dangerous, Hannah. The drug dealer and his mates have contacts in the police, and they may find out where we live. I don't want to be a sitting target if they show up. Who knows what they'll do? They're all fucking homicidal nut cases! Look, I'll drive it just away from the hospital, and you stop in a side street where we can dump it. I'll come to you, and you can drive home. How about that?'

'Okay. Let's go.'

I got out of the car and walked back down the stairs and straight to the Commodore. Hannah set off out of the car park. There was a parking ticket on the windscreen, which I pulled off and tossed into the car as I sat in it. The thought of Glebbo receiving a fine for illegal parking brought a smile to my lips.

I sat in the Commodore, started the engine, and gave Hannah a moment or two to get out of the hospital and onto the main road. Pulling out of the doctors' car park, I drove to the exit and spotted Hannah up the road. As I turned into the traffic, she pulled out ahead of me. We drove through the built-up suburbs of Brisbane, out towards Samford. We hadn't driven far when I noticed that the little red hatchback from this morning was following about four cars back.

Hannah turned into a side road that had cars parked outside the houses. She flashed her hazard lights at me, and I pulled into a space and parked. I pulled the two guns and phone out of their hiding places, put the phone in my pocket, tucked one gun into my belt, and the other I put up under my arm inside my shirt so I could clutch it against my good ribs. I pulled my shirt down over them and checked in the mirror to see if Hatchback Man was still following—he had pulled in near the turn-off from the main road. I would have to do something about him.

I walked along the road and hopped into the front passenger seat of the ute, and Hannah pulled out. I drew the bigger gun under my arm out from under my shirt and laid it on the footwell. One thing was certain: we weren't going to outrun or outmanoeuvre a hatchback in a ute. I leaned right forward so I could see in the door mirror—the red hatchback was behind us. I told Hannah about him.

She said, 'We'll have to lose him, or he'll follow us home.'

'Yes, pretty soon, too. We don't want them to get even a sense of where we live. Although, with contacts in the police, they can probably find out very easily.'

I didn't realise then how true those words would be.

My phone rang. I looked at it, and the number was 'Unknown'. I touched the button to send it to voicemail. A few seconds later, the phone pinged to tell me I had received a voicemail message. We listened to the message on speaker. It was Senior Constable Golni Gadma from the Queensland Police. Gadma wanted to talk to me about an incident earlier that day at the Woolooma shops. She believed I may have been there, perhaps had seen something, and would very much like to talk to me. She left her number.

'How do you think they got your number?' asked Hannah.

'They probably traced it through my car rego. Maybe they are calling all the people whose cars were nearby this morning.'

'What are we going to do about the red hatchback? He's still behind us.'

'Pull into that car park in front of those shops. Make sure he is following and go slowly.'

Hannah drove along one row of cars. I said, 'Okay, turn right at the end and stop. Then go and park. Count slowly to fifty, then leave as fast as you can. I'll call you when I've sorted this bloke out.'

I opened the glove box and pulled out a folding multi-tool we kept there.

'What are you going to do?' she asked.

'I have a plan,' I said and quickly dropped out of the ute below the level of the windows and hustled between the cars so I was on the blind side of Hatchback Man.

Hannah moved forward, turned right again, and manoeuvred into a parking space. Hatchback Man stopped sharply—he didn't want to get too close. He reversed up and into a spot.

Crouching, I ran as quickly as I could with my ribs complaining, around the outside of the parked cars until I was near to his car. I peeked over the boot of the car next to me and saw the Hatchback Man sitting watching Hannah. Keeping low, I crept along the cars until I was behind the car immediately next to Hatchback Man and opened the knife blade on the multi-tool. He was, I hoped, too engrossed in watching Hannah to notice me in his door mirror. I crawled around the corner of the car on my left and into the gap between it and the hatchback on my right. The nearside rear tyre deflated with a low pop and a blast of air as I jabbed the blade into the tyre wall. I pulled the knife out, stood up, and ran in the opposite direction from where Hannah was, carefully folding the blade back into the handle.

Hatchback Man had obviously heard and felt the tyre deflate. He jumped out of his car, looked at me, and looked at Hannah, who was just pulling out of her car park space and turning towards the exit. Undecided what to do, he paused for a crucial few seconds. Then, he set off after me.

Now, I was pretty fit for an older bloke. I could run better than six minutes per kilometre for an hour—say, ten to twelve kilometres per hour. Of course, over a short distance, I could go a bit quicker than that, even with broken ribs, especially when there's a paid killer with a gun chasing me!

I reckoned I had a ten-second start on him before he really got going, so two things would be true. One, I was about thirty-to-forty metres away, which should be far enough away to make it unlikely he could shoot me with a handgun—at least, that was my understanding of the accuracy of handguns from the movies. And two, he wouldn't be able to catch me on foot. As I had a forty-metre lead over him, he would have to sprint nearly a hundred metres in twenty seconds to catch me. For anybody who hasn't trained for it, a hundred metres in twenty seconds is pretty quick. From my brief glimpses of him, he looked fairly stocky. I've been overtaken by plenty of stocky, younger guys at my local park run, but I was willing to bet this bloke wasn't an athlete. Unless drinking schooners of draught beer at the pub counts as athletics.

Chapter 9

Senior Police Constable Golni Gadma had been personally selected for her current role. Normally in the police service, as with all parts of the government, selection for a particular position is based on merit. At least, that was how it should work. The person who got the job should be the best person for that job. Of course, it didn't always work like that: favourites, nepotism, 'jobs for the boys', shagging the boss, failure of the system—there were all sorts of reasons the best person didn't get the job.

Then there were the jobs that can't be advertised. You never saw adverts that said, *'Vacancy: Undercover Operative Required for Dangerous Role. Deceive your workmates, watch what they do, check if they are honest, collect evidence against the corrupt ones, turn them in, give evidence in court to try to convict them, and put the scumbags away in prison. No time wasters, please.'*

Jobs like that don't get advertised. The best person for the job goes through a different selection process, one where their behaviour over the years has been monitored by a certain few, where their arrest and conviction record stands as a testament to their policing abilities, determination, and integrity. These people seem to have a very clear line in their heads for what is acceptable and what isn't, exercising their discretion with sure-footedness. Known for refusing to take the envelopes of cash that occasionally appear at their workspace, they often work longer hours than their colleagues and seem to have no life away from work. They will socialise with their work buddies, but they won't mix with the very few who are known, or even suspected, to be on the take.

Gadma had been approached some weeks before by the people who select officers for such undercover work. It was one thing to work undercover in the community; it was completely another to work undercover within the force. There were suspicions that a member or members of a particular section were involved with the illicit drugs trade in the Brisbane and Gold Coast area. Gadma was asked to go undercover in that section to see if she could find any evidence of corruption. This would naturally be in addition to holding down the normal job in the section for which she had, apparently, been selected.

The section under suspicion had a vacancy and, being a very able officer, Gadma got the job. On merit, of course. Although it may have helped that one of the selection panel was from the management team responsible for investigating the corrupt officers. Before she was transferred into the new section, she received a briefing on all the information available at that time. There wasn't much—mostly rumour and hearsay. She also received a little information about other undercover officers working in the same sector of the industry, among them Mick McInerney, AKA Trent Kipek.

Gadma was given the 'safe phrase' with which undercover officers could identify one another.

As part of her normal, routine work, Gadma had been out to the shopping mall where someone had been bashed, and she was now back in the office following up on some leads. As far as she was concerned, the person bashed appeared to be just a member of the public since, at that time, she didn't know his identity. She wanted witnesses and so had noted down the registrations of the cars near where the incident took place. A couple of constables had been tasked with talking to the owners as they returned to their vehicles, but she wanted to check independently to see if any of them rang any bells in the system.

She went to the office kitchen to get a glass of water and then sat down at her workspace with her list of regos. She entered the car registrations in the database and worked her way through the list, trying to find phone numbers for the car owners.

Gadma noted the relative positions of the various vehicles and worked her way down the list, starting with the cars nearest to where the bashed person was found. First on the list was, she guessed, the car that the bashed member of the public was driving. The car was an old Honda with a sun-blistered bonnet, but the police computer system revealed the number plates belonged to a Ford. That was very odd, she thought. Definitely worth a follow-up, and she set that one aside for now.

The next car, right beside the Honda, was a Jaguar F-pace registered to a Tobias Richmond of Samsonvale, Queensland. She tried his mobile phone number. She got no reply, so she left a message on his voicemail for him to call back. And on she went down her list.

Her next contact was a lady who had seen the whole thing, so she said. Yes, she had seen the grey-haired man and the nice lady trying to resuscitate the poor man who had been bashed. Yes, she watched the paramedics arrive. The nice lady and the grey-haired man gave way to the paramedics and backed away into the small crowd of people packed around the car. She couldn't say how many. Ten? No, she didn't remember any of them. Wait, yes she did. A bloke in a yellow hi-vis jacket pushed past her. No, she didn't remember anything else about him. No, she didn't notice anything else that happened. Wait, yes she did. The grey-haired man helping the poor bloke who had been bashed went off with the bloke in the hi-vis jacket and another bloke. That was all she remembered. Yes, if she remembered anything else, she'd call.

As she was talking, Gadma checked her emails to see if there was anything urgent. There was one from the forensic lab about the bloody hammer they'd found by the victim. *Please ring—there's significant news.* Once she'd disconnected from the nice lady, she rang the person whose signature block was at the foot of the email.

'Yeah, well, mixed news, I'm afraid. First, the identity of the person who was beaten half to death is Trent Kipek.'

Gadma almost choked on her water. 'Say that again?'

'Trent Kipek. Do you want his address?'

'No, no, I'll get it later. Okay, go on.'

'Do you know him?'

'No,' she lied. 'Some of my water went down the wrong way.'

'The good news is that all serving personnel in the Australian Defence Force, the Federal Police, and the State Police services have to have their fingerprints and DNA samples taken when they join so they can be identified if only body parts of them are found. So we've identified two of the three sets of prints. I think you can guess where I'm going with this. Unfortunately, the evidence may have been compromised.'

'How?' she replied.

'Well, Golni, there are lots of fingerprints all over the hammer, and they come from at least three people, as far as we can tell. But one of the prints is from a cop who must have touched the hammer. He must have been really sloppy when the evidence was being collected.'

'Got a name?'

'Yeah, Cyril Cooper.'

'Oh, what, seriously?'

'Yeah, why?'

'He wasn't at the incident at the shopping mall. At least, that's what we thought. He was in the shoot-out at the house in Woolooma, was stabbed by somebody, we don't know who at the moment, and was arrested for shooting the police officer. Any news on him, by the way?'

'Yes, I'm afraid he subsequently died in the ambulance. Was pronounced at the hospital.'

'Oh, what? Who was it?'

'Erik Eriksson.'

'Oh, no!' Gadma was horrified. Erik Eriksson was her direct line manager and 'handler' for her undercover work. She fell silent as she tried to compute what all this might mean.

The forensics guy said, 'So, sounds like you knew him?'

'Yeah, well, nah. Knew of 'im.'

Gadma dragged her concentration back to the phone call.

'Cyril Cooper's now in hospital under police guard. And you say his prints are on the weapon that put this … Trent Kipek in the hospital?' She paused slightly at his name to make it sound more as if she didn't know him and was checking her notes for his name.

'Yes.'

'What's the other name you know?'

'He's a serving member of the Royal Australian Air Force. Flight Sergeant Gleb Orlov.'

'Fair dinkum?' Golni checked her notes to confirm. 'Okay, he was in the shoot-out as well. And he was shot twice. He finished up in hospital under arrest and under guard. What about the third person?'

'Can't help you there, except his prints were probably the last ones on the hammer because they were only in the blood and were as clear as.'

'Okay, thanks, mate.' She hung up.

My God, she thought. *What does all this mean?* Trent's cover must have been blown, and perhaps Eriksson's as well.

She always thought of Trent as Trent rather than Mick so she wouldn't use his real name inadvertently. How did they find out about Trent? What gave him away? And Eriksson. Why was he there? Was it just coincidence? Or did Cooper and Orlov know his real job and lure him there to take advantage of the situation and kill him?

That accounted for the Honda with the Ford number plates. She knew that was what some undercover police officers did—drove cars with fake plates because it was like a badge of honour with the underworld crims. It had the added benefit of not being traceable back to his real identity.

Gadma thought about the train of events. A hammer with Cyril Cooper's prints on it was used to beat Trent Kipek almost to death at Woolooma shops. She knew Trent. Not exactly a friend—people in her line of work tend not to form strong friendships. But he was as much of a friend as undercover cops can have friends—and, in fact, she was working with him on this undercover operation. Soon after Trent was bashed, Cyril Cooper was involved in some trouble in a house a few streets away, where he got knifed. Then he killed another police officer and was arrested. Plus, there was that strange report from a woman who reported a guy in her office car park with his finger cut off—did that fit in with any of this?

She rang forensics again.

'Yeah, Golni,' he replied.

'Can you ask whoever is working the scene at the shops to call me when they have a moment, please?'

'No worries.'

'Thanks.'

A few moments later, her phone rang.

'Golni Gadma,' she replied.

'G'day, Golni, it's Jake from the forensic lab. I'm at the Woolooma shops.'

'Hey, Jake, thanks for calling back so quickly. What's the news?'

'Not much to say, really. As you know, we found the hammer that will probably turn out to be the weapon. It's being examined now.'

'Yes, they got some prints off it. What I'm interested in is the cars.'

'Well, we're going to take the Honda back to the lab for a proper look. The owner of the Jag just came back—'

'What? Has he been at the shops all day?'

'No, it was a "she". She was here not five minutes ago. She said her husband had been called to an urgent meeting before he could get his car out from the crime scene, and she had collected him. Her name is Hannah Richmond. Do you want her number?'

'Yep.'

He read it to Gadma.

He continued, *'She took the shopping we had kept in our van. We found it near the incident, but nobody claimed it, so we just stashed it. Then she got something out of the back of the Jag, and left.'*

'What did she get out of the Jag?'

'I don't know, something small. Looked maybe like a USB memory stick?'

'Thanks again, Jake.' Gadma rang off.

Gadma went down the office to her boss's office and knocked on the door.

Danal waved her in. 'Howyagoin', Golni?'

'The bloke bashed in the car park at Woolooma shops is connected to our Cyril Cooper and the shooting incident at the house in Ladar Street.' She explained what she had found. 'This chap, Tobias Richmond, plays good Samaritan, helps save the life of a stranger, and then is seen disappearing off with two other blokes. The witness says one of the guys is wearing a yellow hi-vis jacket. Cyril Cooper was arrested wearing a yellow hi-vis jacket. But Richmond's wife says Tobias didn't stay because he had to go with her to an important meeting. If you were Richmond, wouldn't you want to know what happened? Even if it meant getting to your meeting a few minutes late? And if he's a fine, upstanding member of the community, you'd think he'd want to give a statement to us. This Richmond smells wrong, boss. I want to bring him in now and see what we can shake out of him about all this.'

'Definitely. Where is he now?'

'Well, I suppose he's at home.'

'D'you know where he lives?'

'Yeah, 340 Goondiwindi Close, Samsonvale, which is out beyond Samford.'

Gadma's boss considered this for a moment. 'Okay, Golni. That's out in, like, Woop Woop, so it's a bit of a trek, and in that area, it's likely to be, you know, on a few acres of land. House number is 340, so he's three-point four kilometres up a street that is a "close", so there's only one way in and out.'

'I think he's, you know, not going anywhere for now. We'll leave it until the morning because I don't have any bodies left over to go with yous—they're all working on the Eriksson shooting—and I don't want you trying to bring this bloke Richmond in on your own in case it turns, you know, ugly. I'll put someone on it with yous tomorrow, first thing.'

Gadma started to move to the door, but her boss stopped her. 'And. I want to know who he's talking to and where he is. So, start the paperwork to get a warrant to, you know, like, monitor Richmond's phone.'

'Okay, boss.' Gadma hesitated. 'And one more thing, boss. Not sure what it means at this point, but Richmond's wife came back to the car and took what looked like a USB memory stick with her.'

Danal thought about this and, apparently, drew no conclusion. 'Okay. Keep me posted.'

She walked back from her boss's, wondering how she could move this investigation along and maybe jump a few steps ahead. They seemed to be behind at every turn and always on the back foot. She wanted to get on the front foot, take the initiative away from the bad guys. It felt as though whenever they learned some information, the bad guys already knew it.

Danal had told her to get a tap on Richmond's phone. She called up the appropriate form on her computer and filled it in, requesting a tap, location tracking, and any history or recordings for incoming and outgoing calls for the last seven days. That should give her some idea of the normal phone usage and, by implication, what had changed in the last few hours—who had he spoken to since this all blew up? She emailed it off to Danal for countersignature.

Chapter 10

Hatchback Man bolted after me and made a good fist of it for about twenty metres. He was gaining fast, but he quickly ran out of steam and gave up. I ran down the line of cars, grunting with pain every time my right foot hit the ground, looking for some way out. Glancing back, I saw him aiming his gun at me. At that range, I thought he would miss, but I wasn't so confident I'd bet my life on it. I ducked down behind the nearest car and crouched, looking through the windows toward where I last saw him. He had his eyes fixed on the spot where he had last seen me. I scuttled from car to car, zig-zagging at right angles to the direction I had been running. Pausing again, I risked a look through several car windows. He was jogging to the place I had first hidden. I stopped behind a van and lay on the ground, looking under the van to watch which direction Hatchback Man's feet were moving. Realisation quickly dawned that if he did the same thing I was doing, he would see me immediately. So, I decided to keep moving as low as I could as quickly as I could. The trouble was, he could move a lot quicker than me because he could run upright.

The window of a car beside me shattered, and I heard the crack of the gun at the same instant. *Okay,* I thought, *that has upped the risks of the police being called, so I'll have to find a longer-term solution as quickly as I can because I can't outrun him.*

I noticed an open-topped 4x4 a few rows away and made my way carefully to it. Tentatively peering through the windows of the car next to the 4x4, I saw Hatchback Man a few rows away, jogging towards me. I wouldn't be able to climb in because he would see me, so I dropped to the ground and slithered quite easily under the 4x4, which had raised suspension and fat, knobbly tyres for off-roading. I opened the spike blade of the multi-tool. My old dad would have said it was for taking stones out of horses' hooves—you think of crazy things at the strangest moments! Then I rolled up on my left side. I saw Hatchback Man's feet walking in a zigzag as I had done between the cars. He turned to creep slowly down the side of the 4x4 under which I was hiding—I sensed he knew he was close. I hoped he wouldn't choose this moment to look under the cars. I measured his steps and, at the stride when his leg would be stationary nearest to me, I jammed the spike into his calf muscle with all the might and leverage I could muster—which wasn't much from under the 4x4 with cracked ribs. However, it pierced his calf and stopped suddenly as the point hit a bone. He screamed in agony. I groaned with pain from the kicking to my ribs, let go of the multi-tool, and rolled out from under the 4x4 as quickly as I could on the other side. I pushed myself to my knees and glanced over the side of the 4x4 by the rear wheel very quickly, just up and down. He didn't see me. He was still shouting and grunting, head bent low, looking at his lower leg, mouth open with shock and horror on his face. Then he stood upright and started firing his gun. A couple of shots went almost straight down into the 4x4, then several more through the 4x4's seats and the bottom of the car ricocheting off the surface of the car park in all directions. Fortunately, none of them hit me.

I lost count of how many shots he fired—I didn't dare move in case he just swung his arm up and shot me. He must have emptied the magazine into the 4x4 hoping he would hit me underneath it, because I heard the click of the trigger being pulled and nothing happening. Time for me to leave!

I stood up and ran as fast as I could before he could reload. After a short distance, I checked behind and saw he wasn't following. I slowed to a more sustainable pace for another couple of hundred metres and checked again. No, he was nowhere to be seen—I was certain he was not following me. I ducked into a shop. I rang Hannah, told her where I was. She arrived a few moments later, and I got gingerly back into the ute, my ribs complaining.

As soon as she had the car moving, she said, 'Were those gunshots I heard?'

'Yes.'

'Oh, Toby! This is nuts! We have to get the police involved in this; we can't do it on our own!'

'I'd like nothing better, but do you know which cops are crooked and which aren't? We could easily report it, and the officer who comes to help us could be one of Smith's thugs. No, for the moment, we have to keep clear of the police and Smith's henchmen.'

'Where are we going?' she asked.

'Let's go to the Woolooma shops and pick up my Jaguar. We need to recover that memory stick.'

'You're not driving, Toby.'

'Two cars, two drivers. No worries.'

'You're not driving. We'll leave my ute there, and I'll drive you in the Jag.'

We circled the car park at the shops and quickly realised that taking the Jag wouldn't be possible. There were several police vehicles dotted around, some with blue and red lights flashing. My car was cordoned off with police tape, and forensic operatives worked the area. We parked and agreed that Hannah would go and see if she could take the car—it looked doubtful. I gave her my keys.

I stood next to the ute and watched as she walked towards my car. There were several people inside the police tape looped around cars in a big rectangle three or four away from mine. One of the officers was walking up and down the rows with a thing that looked like an iPad mounted on a handle with a small, rotating cube on the front. I guessed it was some sort of laser or lidar scanner to record images of the crime scene.

Hannah ducked under the police tape, walked to the Jag, and I could see her talking to one of the people dressed in a one-piece white suit. The person in the white suit wrote something in a notebook. I watched them walk to a nearby white van, and a few seconds later, she moved to the Jag. She opened and closed the boot and returned with the shopping, and put it in the back seat.

'Did you get the stick?' I asked.

'Of course I did; don't tell me my job!' She laughed, holding up the stick for me to see. 'They wanted to know where you were. I told them you hadn't been able to stay, as you had to get home for an important video meeting, and I had picked you up because you couldn't get your car out during the incident. I asked if they knew what happened to the shopping you bought. They had, very kindly, stashed it in their car. I asked if I could retrieve something from inside your car, smiling sweetly. As it was inside the car and the car had been closed up the entire time, and I could open the boot remotely without touching it, they didn't mind, and here we are! They said the police want to talk to you about the bloke who was bashed. And what you have to do to get your car back.'

'And they believed all that?' I asked, slightly incredulously.

She looked indignantly at me. 'Of course! Now, let's go home. I need a glass of sav blanc!'

Chapter 11

After Gadma had left his office, her boss, Danal, considered what he should do with the information about the bashing at the Woolooma shops and the shoot-out at the house nearby. Danal was forty-five years old, 1.76 metres tall, and average build for an Aussie of his age and height—which meant he was somewhat overweight. However, when he stood in front of the mirror in his jocks that morning, he deluded himself that he was still a fine figure of a man. He dialled the number of his boss, Senior Sergeant Smiggins; a smarmy bastard—Danal never liked him. Always so prim and proper in the way he dressed and talked. Bright-coloured shirts and flowery language that Danal didn't understand half the time.

When Smiggins answered, Danal said, 'Sir, it's Danal. You asked me to keep yous updated on the Woolooma shootings and the bloke that was bashed at the shops—seems they may be connected.'

After Danal had briefed Smiggins, he noticed Gadma through the glass panels of his office approaching—he waved for her to come in. She wanted the phone tap on Richmond approved, and she just wanted to remind him to look at his emails for the link to the approval that needed his authorisation so she could send it to the legal branch for processing. He logged in to his computer and gave it the electronic approval. Legal might take fifteen minutes if he hurried them along—if he told them it was, like, urgent, an investigation in progress. They should have the information from Telstra downloading in no time.

Having dealt with Gadma, Danal stood and moved from his desk to shut the door so his thinking would not be interrupted and his phone calls would not be overheard. No matter how colossally dull Danal thought Smiggins was, he realised that Smiggins was an effective manager of the Cannibals Motorcycle Club and worked the distribution network of drugs on Brisbane's south side and down the Gold Coast. Danal knew a bit about the ring of pushers and dealers that Smiggins was running, but he needed to know more. He concentrated, trying to put together the bigger picture of all the titbits of information he had gleaned from various sources over the past weeks about that sneering toerag Smiggins's drug operation.

Danal also had a little info that would benefit the Dogs about a potential drugs bust-up in Mooloolaba.

Danal had been building a relationship with the leader of the Rabid Dogs Motorcycle Club. Danal thought the use of the words 'Motorcycle Club' in their name was big-noting a bunch of, you know, like, fucking lowlife bikie thugs who'd kill and eat their own grandmothers for an oil-stained leather jacket. *Well, they are cannibals,* he thought and smiled at his own joke. He had been tipping off the leader with useful information about, like, proposed police action against the Dogs, which had been greatly appreciated by the Dogs, allowing them to avoid some situations that could have proved very tricky.

Danal didn't like the bikies one bit. But he knew he needed the Rabid Dogs because he had been planning to, like, take over the Cannibals' operation, and he needed the Dogs for their intimate knowledge of the functioning of a drugs network—theirs was on the northside of Brisbane and up the Sunshine Coast—and he needed their irrepressible enthusiasm for violence and bloodshed, especially where the Cannibals were concerned.

'Irrepressible enthusiasm'? Where did that come from?

He thought, *I've been mixing with that sneering toerag Smiggins too much.*

Danal knew the Dogs were always up for any chance to take over Cannibals' turf, which was why he had taken the leader of the Rabid Dogs into his confidence regarding a, like, coup. Wasn't that what they called them? Coups? Danal was planning to get rid of Smiggins and take over his role with the Cannibals.

He decided to discuss with the head of the Dogs the information he had gleaned from various sources over the past weeks about Smiggins's drug operation. The leader of the Rabid Dogs liked to call himself the Big Dog, which Danal thought was a bit wanky, although he would never tell him that to his face—Danal wanted to keep both his legs in working order.

He looked up and glanced around the office to confirm nobody nearby wanted his attention. Dialling the number on his own mobile, he spoke quietly.

The Big Dog was suitably grateful for the information and that Danal had shared his thoughts on the coup. In return, the Big Dog had confided in him about someone he had planted in the Cannibals' hierarchy. It seemed his snitch was servicing Smith's bike when one of Smith's team had stolen a contacts list from a laptop and passed it to some punter in a shopping mall. Apparently, Smith was as mad as a cut snake and desperate to get the memory stick back.

After the call, Danal immediately spotted the connection to the incidents Gadma had briefed him on only a few minutes before. He thought the moment might be just right for the coup to swing into action, or however you start a coup. If he could get the Rabid Dogs to knock off Smiggins, and if he could get his hands on the stick with the contacts list on it, he could use the information to, you know, take over the Queensland end of Smiggins's distribution chain. He could take control of the whole drug supply on the Gold Coast, Greater Brisbane, and the Sunshine Coast, a population of 3.5 million or so. That would really be worth some, like, violence and bloodshed.

He called the Big Dog back to outline his plans, packed up his briefcase and mobile, and left the building. No time to waste. He must get hold of that stick before anybody else.

Chapter 12

Smiggins put his office landline phone in the cradle when Danal hung up. Smiggins didn't like Danal, who he considered to be a rough, crude, old-fashioned plod who placed too much confidence in his gut instinct and not enough on evidence and procedure, his intellect and evidence. He was uneducated in the strict sense but was, how would one describe it? Street smart—cunning like a rat. Not only that, but he had some very aggravating mannerisms when he talked—it seemed as though every other word was either 'like' or 'you know', and he called people 'yous' instead of 'you'. What a bogan.

Smiggins had no sooner hung up from talking to Danal than one of his two personal mobile phones rang. There were no introductory pleasantries. Smiggins knew who it was likely to be, as this particular phone was reserved for his other 'business'. The person calling him knew this, knew that the caller ID was disabled and knew that Smiggins would recognise his voice, so he just started with, *'We are in deep shit!'*

'Okay, how may I be of service?'

'Have you heard about what happened at Woolooma shops?' asked Smith.

'Yes, of course. I've been briefed.'

'That bloke, Trent, who worked in the office here, stole my contacts list off the laptop. The lads think he passed it on a memory stick to some stranger at the shops' car park. This bloody bastard member of the public turns into some sort of ninja, the way they describe it. He put four of my

guys in hospital! I spoke to him just after he'd dealt with the two lads I sent to get the stick, and he's chatting away, cool as you like. Bastard!'

'Well,' Smiggins said calmly, 'it turns out I can help you. The so-called ninja warrior is a gentleman named Tobias Richmond, and he lives at 340 Goondiwindi Close, somewhere near Samford. We're not going out there to pick him up until the morning. He's all yours before that.'

'*Perfect,*' Smith replied. '*That's great news. I knew you'd be all over it. We need to get that stick back as soon as. And any copies he may have made. So the faster you can get out there, the better.*'

'I can't go! If it gets out that I work for you, they'll lock me up and chuck away the key!'

'*I don't give a fat rat's arse—I have plenty more resources in the police, but I'm running short of people at my end because you so-called cops can't catch this bloke Richmond. You go and take some of your local Cannibals with you. And no mistakes!*'

'Can't the lads do this on their own?'

'*I said "no mistakes". If they go without you, there're bound to be mistakes. So you go, tell 'em what to do, and keep them under control.*' Smith rang off.

That really angered him on several levels. He was vexed that Smith wanted him to deal with the memory stick and the Richmonds. It irked him that he would miss the classical concert at the Arts Centre, particularly as it was Rachmaninov—one of his favourites. He was meant to be meeting his wife in a few minutes, so she would also be pissed off with him. He would get shit from her for missing the concert, which pissed him off even more. *But oh, yes,* he thought, *the silly bitch didn't mind the money that allowed them the best seats in the house.* And what rounded out his pissedoffedness was that he would have to use the Cannibals. If Danal was rough and crude, he was like a polished diamond compared to the dirty, scruffy bikies. They all needed a good shower and shave and a change of clothes!

He phoned around to enlist the assistance of some of the Cannibals and gave the bad news to his wife. For this, predictably, she gave him an earful.

He worked on for a while. He had plenty of time before he was due to meet up with the Dogs. The later they arrived, the better, really. The Richmonds would be all tucked up in bed, and he and the Dogs would have the element of shock on their side.

Chapter 13

Smiggins left the office and drove home to get changed out of his suit and collect his own gun, one that was not traceable to him.

From home, he drove to Samford, where there was a café popular with the motorcycle fraternity with a wide asphalted area used as a car park outside. They congregated there most days, but at the weekend, the car park was packed with people who rode out from Brisbane, and it heaved with people standing around looking at, and chatting about, bikes.

He stopped the car next to four or five motorcycles whose riders were lounging around in a group nearby, and they all turned to look at him as he got out of the car. *A splendid turnout at such short notice,* he thought. He supposed the chance to break a few heads and settle some scores with the Rabid Dogs was a big drawcard.

They were all dressed differently, but all looked, recognisably, the same: jeans and heavy motorcycle boots, some in full black leathers, others just with leather jackets. Black helmets for all. Facial hair was, apparently, compulsory, but the style was left to the individual— moustaches, goatees, full beards. One had shown the initiative to shave his face but for a small circle at the point of his chin—it looked as though he had a small dish brush stuck to his chin. Any unexposed skin was heavily tattooed, and even those followed the Cannibal bikie theme. Show allegiance to the clan. One of them, a barrel-chested, fat-bellied, middle-aged bloke, detached from the group and stepped towards him.

'G'day, Smiggo!'

'Don't call me Smiggo, Dennis,' he replied, sneeringly emphasising the 'Dennis', which he knew would make his point. Dennis preferred to be called by his gang nickname, 'Dezza'.

Suitably chastened, Dezza replied, 'Yeah, righto.'

'First of all, is this all that are coming?' Smiggins nodded towards the group.

'Nah, we're expecting a few more. Maybe two or three.'

'All right, let's go in and sit down while we wait. We'll give them a half-hour or so.'

They all trooped into the café, which was a rev-head's heaven. The whole place was decorated as a tribute to fast cars and fast bikes. The tables were fabricated out of old car doors flattened and welded to legs. The walls were covered in memorabilia: posters of Peter Brock and Casey Stoner, movies like *Bullet* and *Easy Rider*, and superbikes and V8 Supercars from the past. There were old number plates around the shelves, bits of bikes as table ornaments, and some TVs dotted around up in the corners showed old MotoGP and TT races.

The café was a convenient rendezvous, but Smiggins thought the whole place was, to put it bluntly, a tacky-looking shithole. It reminded him of Las Vegas twenty years ago—somewhere you had to visit just to experience the appallingly bad taste. He was hungry and would have liked a snack, but the food, regrettably, was not to his taste either: the hot chips came with too much salt and a small bowl of gravy, and the cakes all looked as if they had been made in a factory from petrochemical by-products. He ordered a couple of pieces of toast and Vegemite and a bottle of water—*Safe enough,* he thought.

Dezza said, 'So, Mr Smiggins, we want to get stuck into these Dogs. Where are they? How many of 'em are there? We're ready for 'em!'

'Well, Dezza, they are at an address not far from here. I don't know how many there are. I have a source in the police control room who I pay a little retainer for such intel. He informs me there may be several, but there is at least one. Though that one may put up a fight.'

'Oh, yeah, we hope so!'

'You are welcome to do to the others, if there are any others, whatsoever your little hearts desire.'

'Can we kill 'em?'

'Yes. Certainly. Kill them all. But, I must emphasise, leave the leader for me. If it is who I think it is, I want him. Do you understand me?'

'Yeah, mate.'

'Make sure your confederates understand, too.'

'My what?'

'Confederates, Dezza. Accomplices, acolytes, collaborators.'

Dezza still looked puzzled.

Smiggins waved his hand around in an arc towards the bikies. 'This group of fine gentlemen who are a panegyric personified, an encomium to the Australian free-spirited, free-wheeling motorcycle rider.'

Dezza looked at him blankly.

Smiggins said tiredly, 'Your mates, Dezza. Tell your mates.'

Dezza brightened. 'Oh, yeah. No worries, Mr Smiggins. What are we looking for?'

'A USB memory stick. I'll handle that part.'

Some more of the 'motorcycle club' arrived. Smiggins said to Dezza, 'Is this it now?'

'Yeah, I reckon. Boggo said he probably wouldn't be able to make it because he and his missus had tickets for some fancy-pants piano thing at the Arts Centre, and she would skin him alive if he didn't go.'

'Oh, yeah, that'd be right,' Smiggins said wearily. 'Let's go. You all follow me.'

They set off from Samford for the Richmonds' place.

Chapter 14

It was dark by the time we pulled around the house and into the carport at the back, which was out of sight from the road. In the car, Hannah and I agreed to tell the boys what had happened—they were adults. It was great to be home—the comfort, the familiarity, the security, the family around me.

We brought in the shopping, the stick, and my new collection of guns and phones. I laid them all on the table, which brought a barrage of excited questions from our sons. I really wanted a glass of shiraz but decided I probably needed to stay sharp, and it might react badly with the painkillers.

I was also desperately tired, and a glass of red wine would knock me out before we finished our story. I wanted a shower and a change of clothes but decided to leave it until later. I did clean my teeth, though. They still felt disgusting from when I had vomited, as though they had fur all over them—seemed like months ago, not just a few hours. Afterwards, I brought my laptop and an external hard drive from the office at the back of the house and fired it up while we sat at the kitchen table and told the boys what had happened during the day. I plugged in the stick and started opening files, and Hannah related the story, with me adding an occasional comment.

Hannah announced, 'Now, about that sav blanc I promised myself!'

'Do you think you ought to? We may need to drive again tonight,' I offered slightly tentatively.

'Really? Why? Where are we going?'

'Well, I don't know yet. But we might need to go out again. Let's just talk it over before we settle down for the evening.'

Hannah started making the supper and sent Will onto the veranda to barbecue some snags.

I spent a few minutes looking at thirty or forty files from the stick. By then, Hannah had finished the mash and veggies, Will was back with the sausages, and I had a pretty good idea of what the information on the memory stick was all about. I had jotted down some of the numbers of contacts that caught my eye and looked up at my son.

'Ollie, please will you do a reverse number lookup on your phone for me? Which country is +441624?'

A few seconds later, he said, 'Isle of Man. Never heard of it. Where's the Isle of Man?'

'Hold on,' I said. 'What about +441481?'

'Guernsey.'

'+352?'

'Luxembourg.'

'+41?'

'Switzerland.'

'How about +93?'

'Afghanistan.'

'+9714?'

'Dubai, UAE.'

'And +98?'

'Iran.'

'And finally, +1284?'

'British Virgin Islands.'

'Okay, the undercover cop at the hospital who gave me this stick said it was related to drug dealing. So here's what I think. If you were a drug dealer, where would you get your supplies of drugs or base chemicals?'

'Afghanistan?'

'Agreed. And then you need to transport them to Australia. The journey could be overland to the Iranian coast, across the Straits of Hormuz by boat to the UAE. They've been smuggling everything imaginable across there for centuries. I bought a Persian rug in Bahrain that had arrived like that. Back in the day, it was Persian rugs—now it's Persian drugs. The UAE number has an address at a place called Minhad, which, I know from my time in Bahrain, is an air force base near Dubai.

'Okay. Then at this end, we have several at addresses in Ipswich, which is near the air force base at Amberley. Now, you need to do something with the profits. That's where the British Virgin Islands come in. I heard once that there are more international companies registered in the BVI than any other country on Earth.'

'Where is the BVI?' asked Ollie.

'It's a little group of islands in the Caribbean, former British Colony, one of what they now call the UK Overseas Territories. They are effectively an independent country, but they still rely on the UK for big stuff like defence. You can register your company there and pay no taxes, register your superyacht on their shipping register, your executive jet on their aviation register, and so on—they offer the whole lot in one financial package. Same for Guernsey and the Isle of Man, also both British. Guernsey is one of the Channel Islands near France, and the Isle of Man is in the Irish Sea between the UK and Ireland. Luxembourg and Switzerland will both let you have so-called numbered bank accounts. They don't ask where your money came from, and more importantly, they won't answer any questions! So when the Australian Taxation Office says to them, "Does Ollie Richmond have an account with you?" they shrug and refuse to comment.'

Ollie smiled.

Hannah said, 'I suppose the drugs are coming from Dubai, that air base called Minhad, to Amberley, which is right next to Ipswich, and the drugs boss, Smith, is using RAAF personnel like Glebbo to bring it off base. It then goes through the distribution network from Ipswich, and all the profit goes to offshore bank accounts. The whole operation is right there in that contacts list!'

I told the others, 'Yes, there are contacts in the Middle East, presumably the suppliers and labs where they make the drugs, the transport chain to Australia, the distributors in Australia, maybe more labs, transport and logistics people, dealers, looks like several in the Cannibals bikie gang, and lots more … I don't know what they do—it doesn't say, and they are using what looks like code names or nicknames.'

'It would certainly mean the end of the drugs operation when it got to the police—the non-corrupt police,' Ollie said.

I saved the whole lot from the stick onto the hard drive in my MacBook. Then I copied the folder onto the external hard drive and, when it had finished, ejected the external hard drive. I then copied the folder to my cloud account. That was a relief because, even if someone took the stick from me, I had backup copies on the computer's hard drive, the external hard drive, and on the cloud account, which would be a server in a cave in a Norwegian fjord or somewhere equally secure.

I double-bagged the external hard drive inside two plastic bags and asked Ollie to put it in the big tool chest in the shed.

I sat and considered where else I might hide the file that was even less likely to be found and yet still accessible. I had a website that I built myself, and I recalled that it was possible to publish pages on it without them being accessible to the public. After a little stumbling around in the web-builder app with new pages and permissions, I published a password-protected page comprising the contents of the contacts list. And the page wouldn't show in search results if someone googled it. I opened my mail app, opened a new email, wrote the password in the email, and sent it to myself.

When Ollie came back in, he switched on the TV in the kitchen. 'Let's see what the news is saying about your gunfight, Dad!'

It was on every channel. They described, in energetic and breathless terms, the shoot-out. There were interviews with onlookers.

'I didn't see any onlookers!' I interjected. 'Where were they when I needed them?'

There was an interview with a police spokesperson, who described what the officers had encountered when they arrived. Apparently, the alleged gunmen fired several times upon the officers, who returned fire. More police officers arrived, and the exchange of fire continued until the perpetrators surrendered and were taken into custody. Three of those arrested were taken to hospital, where they were under guard. He sombrely reported that a police officer was fatally shot. As his next of kin had already been advised, he could reveal that the heroic officer's name was Erik Eriksson.

I went still and stared at the TV.

Hannah looked at me and noticed the shock on my face. 'Toby, what is it?'

'Erik Eriksson was Trent's handler. The only person he could trust, he said. Now he's dead.' I asked, 'Hannah, what does your employer do when someone dies while they still work for you? Do they freeze their email account?'

Hannah replied, 'Yes, I think they have all the connections, email, the internal messaging system, and so on, diverted to someone in the Human Resources area. If they have a company phone and car and any other company-provided equipment like a laptop, those are recovered from the family, and I think they do the same with the phone—it's monitored, too. They answer the calls, texts, messages, and emails and respond appropriately.'

'Okay, so let's say the police do the same with Erik Eriksson. There's no guarantee that if I send an email to him with the password to the hidden webpage, it won't be forwarded to be dealt with by someone who is in Smith's pay.'

'Yes, you can't email Eriksson in the hope that it will go to a clean cop. You have no idea where it will go—much too risky.'

We discussed options for identifying someone we could trust in the police and getting the stick to them.

Will said, 'I don't think we can trust anybody in the police.'

'Why not, Will?' asked Ollie.

'Because you can never be sure that the person you pick is, like, clean. Smith had at least one police officer on his payroll, and Dad, you said the undercover cop, Trent, was concerned that there were others. If Smith had one, he may well have had others. What grade or rank would they likely be? And d'you know what? It could go, like, right to the top, couldn't it?'

'Yes, I suppose they could be any rank—people who would be in a position to look the other way to the drug dealing when looking the other way was required,' said Hannah.

'Okay,' I said. 'So, no police for the time being. Who then? Any ideas? What about going straight to the top—the chief of police, or whatever he or she is called?'

'Would it be useful for Smith to have someone in authority on the payroll? Yes, of course. So, in principle, we can go to nobody in the police, in my opinion,' said Hannah.

'Agreed,' I replied. 'What about the Australian Federal Police?'

Will chipped in, 'Would they be interested? Is it part of their job? The Brisbane drugs scene doesn't sound very, like, "federal" to me.'

Ollie said, 'Don't the AFP deal with international crime? At a federal level? I would have thought they would be interested.'

Hannah continued, 'There is an element of urgency here. We need to get rid of this by giving it to someone who will pick it up and hit the ground running. Our lives are at risk— sorry, boys—but our lives *are* at risk while we have this stick and Smith thinks he can take it from us and solve his problems. Especially if he thinks by killing us all, the trail will go cold. Do you think the AFP will be able to deal with this urgently? They always seemed to me to be sort of governmental, bureaucratic police rather than operational, on-the-beat-type cops.'

'Well, yes. You're absolutely right,' I said. 'We need someone who can take this over and give us protection immediately. In Canberra, the AFP are the beat police, like normal police in the other states, but we're not in Canberra. And don't you think they would want to know a lot more from us before they provide us with any useful information about their operation in Queensland? Like, would they tell us whether they have an active police presence in Queensland rather than administrators, or where their nearest office is and whether it is open at this time of night? You know, I think they are far more likely to say, "Okay, mate, you tell us your problem, and we'll decide if we can help." While we're being shuffled from one Canberra bureaucrat to another, hours could go by. I just think we don't have time to discuss it with them. I think we need an organisation we can present ourselves to in person and get their protection merely by being in their office while we explain the problem. Let's move on. Who else?'

'What about a politician—our local member?' suggested Ollie. 'Or the media—the local TV station?'

I replied, 'They would be very helpful if we were in a position where, for example, we had to bargain with Smith, but they can't provide us with the physical protection we need in the meantime. And don't get me started on federal politicians—they're all about as useful as tits on a bull.'

'Okay, Toby, that's enough of that language,' said Hannah. 'What about the Australian customs, Border Force, or whatever they are called? They deal with drug runners all the time.'

'I'll have a look online and see what it says about them,' volunteered Ollie.

'How about the Australian Defence Force?' I put forward.

'What good would they be?' asked Will.

'Well,' I said, thinking out loud, 'they have skin in this game, with at least one of their staff involved. Presumably, there are others at Amberley involved, too. They have their own military police, independent of

Queensland Police and the AFP. They'll have jurisdiction on the base—I'm pretty sure the Queensland police won't.'

'What do you mean, "jurisdiction"?' asked Will.

'The military, in this case the Royal Australian Air Force, will have authority on the base. It'll be like a separate little country or state—everything that happens on the base will be dealt with under military law. The regular Queensland Police Service probably won't even be able to go onto the base without permission from someone pretty senior in the RAAF. Outside the base, the local police have jurisdiction. That's why the RAAF has their own police force: so they can enforce the military rules on the base. But they won't have any powers off the base.'

'But how can you be sure the argument for the chief of police being corrupt doesn't apply to the senior bloke on the base as well?' asked Will.

'Yeah, well, that's a good point, Will,' I replied.

'I can't find much on the Australian Border Force,' said Ollie. 'The government agencies that we have talked about all have their headquarters in Canberra and only a Canberra phone number. I suppose, when you ring them, they find out what you want and then farm it out to the appropriate place to handle it.'

Hannah asked, 'Is there any sort of command structure, you know, in the "About us" page?'

'No, there's a little bit about what they do, but no real help to us.'

'Can I have a look, please, Ollie?' I asked.

He passed me the laptop, and I viewed a few pages.

'No, there's no command structure, no names of local contacts, no list of office locations, so we can't just go to their office and walk in. They really want to control all initial contacts through the one phone number. What about ASIO?' I suggested.

'What's ASIO?' Ollie asked.

'Yes, good question,' I said.

'And what's a good answer?' he replied.

'The Australian Security ... something or other, not sure. It's the Aussie spies. Let me look it up. Here it is—ASIO, the Australian Security Intelligence Organisation. They do counter-terrorism, among other things, so they must have people on call ready to go to terrorist incidents.'

'But this isn't terrorism,' said Will.

'No, and it's the same deal for contacting them. One phone number for all states. Anyway, they would probably just toss it to the local police, and we don't want that!' I continued, 'I think we have the same problem with all these non-police organisations—we need help tonight, and I don't think they can provide it. The only organisation that can provide the help we need, with the speed we need, is the police, and we can't trust them. Looks as though we are on our own.'

In the quiet pause as we thought about our predicament, we finished our meal, and I cleared the plates into the dishwasher. My hand throbbed, and my ribs ached. I opened the box of painkillers they had given me and swallowed a couple of them with a swig of water.

'What if we give it to several of them at once? They can't all be, like, stereotypical government organisations—"wheels grinding exceeding slow"—can they?' ventured Ollie, making inverted comma signs with his fingers.

Hannah replied, 'No, that's true, Ollie, but then we'd have no way of knowing who is doing what. And when the crooked police find out, we wouldn't know who told them. Not only that, but we might have to deal with several different agencies, and it could get very complicated and go very badly, very quickly. We might have to coordinate with lots of people who are all telling us to do different things. We'd spend all our time on the phone. I vote we make a plan on our own to start with.'

'I agree with Mum,' I added. 'So what are we going to do? What is our first priority?'

'Safety,' said Will.

'Agreed,' said Hannah.

Chapter 15

Gadma decided she would try to find the numbers for other phones at the Richmonds' address: his wife's, maybe parents' or kids'. If Tobias Richmond decided to leave his phone there or, more likely, turned it off, it might be helpful to track the other phones at the premises.

She filled in another form requesting Telstra report all mobile phones that were frequently located at the Richmond address on Goondiwindi Close. Her direct superior, Danal, had already left, so she sent it to his boss, Senior Sergeant Smiggins, for approval, and copied it to Danal. She thought Smiggins was an obsequious, slimy reptile; he made her very uncomfortable. Whenever she spoke to him in person, he would stare at her breasts. Bloody creep.

She started researching Tobias Richmond to see what she could learn about his life. She started with the internal database that combined information from a variety of government databases, things like the registry of births, deaths, and marriages, electoral roll, driving licence and car rego information, military service, national census, and criminal record. Some information she already knew, like the car rego and his date of birth, but other stuff was new, although not particularly interesting—he had a 'blue card', which meant he was able to work with children and vulnerable people. Of more interest to Gadma was that his wife's name was confirmed as Hannah, and he had two boys, Oliver and William, sharing the same date of birth—so, twins—twenty years old. Both Tobias' parents were dead. She searched Hannah and found that her parents were both still alive—she noted down all their details. The electoral roll told her the four of them were the only voters at the address. In Australia, voting was mandatory for every adult, so if there were no other voters listed at the address, in theory, there were no other adults living at the address—at least not permanently.

Facebook, Twitter, and Instagram didn't reveal much. She was looking for his account and then contacts, friends, comments, 'likes', and so on. Anything she could find about him that would build up a bit of a picture of the person she was seeking. There were plenty of Richmonds on Facebook—but she couldn't be sure which one was him. Possibly, he didn't have an account, but without opening every single one, which might take a while, she couldn't think of a quick way to pull out the one she wanted. The trouble with these social media sites was that anybody could use pretty much any name, so he may not even be on Facebook as Toby, Tobias, or T Richmond.

She tried LinkedIn, where he was more likely to use his own full name. She found him and his contact details, which included the mobile phone number, but it wouldn't let her get a list of his connections.

Having exhausted all the easy avenues, and with her tummy starting to rumble, she decided to go to find some food. She left the building and went to the Thai place across the road, where she ordered a short soup and a pad thai to take away. She returned to her desk, pushed off her shoes, drew her legs up under her on the chair, and settled down with her meal.

As she ate, she googled Tobias Richmond and went several pages down the returns, hoping to find something useful. Nothing jumped out at her. She wondered why he had left the scene of that bashing in the shops' car park. And why did he allegedly leave the shops with Cyril Cooper? Cyril got himself stabbed later and taken to hospital. Did Richmond stab him? Was that why he was making himself scarce? And what was the significance of the USB stick? Why did Richmond's wife pick that up? Causation or coincidence?

She considered the arrest of Richmond in the morning and called up Google Earth to look at the premises and then 'Street View' for a, well, view of the street. The boss was right. The house was up a long cul-de-sac, a reasonable-sized house with a pool and a horse-riding arena at the back. There were a couple of sheds and some fences dividing up the property into paddocks. Plenty of room to pull in off the road up the driveway, but not the sort of place to try to arrest someone in the dark—there seemed to be loads of places to hide. Good plan to do it in daylight. One final check of the phone tracker to see he was still at home, and she reached the end of what she could do easily that evening on the Richmond case, so she moved on to tidy up a few emails.

Chapter 16

I wanted everyone to work through the problems together. That way we all, as they say in management-speak, 'took ownership'. So, as we ate our meal, I tried to lead the conversation with some more questions. I started with, 'Are we safe enough here? Do we have to go to a hotel or somewhere else?'

'Who knows we're here?' asked Ollie.

Hannah replied, 'The police. They have your dad's car rego, and they can get the address from that in seconds. And if the police know, then Smith may know.'

'Of course! So we had better leave. Where to?' I asked.

'I don't think we ought to go to a friend's house because we don't really want to draw any of them into this, in case there is trouble,' said Will. 'So I suggest we go to a hotel.'

'What about the beach house?' Ollie offered.

'Noosa's pretty far away,' I replied. 'It's nearly two hours to get there on a good day on the highway. Also, there are really only two roads in and out, and they are both heavily built-up and busy. I think I'd rather be somewhere where we have travel options.'

Ollie, not to be put off, then suggested, 'Why don't we stay here? We know the place inside out, there are multiple ways to get out, we have all we need here—food, water, power, computers, phones—we've got the dog as a warning system, and you can't move without the floorboards creaking.'

'Yeah, all very good points, Ollie.'

Will decided to put forward his opinion. 'I agree with everything Ollie said, except I think this is, like, the first place they are going to, like, look for us. If we want to reduce the risk of them finding us, then we should go somewhere else—I mean, *we* don't even know where we'll be! And there is only one road in and out of here. I think we'd be better off on the road or somewhere else a good distance from here. We can always sleep in the car.'

'Okay, Will, I'm convinced; we have to leave. Get a bag each, put a few clothes together, the laptops, chargers, and so on, anything else you think you may need for, literally, only a couple days. All the guns—how many do we have now? I'm not sure. Anyway, round them up and bring them. Bring all the cash you have, and be ready in five minutes!'

Having collected together the clothes I thought I might need, I stuffed them into a backpack along with my laptop, iPad, the travel extension lead, and a variety of chargers and cables. Taking off my spectacles, I put them into the hard case, which I stuffed into my pocket. My black briefcase was in the kitchen, and I picked it up as I headed out of the house to the ute.

Ollie appeared, carrying a small shoulder bag.

'Ollie, if you are ready, please will you put together some stuff for Merlin? His lead, food bag, bowls, bed, that sort of thing.'

As I put my gear on the floor near the front door to take as I left, I shouted, 'Come on! Let's go!'

I hurried to the back of the house, where Hannah had filled a bag of her own stuff.

'How's Will doing?' I asked.

'He's ready.'

I turned, and Ollie was right behind me.

'Ollie, Merlin's stuff in the back of the ute near the tailgate and load our stuff towards the cab. Quickly! Will, grab the bushfire "go-bag"—it's got useful stuff in it like torches and batteries. And pull four sleeping bags out of the cupboard in the spare room and as many camp beds as you can find in the shed—hurry!'

We congregated back in the living room. Merlin was looking stressed; his head hung low, and he was drooling a little—he didn't like it when we packed bags and loaded the car because he knew he was going to be taken out of his comfort zone.

Suddenly, he came to attention and made a gentle bark. Not even a bark, just a sort of guttural, low-voiced, tentative, *'Oof,'* as though to say, 'Did anybody else hear that? Should I be worried? Do you want me to give them the full business?'

He was standing in the middle of the room. His hackles along the ridge of his shoulders were up, tail pointing out straight, and he was looking at the front door, brow furrowed, tilting his head left and right. At fifty-two kilograms, he was big for a Rhodesian Ridgeback and the gentlest, quietest, most good-natured animal you could wish to meet.

Hannah said to him, 'Who is it, Merlin? Good boy! It's just Will coming back,' as she walked down the corridor towards the front door.

Will ran up the steps of the house and closed the door quickly behind him. 'There's someone here,' he said urgently, 'just parking by the shed.'

Chapter 17

About half an hour after leaving his office, Danal pulled into a servo, parked, and walked into the shop. He put a hot meat pie from the cabinet carefully into a bag with the tongs provided, pulled a bottle of Coke from the fridge, and went to the desk to pay.

The young lady behind the desk said, 'Any fuel tonight?'

'No, just these, thanks,' replied Danal. He waved his card over the payment machine and walked out to his car, tucking into the pie as he went. He sat in his car and waited. He rang Gadma. 'Any location information from Telstra on Richmond?'

'Yeah, boss, he's tucked up at home, by the look of it. He was at the shops where Trent Kipek was bashed, he was at the house during the shoot-out, and he spent the arvo at the hospital. So I'm guessing he was injured at some point, badly enough to warrant treatment. A couple of calls between him and a Richmond, first name Hannah—guessing his wife. Went home via the shops. No calls since he came out of hospital.'

'Okay, thanks. Let me know if he moves.'

A crappy old, scratched-up Harley Davidson Softail from about 2002 came chugging onto the forecourt and stopped next to him.

What a piece of shit, he thought. *Looks as if it's been hand-painted with black emulsion paint.*

The rider dismounted, and Danal wound down his window.

'Shall we take your car?' asked the dishevelled-looking young rider. Across the front of his Nazi-style helmet was the word 'Rabid'.

Presumably, on the back it said 'Dogs'. He pulled the helmet off as he got into the car. His shoulder-length, reddish-brown hair needed a good wash, and his long goatee beard looked as though it hadn't seen a comb in months. He wore a black T-shirt with a washed-out death-head motif, jeans that were more oil than material, and black boots with scuffed toe caps exposing the steel.

Danal looked him up and down with distaste, but the lad was oblivious.

'Yes, get in,' Danal replied and took a long swig of his Coke.

The young man dropped into the seat next to him and said eagerly, 'Where we going? What we doing?'

'I'll tell you on the way.'

They both belted up, and Danal pulled out of the servo into the traffic, leaving Brisbane to the northwest towards Samford.

He had considered waiting for more Cannibals to back him and the lad up, but two things made him press on: first, he wanted to get the stick as fast as possible—faster than the time it would take to get significant numbers of Dogs out there. And, second, the lad sitting next to him might have looked like a scruffy urchin, but Danal knew from experience that he was a very tough, reliable little bastard who, literally, punched above his weight. He was confident the two of them could handle some retired old bloke. However, to be on the safe side, he had asked the Big Dog to round up some of his lads as soon as he could and send them over. You never knew …

Chapter 18

Will hustled into the house past Hannah, who flicked the lights out with a sweep of her hand and then turned the key in the lock. Encouraged and emboldened, Merlin could sense the change in atmosphere. He made another couple of *'oofs'*—a bit louder, as though to say, 'Told you so.'

I said with some urgency, 'Okay, boys, you go into the en suite at the back. If anybody comes into our bedroom through the robe area, you go out through the study. Or vice versa. Hannah, you take this gun and go with them. Try to get out through the back door—you can go left out onto the road or right off the deck down into the big paddock.'

I racked the slide to cock the Glock, the one with the silencer, and handed it to her. 'It's loaded and cocked—just pull the trigger. Keep your finger off the trigger unless you're going to fire the gun. It's a semi-automatic—just keep pulling the trigger. It's got fourteen bullets in it. That little button switches on the LED light, see?'

I flashed it on and off. I grabbed the head torch from the basket on the kitchen worktop and gave it to her.

'What are you going to do?' she asked incredulously. 'Surely you're not going to try to fight them?'

'We'll see. I've got the stick in my pocket. If I get caught, I'll give it to them. I may be able to persuade them to go. Take Merlin and hang on to him.'

Merlin started to bark—proper barking this time, with one bark running into the next in a continuous *'Woowoowoowoo'*.

He sounded very big and frightening—luckily, the intruders didn't know what he was really like!

I followed the others to the back of the house and said to their backs, 'Put the lights out so your eyes have a little time to get accustomed to the dark.'

Hannah unlocked the back door, left it standing ajar, and went into the bedroom.

I followed her into the bedroom and retrieved my little LED head torch, which I strapped around my forehead but didn't switch on. I racked the slide on the gun to cock it and then picked up the baseball bat I kept beside my bed. It was a proper bat, but a smaller version for juniors that we bought one of the boys when he was small. It was printed with the name 'Tee Ball' and 'Louisville Slugger', and the wooden bat hefted nicely in my hand. It made a very good club, which is why I kept it there. Just in case. Never really expected to need it.

There were a couple of heavy *thumps* from the front door, followed by a huge crash as its latch gave way. From the rear of the house, I heard Merlin go completely mad again with his barking. I walked through from the back of the house, the Glock in my left hand, flipping the lights out with my right thumb as I went while holding the bat.

Pressing myself flat against the wall to the side of the kitchen door, I raised the bat above my head with only a slight twinge from my ribs.

I listened as hard as I could. The adrenaline made my body feel as though it was bursting with excitement. I tried to breathe as quietly as I could through my mouth—I wanted to gasp for breath, but I stood, listening, trembling with fear.

I heard the floor creaking gently as one person moved slowly towards the kitchen door where I waited. Then I heard another person out on the veranda, on the side away from the road—presumably so they wouldn't be highlighted by headlights if a car went along the road. The person in the lounge, just out of sight, slowed as he or she approached the kitchen door. I had the benefit of the dark room on my side, and the person was lit from behind from the lounge. I saw the barrel of a gun in the doorway. Slowly, gradually, the barrel came into the room, followed by the rest of the gun, a hand, and arm holding it. The person switched the lights off in the lounge, and I thought, *Now's my chance.* I swung the bat down as hard as I could on the person's wrist. I heard both bones in their forearm snap, and their gun dropped onto the floor with a clatter—I didn't know where it went in the darkness. My eyes had had a few seconds to adapt to the dim light, and I raised the bat again. While the person yelled and swore and clutched at their wrist with their left hand, I stepped into the doorway and swung again at his head—it was a 'he'.

I could hear him now, cursing, 'Fuck! Fuck! Fuck!'

I caught him high on his shoulder at the base of his neck. I went again and again at him, swinging almost blindly, following the sound of his shouts. As he retreated into the lounge, he put his left arm up to protect his head, so I pounded at his left-side ribs. I caught him again and again.

He fell to the floor, curled into a ball, and gave up, shouting, 'Stop! Stop! Stop! Fuck's sake, stop!'

I stopped and looked around for the other person. There was sufficient moonlight and starlight that I caught sight of him to my left, immediately outside on the veranda by the French doors about five metres away. I tossed the bat onto the settee and swapped the gun to my right hand.

I quietly warned the bloke on the floor, 'Don't move, or I'll shoot you.'

I crept slowly towards the French doors with the gun aimed, in the best TV tradition, with my two hands stretched out in front of me. I knew I had two opportunities to shoot this man. Now, straight through the glass doors. If I missed, he would have to run around to the front veranda and down the front steps. From where I stood in the lounge, I could step back one pace and have a shot down the hallway through the front door, which was standing open, to the front steps. I would be able to shoot him in the back. I have always considered myself a man of principle and integrity. Would I be able to shoot him in the back? This bastard and his mate had come armed, ready to kill me. Maybe to kill us all. Was there a primal instinct in some deep part of the brain to protect home and family? Yes, I thought I could shoot him in the back. *However, let me try in his front first.*

I didn't switch on my head torch because I didn't want to dazzle myself in the windows or warn him. I took careful aim at the chest of the shadowy figure outside and squeezed the trigger. The gun made its deafening *crack* and jumped in my hands. The glass of one small pane in the door shattered, but the man didn't move. *Oh, bugger,* I thought. *Missed again.* Before I could fire another shot, he had jumped to his right to hide behind the wall beyond the windows. Okay, still no way out from there except around the veranda past me or over the side of the veranda down a drop of about two metres. But he didn't know how far down it was.

I moved quickly down the hallway to the front door and swiftly glanced around the corner to my left, where he would appear if he was coming. No sign yet. I stood in the hallway with my right arm along the wall of the front of the house and my right eye just out far enough so that I could aim the gun along the wall. I waited. If he jumped, I would hear him. If he didn't, I would see him.

I heard the creaking deck boards as he moved, but he didn't appear. I heard the thump. He must have dropped over the side of the veranda. He obviously realised he would be silhouetted if he tried to pass the windows and decided discretion was the better part of valour. I had all the external light switches near me and flipped on the corner light that shone down in the direction I thought he would go. And there he was, running with a slight limp towards the darkness. I fired a shot at him and missed again. I set off down the steps and, at a gentle trot, circled the outside of the pool fence, the other side from where I saw him, in the hope that I would cut him off before he got to the road.

It worked perfectly; he was in the dark and didn't know the lay of the land. I spotted him looking around, trying to get his bearings. Pausing behind a tall fig tree, again trying to control my breathing, I raised the gun and took aim. He hobbled quickly towards me. When he got to about ten paces away, I shouted at him, 'Stop, or I'll shoot!'

He stopped. Now what? I wasn't sure how to deal with this. Should I shoot him anyway? Should I try to wound him in the leg? I felt absolutely fried—I was panting, and my hands were shaking. My mind was going at the speed of sound, and yet I couldn't think of what to do except shoot him or run away!

Emerging slowly from behind the tree, I cautiously walked towards him, keeping my eyes firmly fixed on him for any sign of a sudden move. I told him, 'Lie face down on the track with your hands behind your head.'

He complied.

I told him, 'Holding the barrel, toss your gun over here.'

This he did.

I took a couple of steps to stand next to him; my intention was to shoot him in his calf muscle. I thought that would be sufficient to stop him moving around, but not enough to kill him. I was too naïve and not careful enough. As I stepped towards him to retrieve the gun, he kicked out sideways and caught me just behind my knee. It wasn't hard, and it didn't hurt, but it was enough to make me stumble. Before I could bring my gun to bear on him again, he was up in a flash and punching and kicking me in a flurry of blows. He kicked the gun out of my hand, and it fell a metre or so away. He dived towards it. I tried to intercept him and drove him sideways away from the gun. I fell on top of him. He scrambled to get the gun; I was almost riding on top of him, trying to pull him back with my arms around his neck. It was not going well. He was much younger and stronger than me.

We rolled around, first me on top and then me underneath with him on top, but both on our backs. He elbowed me in the stomach, which hurt like hell—much more than it would normally because of my two cracked ribs. That was all he needed. I grunted and relaxed my grip on him a fraction, and he pulled my hands away from his neck. While I still writhed in pain on the ground, he got to his feet and swooped on his gun. He swept it up and pointed it at me.

'Where's the fucking stick, you fucking dickhead?' he shouted.

'Here! I have it here!'

'Where?'

'In my pocket. Let me get it for you.'

There was a *crack*. Not loud; a bit like a can of beer opening. In the same instant, the man's chest exploded in front of my eyes. A spray of bits of bone and lung and a mist of blood flew through the air and covered me from waist to head. He toppled as he fell in a short arc to land on top of me. In the semi-darkness, about ten metres away, Hannah crouched with a gun pointing at where the man had been, a small curl of smoke drifting from the barrel. She lifted her arm, still holding the gun, to put her forearm across her open mouth, horror on her face.

I pushed the bloke's body off me and wiped the spots of blood and viscera from my eyes. I eased myself up to a standing position and slowly walked over to Hannah.

'Point the gun down, Hannah,' I said.

She lowered her arm to her side. I reached around her and took the gun. I asked her, 'What happened to the other guy?'

She looked past me, staring mesmerised, at the man on the ground she had just killed.

'Hannah,' I said gently but urgently, looking up towards the house. 'Where's the other bloke?'

She tore her eyes away from the mangled, bloody body to look at me. 'What?' she asked.

'The other bloke. Where is he?'

'The boys are guarding him with the baseball bat and his gun.'

'Okay, come on.' Nodding back over my shoulder, I said, 'They mustn't see this.'

I picked up my Glock and placed my arm across her shoulder as we walked back to the house. 'Thank you for saving my life.'

'I thought he was going to kill you.'

'I'm sure he would have done once I gave him the stick. I was quickly running out of ideas about what to do next.'

'Oh my God, Toby, I killed a man!' she cried.

I hugged her with my arms wrapped around her, her arms down by her sides. She stood stiffly, in shock and horror. After a few seconds, she started to relax, her shoulders sagged, and she tucked her head into my neck. I lowered my head. Her beautiful long hair tickled my face, she lifted her arms around my back, and we held one another tightly.

I whispered to her, 'Don't worry. We'll get this sorted out.'

Chapter 19

We walked back up the steps and went into the house.

I said, 'Boys, one of you go into the study. On the shelf near the toolbox, there are some cable ties. Bring me a few, please.'

They looked around at me together and both said, almost in unison, 'Oh, my God, Dad! Are you okay?'

'Yes, I'm fine,' I replied, looking down at my bloodied shirt. 'It all belongs to the other chap.'

'What happened outside?' Ollie asked. 'Are you all right, Mum?'

'Yes, we're okay, but you are not to go out there.'

Will turned and started towards the study.

'What happened to the other bloke?' asked Ollie.

'Your mum shot him. She saved my life.'

'Mum, are you okay?'

'She's very shaken. Ollie, will you put the kettle on and make your mum a cup of tea, please?'

'What happened to him? Did you kill him?'

'Yes,' she replied quietly.

'OMG, Mum! You're, like, awesome!'

'I had no choice!' she said defensively. 'He was going to kill Dad!' She sat heavily down on the sofa behind her and cried. The tears rolled down her cheeks as she sobbed, her shoulders shaking and her bowed head nodding.

I took her by the hands, pulled her gently up to me, and hugged her again. Then I led her to the rear of the house into our bedroom, and we hugged one another again. She continued crying, and I said quietly, 'Sit down here on the bed, darling.'

She sat and put her face in her hands. I dampened a face cloth in the en suite and gave it to her. She took it and wiped her face.

'I'm okay,' she said. 'Just feeling very wobbly. The adrenaline is wearing off, I think, and the shock of killing that poor man is setting in.'

I wiped my face with the cloth.

'You did a very brave thing, and if you hadn't, I would probably be dead by now.'

'That's why I shot him. I couldn't think of another way to deal with the situation quickly. What will happen to him? What will happen to me?'

'Well, I suppose the police will deal with his body and the other arsehole in the living room. I expect this will be a crime scene, and it will be crawling with forensic experts in no time. I can't tell you how grateful I am and how much I love you. Thank you, Hannah, for saving my life.'

'But why did his body explode like that?'

'There are different sorts of ammunition. The ones I fired today at that bloke in town must have been different because they didn't do anything like the damage the one you fired did. They used to be called dumdum bullets, and I think they were outlawed for use in war back in the 19th century because they did such appalling damage. They have soft or hollow points, I think, which makes them expand on impact. I suppose the Geneva Convention doesn't apply to drug wars.'

'But what do you think will happen to me?'

'I don't know, but I would have thought that there would have to be provisions in the law for people to defend themselves with extreme measures when they are in extreme danger, which this obviously was. If past performance is anything to go by, those guys would certainly have killed us. I think there is little doubt that we took the only course of action available to us. We'll get through this together.'

'Thanks, Toby.'

I tried to lighten the mood and said, smiling, 'And don't worry. I'll bring the boys to visit you in prison.'

She looked up sharply and then realised I was teasing.

'You bastard! You'd better. And remember to bring a file baked in a cake!' She stood up and decisively said, 'Right, let's get on with this!'

We walked back to the living room holding hands. I put the Glock on the worktop as we passed. Ollie handed Hannah and me a mug of tea each. Will came in and handed me the bags of cable ties.

I said to Will, 'Pick up the baseball bat and give him a smack in the head if he tries anything.' And to the bloke on the floor, I said, 'Roll onto your front and put your hands behind you.'

'I can't!' he moaned. 'You've busted my fucking wrist!'

'Oh, eat some cement and harden up, you sooky lah lah. Sit up and hold your hands out.'

He held his hands out. I wrapped one cable tie around his right wrist as close to the hand as I could and tightened it. He grimaced but said nothing. Then I made him put his left hand under his left knee, looped another tie around his left wrist, looped it through the right cable tie, and pulled it as tight as I could.

He grimaced and spat, 'Oh, fuck! That hurts!'

'Oh, stop your whingeing. You only have to worry about whether you will ever have the use of your right hand again. At least they'll use an anaesthetic when they operate, which is more than your pals did for me when they cut off my finger.' I held up my bandaged hand in front of his face. 'Come to think of it, my ribs are a bit sore. Where did I put my painkillers? Would you like some?'

'Yeah, thanks.'

I laughed. 'Well, tough shit, arsehead! You were going to kill us all. You're lucky I don't just drag you outside and shoot you like your buddy.'

'Have you killed him?' he said incredulously.

'Yep, he's as dead as. So, you see, we have nothing to lose now, so I strongly recommend you do as you're fucking well told!'

The cable ties weren't long enough to go around both ankles, so I did the same arrangement as his wrists, putting one around each ankle and looping them tightly together. I pulled his knees upwards so his heels were close to his hands and secured another cable tie through the loop around his left foot and his right hand, near where it was smashed. That would really hurt if he tried to move far. I started going through his pockets and found his wallet. This was becoming a habit for me. *Okay, who do we have here?* I thought as I pulled out a bunch of cards. *Sergeant Danal, Queensland Police: With Honour We Serve.*

Well, what a surprise, I thought. *Another cop.*

I walked back into the kitchen. 'Listen, if anybody has heard the shots and reported them, which is possible since it's been like the St Valentine's Day Massacre 'round here, I reckon we have about fifteen to twenty minutes before the police arrive. Let's get everything we've put together loaded in the ute and get out of here.'

'What are you going to do?' Hannah looked concerned.

'I'm going to check the bloke outside for any identification. I'll be back in a minute.'

As the others turned to busy themselves, I trotted through the house and out of the front door, switching on my head torch as I went. Once I got to the body, I was shocked again by how much damage one bullet had done to him. I didn't know what sort of bullet it was, but I found a small hole in his back, where I guessed the bullet had entered, and a huge hole in the front of his chest where it left. He was a young chap, maybe early twenties, in jeans, boots, messy hair to his shoulders, a straggly, ginger goatee beard, and the remains of a black T-shirt that was dirty even before it was covered in blood. I found his wallet and opened it. *Please, not another copper,* I thought. No, not this time. One Sam Brown, address in a suburb I'd never heard of, Queensland. I looked at the credit cards and the cash. Should I take it and stoop to their level?

Fuck it. It might come in handy later. I took a credit card and exactly $200 in cash. I thought, *Stealing from the dead now, eh, Toby?* My principles had slipped even further. I stuffed them in my pocket. I put the wallet back in his pocket where I had found it, picked up his pistol, and jogged back to the house.

I put on my reading glasses, dialled voicemail on my phone, listened to the lady police officer's message, and jotted down her name and number. I asked Danal, 'Where's your phone?'

'In my left pocket.'

I pulled it out.

'What's the code to unlock it?'

'Why?'

'Because I want to make a call, of course.'

'You just swipe up and hold it in front of my face and it will unlock.'

It opened and I dialled Gadma's number using Danal's phone.

She answered, *'Hello, boss. What's up?'*

Unable to stop myself, I repeated, 'Hello, boss?' I paused, confused, and then rang off. For a few seconds, I just stood looking at the phone and thought about the implications of what Gadma had just said.

Danal interrupted my thoughts. 'Who was that you just rang? Was it Gadma? She's too fucking smart for her own good, that one.'

I dragged my thoughts away and looked at Danal. Why would he be threatened by a junior copper? I was comforted that he felt threatened by her. I hoped that was because she was a straight copper.

I dialled the number again, and as soon as she answered, I said, 'Write this down. My name is Tobias Richmond. I've got a colleague of yours here with me at 340 Goondiwindi Close, Samsonvale. His name is Sergeant Danal. He has a badly broken wrist from me hitting it with a baseball bat, and he's in considerable pain. He'll need to go to hospital, but there's no rush. In fact, take as long as you like. He and his sidekick, Sam Brown, came here on behalf of Alan Smith, who is a corporal in the Royal Australian Air Force at Amberley and is also some sort of a drug dealer kingpin. They think I have something that Alan Smith wants. Anyway, these two lowlife bastards came here to our home prepared to kill my family and me to get it. They very nearly succeeded. Unfortunately for Sergeant Danal, as I said, it didn't work out so well. It was even worse for poor young Sam, who is lying dead on my front lawn. If you work for Alan Smith as well, you'll now know not to underestimate me like these two pieces of shit and the other four I put in hospital earlier today. If you are an honest police officer, which seems increasingly unlikely as this day progresses, then you'll need to up your game. You have a broad selection of corrupt coppers working in your police force, and there may well be more. Either way, Gadma, watch your step.'

I rang off.

I stood and looked at Danal's phone. I thought it might come in handy—you never know—so I changed the passcode to one of my own and put the phone on the kitchen benchtop next to Orlov's. Seeing both phones side by side, it struck me that if one is handy, two must be doubly handy. I unlocked Orlov's phone and changed its passcode as well. I wrote the passcodes on strips of masking tape and stuck them to the back of the phones. Now we had two phones we could use.

I shouted, 'Okay, everyone. Let's finish loading the ute and get out of here!'

The family, carrying final bits and pieces, dashed down to the carport where the ute was parked, and any moment, I thought we would be able to leave.

While the others loaded the ute, I walked around the house and collected the four guns and three phones: mine and the two I had confiscated.

Chapter 20

Having finished her meal at the office, Gadma was still working when her work mobile phone rang and the name of her boss, 'Danal', showed on the screen.

She didn't expect him to be ringing at this time of night, but she answered with a cheery, 'Hello, boss. What's up?'

She listened for a few seconds, and the line went dead. She looked at the phone and started to unlock it to ring her boss back. The phone lit up again with his number ringing.

'Hello?' she said, more tentatively.

The person on the other end started talking as she got the phone to her ear. She jotted some notes furiously. As she was about to speak, the connection was cut, and she looked down at the phone for a second. Well, that answered a lot of questions about Tobias Richmond, she thought. But it posed a hell of a lot more. That wasn't Danal; it was Richmond himself using Danal's phone. He had given Gadma a great deal to think about, not least of which was that he told her that her boss was working for a drug dealer called Alan Smith, and others on the force were also bent. Well, that wasn't news to her in general, but it was as far as Danal was concerned.

She sat and pondered what the hell was happening. She had only been in Danal's office, it seemed, a few minutes ago—when was that? She checked her emails and found that it had been about two hours ago—time flies. Why had Danal gone to Richmond's house? What had he been doing—was he really trying to rob Richmond? How had Richmond overpowered him? Who should she tell up the line of command to get some direction on what she should do next? She didn't think about it for more than a few seconds because she wanted to get out to the Richmonds' place and take a look for herself. She went to her car, programmed the Richmonds' address into the GPS navigation app on her phone, set it into the cradle mounted on the windscreen, manoeuvred her car out of the car park, and headed for Samsonvale.

Once en route, she used the display on her dashboard to dial the number of Senior Sergeant Smiggins—her boss Danal's direct line manager.

'Hello, sir. This is Golni Gadma.'

'Aaah, hello, Senior Constable Gadma. What a pleasant surprise. What can I do for you this fine evening?'

'Some guidance and some help, sir, thanks.' She apprised him of the situation as far as she knew it and asked for assistance out at the Richmond house. She explained that her constables were off duty and, although she had tried to contact them, neither had replied to her yet. He sounded as if he was suitably horrified that Danal was possibly, probably, crooked, but she couldn't see him to watch his body language. He told her to find someone else to come and meet her out at Samsonvale, and he would authorise some backup from the city.

Gadma immediately dialled the number of her friend, Simmo. She'd worked with him on many occasions. He wasn't involved in the undercover group she was in, but she did trust him to the extent that she didn't have any evidence that he was on the take. And she did like him and trusted him to drop everything and help her if she asked.

He did.

'G'day, Simmo, it's Golni. You got this evening spare?'

'No, I'm very busy having an evening off, eating my meal with my feet up, watching TV, and then I'm going to have a substantial quantity of chocolate ice cream.' He knew what was coming. 'So, what is it that's gonna make my pizza go cold?'

'Pizza's always better cold the next day, Simmo. Didn't you know that? Look, I need you at 340 Goondiwindi Close, Samsonvale, right now. I can't find anybody else on my team to help me. I'm going to be there in fifteen minutes or so. Get in your car and call me when you're on the road.'

'I'll just clear it with my boss and be with you in a moment.'

A few minutes later, Simmo rang. 'So, what's the big hurry to get to Samsonvale?'

'We're going out to the home of Tobias Richmond, who rang me earlier. He called me on my boss's phone.'

'Interesting. Why did he do that?'

'Because he had just broken Danal's wrist—he claims Danal was trying to rob him and maybe kill him and his family in the process. Richmond also admitted killing someone named Sam Brown, who was also there with Danal.'

'Well, that's not bad for a quiet afternoon at home, eh?' he replied.

'Oh, no, Richmond hasn't had a quiet afternoon at home. He has spent the day putting people in hospital. Shot, stabbed, run over. I believe Richmond was involved in the bashing of a bloke at Woolooma shops, or, at the very least, he was at the scene.' She didn't mention Trent's name because she didn't know how much Simmo knew about the undercover operation. Nothing, she hoped. 'Then, he says he was at the scene of the gunfight today, where a member of the public was shot, a police officer was stabbed, and another police officer, Erik Eriksson, was killed. Then there was a fourth, or is that fifth, person run down in the street. This bloke Richmond has certainly had a busy day! Where are you?'

'I'm about twenty-five minutes away. You're not going to go in there before I arrive, are you? He may still be there, and if he is, it sounds as if we need all the eyes and ears and guns we can get as we go in.'

'Yeah, totally. I'll wait for you just down the road so I can keep an eye on the house. There's obviously only one way in and out of Goondiwindi Close, so I'll see him if he tries to leave.'

'My guess is, he's already gone,' said Simmo. 'So, who was the officer stabbed, and who was Eriksson? What part of the force were they in? I never heard of Eriksson.'

Gadma feigned ignorance. 'It's possible Cyril Cooper, the stabbee, was involved in a drugs ring—not in a good way. And Eriksson was in the drug squad, apparently. Draw your own conclusions.' She changed the subject. 'I'm with you—I think they will all have scarpered by now. They may be sitting on their couches with a stiff drink waiting for us but, most likely, they will have run for it. I mean, he's admitted to putting five of them in hospital and one in the morgue. But he didn't say that he had bashed the bloke at the shops or killed Eriksson. Maybe he lost count. I don't know, but I believe him. He sounded as though he was telling the truth. Just an innocent bystander. Wrong place, wrong time—the car park at the Woolooma shops. Out of his depth. Correction: possibly not out of his depth, the way he has dealt with the weird shit he's faced today. Anyway, you can't rely on what he said alone, but as much as you can tell over the phone, I think he's fair dinkum. He also claimed that Danal is working for some drug dealer at RAAF Base Amberley.'

Simmo replied, 'What? Two of our guys selling drugs? Bloody hell, that's incredible! Okay, well, look, Golni. We need to be super careful around Danal. If he is dirty, we need to play him exactly by the book. What are the rules? I've never been involved in an internal investigation, have you? Should we put him in handcuffs immediately?'

'No, me neither,' she lied, 'so I don't know. Let's see how badly injured he is and then decide. Apparently, it's a broken wrist. If so, he'll need someone to drive him to the hospital. If we need to cuff him, we could cuff his good wrist to his escort! Let's go hard; that way, we can apologise and back off. Better than going in too softly and having him do a runner.'

Gadma's GPS told her that her destination was approaching. She didn't slow down but kept going straight past the house entrance with the sign '340' on the right—there were lights on inside—did a U-ey at the next junction and returned. Having passed the house entrance, Gadma slowed and pulled off onto the grass verge facing down the road.

She stayed in the car and called on her radio to report her location to the Operations Control Room and ask for an ambulance to come without lights and sirens and wait outside until she gave the okay. She also asked for the on-call forensic crime scene crew and gave a quick outline of what she believed they should expect. They told her there had been a couple of reports of fireworks or gunfire in the area. The reports had come from number 316—just down the road from where she was.

As she waited, Gadma considered her position. Events had been moving pretty quickly, and a lot had happened. She decided to switch on the voice notes on her phone and make a record of dates and times, the conversations she had had, who with and when, what she had been told, what she had done, and her intentions for the immediate future. A clear record might be necessary. Just in case. Keep it all straight for her report later.

She got out of the car, put on her Kevlar body armour, and climbed over the three-bar fence to see what she could see of the house. In the moonlight, she could make out that the house, a big old Queenslander with a few lights on inside, was set about ten metres back from the road. The driveway, just up the slope from where she was standing, looped from the gate around to the back. There were some huge trees dotted around the house. Figs, she thought. She was under one of them and guessed it was a hundred years old. Probably planted when the house was built.

Chapter 21

I quickly examined the two guns we had most recently acquired. Unfortunately, neither was a Glock, so I was immediately unsure how to use them and make them safe. The first was a sandy colour and had 'Smith & Wesson, Springfield, MA, USA' engraved on one side and 'M&P' on the other. I kept the pistol pointed at the floor and pushed the buttons to try to get the magazine to eject. There was a lever that didn't seem to do anything, so perhaps this gun had a safety catch—I didn't want to pull the trigger to see if it locked the trigger in case it didn't and the gun went off! I pressed the small button by the trigger guard on the grip—the magazine popped out. Okay, success. The magazine had an indicator on it, which was small holes drilled through the metal to allow the bullets inside to be seen. There were six holes numbered four to fourteen in twos. I could see bullets down to the number eight. I slid the top part of the pistol backwards—'racking', Gleb Orlev had called it—and the bullet in the chamber popped out onto the floor. I picked it up and pushed it into the top of the magazine. Now I could see ten bullets. Okay. With the magazine out of the gun and the bullet out of the chamber, I pulled the slide back again and looked in the chamber. Good, no bullets. I gently pulled the trigger and heard the click of the firing mechanism. I racked the slide again and switched the safety to the other position, and pulled the trigger. Nothing happened. All good—now I was sure that particular switch was the safety. I rammed home the magazine, racked the slide to load a bullet into the chamber, and put the gun down. Ten rounds, one in the chamber, safety 'on'.

The second gun had 'Walther Arms, Fort Smith, AR', some code numbers, and 'Made in Germany' on one side and 'Carl Walther, Ulm' and 'Read Instruction Manual'. *Yes, good advice,* I thought—if I had the instruction manual. I turned it over in my hands and read the engraving on the other side: 'Walther PPQ'. Didn't James Bond use a Walther PPQ? Or was that a PPK? Or maybe it was a Beretta? Not sure.

Fixed underneath the business end of the barrel was a small black device on which 'XC2 Weaponlight' was written. I examined the buttons and found that there was one for a green laser only and one for laser and light. I touched the buttons—on and off—just to see that they worked. They did. *Well,* I thought, *that will come in handy for night work.*

I went through the same process as the Smith and Wesson to make the gun as safe as I thought I could. The magazine appeared full, with fifteen bullets. I ejected the bullet in the chamber and then wondered how to get it back in there. In the end, I reinserted the magazine, racked the action, which I guessed loaded a round into the chamber, popped out the magazine once more, loaded the spare bullet into the magazine, and rammed the magazine home into the butt of the gun and switched the safety to on. I checked through the steps. *Fifteen rounds, one in the chamber, safety on. Okay, I'm beginning to get the hang of this!*

I took the two new guns down to the ute and put them under the front passenger seat. I gave one phone to Hannah and one to Ollie as they were passing on their way to the ute—spread the resources.

'The passcodes are on the back,' I told them over my shoulder. 'There are two guns under the front seat.'

As I hurried back to the front door, I heard the sound of several motorcycles approaching up the road. I didn't think anything of it for a moment, but then the penny dropped. Bikes? Oh, no, the Cannibals!

I stopped and listened to the reverberations through the night for a few seconds, just to make sure they weren't passing on the main road not far away.

Fuck it! I ran to the front door and switched off the lights on the veranda and in the corridor. As they approached the turn into our driveway, I heard the bikes slow. *What? Oh please, not reinforcements! If they find their buddy, Brown, dead, and Danal with his wrist shattered, they'll kill us all.*

I hustled Hannah and Ollie back into the house and closed what was left of the door, Danal having almost kicked it off its hinges. Half a dozen bikes chugged and blattered, revving their engines, into our driveway and pulled up in a gaggle. *Now what?* I thought. At the front of the group, a car pulled up, and its lights went out—I didn't hear it at all. The bikes' engines were all switched off, which left an eerie silence over the place. A couple had left their headlights on, which were being swept over the house and surrounds.

I kept absolutely still, just peeking around the corner of the door frame.

The bikies dismounted. One went towards the front of the house—the side near the road—and one went towards the rear of the house, past the carports where Hannah's ute was parked. One of the bikies remained with the bikes. They were completely confident; they even left a couple of the bike headlamps on to assist with finding their way up the steps to the front door. Maybe they were friends of Danal, which was why they were bold—nothing to fear here.

Hannah and the boys ran to the back of the house again, and I retreated into the spare room by the front door. I pushed the door so it was just not quite closed. In the darkness, I went around into the corner of the room, hidden behind the wardrobe, out of immediate sight from the door if they switched on the light. I waited and listened. My adrenal glands dumped more adrenaline into my system, and I was again anxious and frightened. It's funny how you don't need a toilet until something like this happens, and then you wish you had taken the opportunity when you had it earlier.

In their heavy boots, I heard several of them stamp up the steps. It seemed to me as though they were deliberately trying to make noise, as though this was part of the plan to intimidate whoever was in the house. *We're coming to get you, and we don't care who you are. We're tougher than you, and we outnumber you.* Maybe that was it: just the sheer weight of numbers. As Bill Slim, the allied commander in Burma in World War Two, said about tank warfare, 'The more you use, the fewer you lose.'

I heard them walk straight in through the front door without pausing. I was really worried now. They had made no attempt to be quiet or hide. Quite the opposite. Now I was hoping that the neighbours *had* phoned the police, but our nearest neighbours were a couple of hundred metres away and may not have realised that a gang of bikies had stopped at our house. If they heard them at all, the neighbours might have just thought they were driving by.

I heard the door to the spare room opposite open and, after a pause, slam shut. Then the door to the room in which I was hiding swung sharply open and crashed against the end of the wardrobe, which was behind the door. I pressed myself tightly into the alcove made by the corner of the room and the wardrobe, hoping they would not see me. The light went on for a second, then off, and the door slammed shut but bounced open—the latch had never been good on this door. The bikie walked on—couldn't be bothered to close it properly.

My mind flew to Hannah and the lads—what would they be thinking? *Just give up quietly*, I hoped. I was already regretting not staying with them. They mustn't start a gunfight with these people—these bikies sounded as though they meant it.

I didn't know what to do for the best. I ran through the options that immediately presented themselves to me, *Give myself up? Would achieve nothing. Try to fight them? I might get myself killed. Also* achieves nothing. Try to get around to the back of the house to my family? I might be seen, which would end badly. Stay here and wait to see what happens? Again, no help to my family. I couldn't see a way to get an advantage.

As my mind rushed through these options, trying to think of the best way to take some action, I heard a shot from inside the house. What the fuck? I could feel myself start to panic. What the hell was that? I hoped against hope that my family was okay.

I crept to the door, trying to tread lightly without making the floorboards creak. I gently opened the door enough to look out to my left, down the corridor towards the living room. I could see nobody left or right, so I crept out of the spare room, out of the front door, and around the veranda to the right. I slowly made my way along the veranda, passed the room in which I had just been hiding, to the first living room window and put my left eye just around the corner so I could see.

The door to the kitchen had been shut, and Hannah and the lads were standing with their backs to the door. They looked basically terrified. Hannah was trying to keep Merlin settled, but he was pulling against the collar she was holding. He was growling and making his disgruntled 'oof' sounds from the back of his throat. The bikies were all carrying weapons; handguns, a sawn-off shotgun, a machete. The two from the car had slipped balaclava ski masks over their heads and faces, and those who arrived on the bikes wore bandanas across their faces with their helmets still on their heads. One had a sawn-off shotgun pointing at Merlin.

On the floor, sprawled in an unnatural position, was the bloke whose wrist I had broken; was his name Danal? He had half his head missing—the blood, brains, and bone of the other half were lying across the living room floor in a vee shape spreading out from his head towards where I was standing.

As I watched, Ollie bent down to his right and vomited on the floor. I crawled under the window along to the side door from the kitchen, put the gun I was holding on the floor near the door jamb, opened the door, and strode in. We rarely locked our doors—didn't see the need to. Until now.

I knocked on the door from the kitchen to the living room and heard the conversation fall silent on the other side. Hannah slowly opened the door and looked at me. She pulled the door wide and fell into my arms.

Chapter 22

Smiggins and the Rabid Dogs made no secret of their arrival at the Richmonds' house. You can't make six Harley-Davidsons arrive quietly—subtle they ain't. They made their way to the house, dropping a couple of guards left and right. Smiggins and Dezza put on skiing balaclava hats that covered their faces except for eyeholes, cut out so that they could see.

They found the front door already standing open, so they strode straight in down the short hallway into the living room. Smiggins, politely, he thought, allowed Dezza to go first—just in case. Dezza presented a much bigger target than him. On arrival in the living room, he found his junior officer, Danal, sitting on the floor, knees up, secured by cable ties, cradling his arms in his lap. Two of the others went on through the house to see if there was anybody else at home.

Smiggins smiled under his balaclava and said to Danal, 'Oh, goodness. Christmas has come early this year.'

Danal knew immediately who was inside the balaclava. He'd been expecting him. He also knew the likely outcome of this meeting with his boss on the force.

'For me or you?' he asked.

Smiggins took two steps towards Danal and placed his gun against Danal's forehead. 'Oh, for me, dear boy. For me.'

Smiggins pulled the trigger, and Danal's head flew backwards; his body rolled over onto its side as his skull and brain sprayed across the floor.

'Yes, very happy Christmas for me. For you? Not so much.'

He turned around as he heard people coming into the room from the kitchen. Dezza came in last, closing the kitchen door behind him. A rather attractive-looking woman, obviously in good physical shape, with long, dark hair with a greying streak running from the right forehead, and lovely breasts, led in two young men. The two young men, he guessed in their early twenties and obviously twins, as they were so alike, stood towering over their mother. She stood upright, almost defiant, in front of her lads, like a mother duck protecting her ducklings. The woman was struggling slightly to hold a very large dog by its collar as it snarled at Smiggins. With her other hand, she pushed the boys behind her. He couldn't help smiling at her proud bravado. And he couldn't help staring at her beautiful breasts under her blouse.

He could see they had all noticed the remains of Danal spread across their living room floor. *That's a good thing,* he thought. *They'll know I am not playing games.*

'Now, who do we have here?' he asked.

'Hannah. I'm Hannah, and these are my sons.'

'Well, excuse me if I, very impolitely, don't introduce myself. I am here to retrieve a USB memory stick for my employer. Hand it over.'

One of the lads said, 'I feel sick ... I'm gonna ... be ...' He didn't finish before he bent down to his right and vomited on the floor near the door frame.

The dog required no invitation and surprised the woman by turning to start eating the vomit. The woman dragged him off. 'Merlin, stop that!'

'"Better out than in," my dear old mum used to say.' Smiggins's rather jovial tone changed to one much more threatening, 'Now, where were we? Oh, yes. Memory stick. Give it to me.'

The woman, Hannah, said, 'My husband has it.'

'And where is he?'

'I don't know.'

There was a knock on the door from the kitchen. Hannah looked quizzically at Smiggins, and he nodded. She opened the door and fell into the arms of the man in the next room.

Chapter 23

I hugged Hannah tightly.

'Ah, how touching,' One of the balaclavas said. 'Get back in here, you two!'

I pointed at the body on the floor of our living room. 'Why have you killed that man? Wasn't he a bikie like you?'

'Oh, please! He's with the Rabid Dogs.' This bloke had a really whiney, effete manner. 'And how does one avoid being bitten by a rabid dog? Well, of course, one shoots the mendacious little fucker. I've done him a favour, really. Although he probably doesn't see it that way.

'Now, then, we don't have time to procrastinate. I want the memory stick with the contacts on it. I want the computer you used to copy the contacts list. I want any other copies you made on any other hard drives. And I want them all *now*!'

'Yeah, sure,' I said. 'You are welcome to them all. They've caused nothing but trouble.'

I pulled the stick out of my pocket and gave it to him. 'There's a copy on the hard drive of the computer.'

'Show me,' he said.

I started my laptop. Within a few seconds, I showed him the file on the hard drive. He told me to delete it. I did.

'Any other copies?' he asked.

'No.' I didn't tell him about the version on the hard drive in the shed. I was trusting that none of my family would volunteer the information if I didn't and that the bikies would not have time to go searching for it. There was the sound of motorcycles in the distance. The second bloke in a balaclava mask said, 'Boss, hear that? Are we expecting anybody else?'

They stood and listened intently for a moment. 'No.'

I said, 'Sounds as though they are on the main road from Brisbane—it passes quite close, maybe five-hundred metres away—but they'll have to go another couple of kilometres to get to the turning for our road. Then it's three-and-a-half k up Goondiwindi Close to get to our house. If they are coming here, they'll be here in three or four minutes.' I hoped that would be sufficient to get them to leave in a hurry.

'Yes, well, look, we'll see about that. Now, I implore you, do not fuck with me, because I enjoy behaving unconscionably. Are there any other copies?' As he said it, he raised his hand and placed his gun barrel gently against Will's cheek. 'As I said, I can be unreasonably menacing. But it's such heady stuff! Open your mouth, dear boy,' he said almost in a whisper, pushing his face up close behind the gun, 'unless you want me to blow your teeth out.'

Will opened his mouth so the bullet might pass through both cheeks and through his mouth without blowing his teeth out. Will's eyes were wide with fear, flicking from me to the balaclava. With the computer unlocked, there was an outside chance one of them might find the version I copied to my cloud account. They were unlikely to find out I had copied the file to an external drive, which we put in the shed, and less likely still to find the locked copy on my website. I thought quickly about the odds. Maybe if I gave up two, they would go without further questions.

'Yes, yes! Wait!' I said. 'There are two more copies. One copy on my cloud account and the other on an external hard drive we hid in the shed!'

'That's better. My word, you have been a busy little bee on your computer. I didn't think a smart person like you would make just one copy. Show me,' he demanded.

I navigated to the browser and then to my cloud account. I pretended to struggle with the technology—not much of a stretch for me. I thought every second I could use would be another second for opposition bikies to arrive.

We rarely hear bikes on the main road except at weekends, so the chances of the ones we could hear in the distance going somewhere other than here just seemed less and less likely. I showed him the file. He told me to delete it. I did.

'Well, that was simplicity itself, wasn't it?' His eyes smiled through the holes in the balaclava.

The bloke who had been on guard by the front door and had gone to check on his mate by the bikes came scrabbling into the house, his boots thundering on the floorboards.

'Boss, there are heaps of bikes coming up the road!'

I said, 'Ollie, show them where you put the hard drive. Quickly!'

I wanted to get rid of them.

Balaclava nodded to the other balaclava-headed thug. 'Dezza, take dear Ollie and collect the hard drive in the shed. And hurry up. We may be about to receive uninvited and unwelcome guests!'

They turned, and Dezza shoved Ollie ahead of him down the corridor, out of the front door.

Balaclava called after them, 'Dezza, then put Ollie in the car!'

'Okay, boss!' Dezza shouted in reply.

'No!' shouted Hannah. 'Don't take Ollie! Why? He hasn't done anything!'

Ignoring Hannah, Balaclava spoke to the remaining bikies. 'Right, gentlemen, let us depart as briskly as we can. Get the others back to the bikes!' And to us, he said, 'Don't follow us. I'm taking your son as insurance against you doing anything stupid, like trying to recover the stick or hard drive. Also, in case the police try to block the road before we get clear. So don't ring those wonderful boys in blue until we're well away!'

'Please leave our son!' I pleaded. 'We have no reason to ring the police—you haven't hurt us, and you're welcome to those bloody files—they've been nothing but trouble to us. Take them and get them out of our lives. Just go, but please leave Ollie!'

'Oh! Bravo! Such an impassioned plea, but I fear not.'

'Well, when will you release him? When you get to the end of the road and you are clear?'

'Not sure, no. I think he could prove efficacious for a while—you know, a sort of human shield. And we have a friend who likes prime young lads like this. Now, kindly fuck off.'

'Where will you take him? At least tell us that.'

He couldn't resist bragging. 'Somewhere you can't even get close, so don't even try. We have our own private security firm, don't we, Dezza? They don't even know they work for us—they're called the Royal Australian Air Force Security Forces Squadron.'

I didn't want to give away that I guessed what he meant because he might realise we had read the file, which might stop him from leaving to check how much we did know or, worse still, just kill us to stop us transmitting the information. I said, 'What are you talking about—the RAAF security? How are they helping you?'

'They prevent little civilian pricks like you from penetrating onto RAAF property!' He hurried to his car.

Hannah, Will, and I followed him out to the veranda and across the front lawn. Merlin trotted along with us, tail slowly wagging now he had decided, maybe, we were going out in the car.

I pleaded with Balaclava again, pulling at his arm as he hurried down the slope, 'Please! Leave our son!'

He flicked his arm and said, 'Unhand me, sir, or I'll shoot the fucking lot of you like that Rabid Dog inside!'

Hannah, still holding Merlin by the collar, shouted at Ollie, 'Ollie, just do as they say. We'll get help!'

'Not happening, gorgeous!' said Balaclava, laughing. 'You won't be able to send help where we're going! Even the police can't get in!'

Hannah was absolutely furious. She gritted her teeth and growled at Balaclava, 'If you touch a hair on his head, I will hunt you down and fucking tear you to shreds, you mongrel!'

As he got in the driver's seat, he said, 'Spirit! I like women with spirit. And nice tits, too! You're giving me a hard-on. Shame I have to take my leave.'

Dezza pushed Ollie into the back seat ahead of him.

Balaclava started the car and accelerated hard to the end of our driveway and pulled straight out into the road, turning left down the hill.

The sound of the oncoming Dogs' motorbikes grew quickly louder as they opened their throttles to come up the hill. One of the remaining Cannibals called out, 'Take cover, must be the Dogs—we're going to have to kill these fuckers on our way out!'

The shadowy figures moved to the various trees dotted about the property near the front gate.

I said to Hannah and Will, 'Get back up to the house, quickly!'

'What are you going to do?' asked Hannah as we ran.

'I'm going to do my best to protect us. Where's that you-beaut gun with the light and silencer?'

'I put both the guns under the mattress in our bedroom when I heard the bikes.'

'You are wonderful. I love you!'

We dashed to the back of the house into our bedroom and retrieved the two guns. I said, 'Probably the safest place will be in the bath—the bullets will go straight through the timber walls but maybe not through the cast-iron bath.'

I didn't know whether that was true, but it seemed the lowest-risk thing to do. In the en suite, I made sure Hannah and Will were as low down in the spa bath as they could get, lying with their heads at each end just below the bath rim and their knees high. Merlin sat by Hannah's head, watching what was happening.

I trotted through the house to the front door, flicking the lights back out as I went. I pulled the door closed enough that I could just see out.

The Dogs, about a dozen of them, came up the hill, slowed, and throbbed to a stop at intervals up the road. They all left about five metres between each other and stopped on the grass verge outside the house. They all switched off their lights, kicked down their stands, and dismounted. Then they sidled slowly to the fence nearest to them and climbed over. There was just enough light from the stars and the distant glow of Brisbane for me to make them out as they stepped to the ground from the fence. This must be some bikie tactic; turn up late at night, make a lot of noise, and hope to frighten the opposition into submission. They stood, bold as brass, as though expecting their opponents to flee, running and screaming into the night. Maybe they were so confident because they were expecting only my family and me to be here. Not happening.

The Cannibals let the Dogs all climb the fence to the inside and then opened fire. The Dogs, obviously taken by surprise, were not so full of swagger and bravado now. They all dropped low and scuttled to find the nearest cover.

I considered whether to put the veranda light to my left on, as it would highlight anyone from that direction—the Cannibals—and just about provide enough light to see anybody from my right—the Rabid Dogs. I thought it might discourage any of them from coming to the house because they would be clearly seen by their opposition, which would make them an easy target. The only drawback was that putting the light on would draw attention to the fact that there was somebody here, and it would spoil my night vision in the darker areas to my right. They would be able to move around to the rear of the house without me seeing them in the gloom. In the end, I left the light off. It would allow me to see better in the dark.

As my vision in the darkness improved, I could see shapes—the Cannibals—moving from tree to tree to my left towards the oncoming Dogs, who were working their way around both sides of the pool towards the Cannibals. Two Dogs passed below me at the bottom of the steps. I kept the door ajar so I could just see with one eye. I let them go. I didn't want to make it a three-way fight—let them kill one another!

As the two Dogs crept past the house, down towards the area where the Cannibals' bikes were parked, a figure stepped out from the corner of the house to my left and blasted them one after the other with both barrels from a sawn-off shotgun. They fell like dropping sacks of laundry, crumpled heaps on the ground. The shooter stepped back out of sight into the darkness behind the corner of the house. More shots were fired down in the trees; some were the cracks of pistols; others were the deeper-throated booms of shotguns.

I wondered whether I should try to get above the shooter on the veranda and try to kill him, but the sure knowledge that the creaking boards would give me away long before I reached him kept me at the front door.

I heard more shots and saw the muzzle flashes in the distance among the trees. I heard shouts as Cannibals and Dogs fought. I heard screams and groans. Shadows ran from spot to spot, guns firing as they went.

To my right, the Cannibal who had been ordered to cover the rear of the house just in case we escaped, very cautiously crept along the fence-line. I heard his mate down to my left, who had killed the two Dogs with the shotgun, call out to him, 'Guido!'

The man to my right stopped and looked to his left, where he had heard his name called from. Obviously unsure what to do, Guido climbed over the fence and crouched down behind the fencepost.

The Cannibal to my left came around the corner, hurried across the patio area below me towards Guido. 'Wait for me, Guido!' he whispered loudly. He climbed the fence also.

One of the Cannibals' motorcycles down by the trees burst into life. The headlight came on and flicked to full beam, and the bike roared down the driveway, spitting gravel behind it as it fishtailed towards the gate. A volley of shots rang out from various positions, the driver fell off the side, and the bike continued upright until it hit the left gatepost and tumbled through the gate towards the road, the engine dying to an idle and the headlight pointing up to the sky. The engine chugged gently at idle for a few moments and stopped with a single backfire. That just left the ticking of the front wheel to be heard as it continued to spin slowly.

To my right, I heard the self-starter of another bike whirring as it tried to make the motor catch. After a few seconds, the motor started. The rider gave it two squirts of the throttle. The bike, without lights, accelerated with a thunderous clatter from its straight-through exhaust, down the hill, past the gate. I heard it changing up through the gears, the noise reverberating through the quiet evening as it charged off into the darkness. Guido and the double-killer, I guessed. They'd decided they were outnumbered and outgunned and wanted to live to fight another day. The pillion passenger was firing guns from both hands towards the trees as they charged past the Dogs near the gate. It was sufficient— they raced on down the hill and away into the night.

Near one of the trees, I saw a figure. As I watched, there was the flash and crack of a pistol being fired twice in short succession. By the light of the muzzle flash, I could see a man standing, pointing his weapon down at another person on the ground. The person on the ground had his arm raised in defence at what he knew was about to happen. After the shots, the person on the ground lay still.

Three or four people, only shapes in the darkness, moved from tree to tree, obviously checking on the people they found. The poor guy they found was the enemy and got two bullets to finish him off.

I saw one of the shapes bend low over another person, and there was a short, 'No, no!', a grunt, and a cough. Then silence.

Decision time: was I going to get the family and run, or should I stay and fight? I decided running was the better option—I didn't want my family mixed up in any more gun battles. I turned and ran through the house, calling to Hannah and Ollie as I went, 'Don't shoot! It's me! Get out of the bath; we're going!'

They were both already standing by the back door as I came through the house to them. 'Let's get out of here, quick as we can!'

Chapter 24

Gadma heard a car approaching, saw its lights, and watched it slow and pull up on the other side of the road. The engine died, and the lights went off. Simmo got out, put on his body armour, and shifted his equipment belt so it was all comfortable as he walked towards her car. As with all officers, his belt was laden with equipment, not least of which were his pistol and his taser. She called quietly to him, and he climbed over the fence and came to her.

'What's happening?' he asked.

'Just exactly what you see. I've been here about three minutes.'

'How long for the backup?'

'Backup? What's that?'

'No backup? Dead bodies to the left of us and dead bodies to the right of us and no bloody backup?'

'Nobody spare.'

'Oh, what, really? I was joking.'

'Yeah, well, I wasn't. No backup.'

They used the massive trunk of the fig as cover and kept watching the house and surrounding area. As her eyes had become accustomed to the darkness, she could pick out more detail: the pool fence, a shed with some equipment inside, a small building—a big kennel? Must be a big dog for a kennel that size. Another good reason not to go barging in!

Over to her right, she could see what little light there was glinting off the chrome highlights of some motorbikes.

Gadma briefed Simmo on what she knew about what they faced in the house. She reminded him that her boss, Danal, might be in there and that he could be working for the opposition.

Gadma decided that Simmo would guard the front door, which was on the side of the house facing them down the hill. She would have a quick recce along the driveway around to the back before coming back to join Simmo in going in through the front door.

They left the dark shadows under the fig tree and walked slowly, well-spaced, towards the house, guns drawn. Gadma went slightly right along the driveway. They had only gone ten metres when Simmo said, quietly but firmly, 'Stop!'

He dropped to a crouch and said, 'There's someone here.'

She could see Simmo moving but not any detail.

He stood, and then he said, 'No, he's definitely dead. No pulse, cold, and a huge hole in his chest. Let's go.'

He crossed the driveway, slowly walked up the front lawn towards the front steps, and waited.

Gadma moved cautiously to the right of the house and spotted a dual-cab ute in the carport with the interior light on and someone moving around in the cab.

Chapter 25

Hannah opened the back door, and we piled out. We quickly descended the steps to the right and made our way around the back of the house to the left to get out onto the road. I suppose it might have been quicker to go over the balustrade of the veranda, but we couldn't even lift Merlin, let alone lower him to the ground.

'Let's get up the road and see if we can get to Marty's house,' I said as we ran. 'If we don't make it, we'll get through the hedgerow and hide!'

We ran up the inside of the fence, through the top foot-gate, and off up the road. It took us two or three minutes to get to Marty's place. We jogged straight to his front door and rang the doorbell. By now, it was quite late. We waited for a few moments and rang the bell again. I heard it ringing softly inside.

'Come on, Marty!'

Eventually, there was some movement inside. A light went on, and Marty, dressed in pyjamas, came to the door. We must have looked a real spectacle—hot, sweaty, out of breath, and armed with a variety of guns. I hadn't had a chance to shower and change, so I still had blood all over me from at least two people.

We all pushed quickly inside, Will closing the door behind him, and I said, 'Marty, quickly, put the lights out!'

'What the fuck?' He shambled blearily to the switch and put the light out.

'Thanks, can't explain now, but I will. Who has a phone?' I asked the group.

'I've got one, Toby, by my bed,' answered Marty. 'Just a sec.'

A few seconds later, he returned with his phone and his wife, Maggie, behind him.

'Here you go.' He opened it and handed me the phone.

I dialled the emergency services number, asked for an ambulance and the police, briefly told them where to go and what they might find, gave them Marty's name and address, and rang off.

Maggie, looking at each one of us in turn, said, 'What are you doing with those guns? Are they yours? Toby, you're covered in … what is that? Blood?' She pointed at the Glocks Hannah and I carried.

'What the fuck is going on, Toby?' asked Marty.

'Okay, the short version …' I explained briefly what had happened that evening at our house. I left out the rest of the day's mayhem. They both burst in with questions—very good questions, like, 'Why do two bikie gangs want to come to your place, anyway?' and 'What have you done to your hand, and why are you covered in blood?' but I interrupted their questions and said that a full explanation would be forthcoming on another day over a glass or two of cab sav. But not now. Now I had to go back to my place to see what was happening. Had all the bikies left? If so, we could get going the ute and our stuff and escape to some sort of safety. I told them I would only be a few minutes and then I would be back to let them know what was going on. I swapped guns with Hannah because her gun had the silencer and torch fixed to it.

Rather than go down the road, I let myself out the back of Marty's and went through the wires of the fence into our top paddock. I picked my way slowly down the paddock towards the house, staying under the trees where it was darkest. Near our property, I could see torches flashing around, lighting up the trees and the outside of the house. There were one or two lights in the house going on and off as people moved through the building. I was still in the paddock but below the house where I had a good enough view of the area to watch the activity in front of the pool area, up the front steps, the veranda, around to the carports in front of me. I stopped moving and held my breath when I realised there was someone close by.

'Is it open?' he whispered.

Another person answered from the far side of Hannah's ute that was blind to me, 'Yes, and it's got loads of stuff in the back.'

The first replied, 'Have a look inside and see if there's a computer, a memory stick, or a hard drive or something obviously to do with a computer. I'll keep an eye out down the drive,' as he moved to the open corner of the carport not ten metres from where I was crouching below the long grass along the fence-line to the paddock.

The ute's door opened, and the interior light came on. I saw the other bloke get into the car and start to look in the various compartments and over in the back seat.

The movement of two dark shapes caught my attention. One picked its way slowly and cautiously towards the house, weapon drawn. The other moved slowly towards me on the driveway. If they hadn't moved, I wouldn't have noticed them. *Now, who's this?* I thought.

The guard in the carport must have seen the one on the driveway, too, because he slowly and quietly drifted back, melting into the darkness. He said nothing to his mate in the car, who was still poking around in the back.

As the person crept further up the driveway towards the carport, they could obviously see there was someone in the car. They continued around the ute, quite close to the open door, and said quietly, 'Police. Get out of the car with your hands empty and put them on your head.' I could tell from the voice it was a female police officer.

The bloke stopped mid-search and gradually came out of the ute backwards. He closed the door so the interior light would go out in a few seconds. He stood upright and turned slowly, raising his hands onto his head. Closing the door to put the interior light out was pretty quick thinking, I thought. However, he didn't know how long the courtesy light would stay on. He could have got himself shot for non-compliance with the police officer's instructions, but he kept her attention by talking to her.

'Stay calm, darl, I don't want to get shot.'

'Turn and face the car, put your hands on the roof, and spread your legs.'

He stood still and looked at her steadily. 'Oooh, I do love it when you talk dirty, you horny little bitch.'

The interior light in the car faded and went out.

'Turn 'round or I'll shoot you now and call it resisting arrest. No witnesses. I'll blow your balls off. You'll be really popular with the other inmates—I'll save them the trouble.' She sounded to me as though she meant it, and the bikie thought so too. He slowly turned and put his hands on the car.

I was again in a quandary. Should I keep quiet and see how events played out, or should I intervene—and maybe get shot for my trouble? I stayed low but just high enough that I could just see through the tops of the tall grass immediately in front of me, and I called out, 'There's someone in the corner!'

The police officer's head snapped around to look at where she must have thought my voice had come from and then back to the corner. She swung her gun towards the corner, but I guessed she couldn't see the person there in the total darkness. I could no longer see the bloke at the back of the carport—he must have been crouching in the corner. But he could obviously see the police officer because he fired a shot across the bonnet of the ute that hit her and threw her backwards, crashing her to the floor. The crack of the shot made the corrugated steel of the roof ring and the flash lit up the scene for a fraction of a second. The other shooter, who was by the car door, jumped around to the front of the ute and crouched down with his mate. They both fired a couple of shots blindly in my direction as they hid behind the bonnet. Groaning, the female officer started to move.

One of the thugs said, 'She's still alive. She must be wearing a vest. Shoot her in the head, and let's get out of here!'

Hesitating, the other replied, 'You go out there and shoot her—the guy in the paddock might be armed!'

Chapter 26

I crawled slowly to my right along the fence-line behind the tall grass that I couldn't reach with the slasher. After a few metres, I got to a position where I could see the right side of the ute, just a slight glint off the metallic paintwork. I aimed my gun at the front of the ute. The instant I saw any kind of movement, I fired at it twice in short succession, aiming at where I thought the two were hiding. One of them fell forward, sprawling on the concrete. The other came running from behind the ute on the far side, firing in my direction as he ran down the driveway. I kept my head well down. I was frightened shitless, having some genuine killers shooting at me. I gave him a few more seconds and then heard a motorbike start and power off down the track and out of the gate.

There was no noise from inside the carport. I climbed through the wire fence and walked quickly to my right to the support post of the carport. I stood and watched. The bloke on the ground was quiet. I went to him, keeping my gun trained on him, and switched on the small torchlight fixed to the underside of my gun. He was a mess. I'd forgotten that my gun had the 'exploding' bullets, as I'd come to think of them. My bullet must have hit him in the stomach, expanded as it passed through him, and lifted out a section of his spine and lungs as the hundreds of fragments ripped through him and departed his body at the back. The rear wall of the carport was covered in blood, bone, and viscera. Small lumps had slid, and rivulets of blood had run, down the concrete and pooled at the foot of the wall.

My mind was numbed by what I was looking at, what I had done to this thing that a few seconds ago was a person. I stared at the carnage. Then my mind became un-numb. My stomach telegraphed to me that awkward feeling—*something is happening down here, and you had better be ready!* My mouth quickly filled with saliva. I tried to swallow but couldn't. I knew what was going to happen and stumbled to the other corner of the carport. On the way, I took a deep breath; my diaphragm gave two or three nudges, followed by a huge push, and I vomited. My delicious supper came out of my mouth and nose, splattering onto the concrete. After a few seconds, it happened again. Then I was empty. I spat a few lumps onto the floor and wiped my mouth and nose with the hem of my T-shirt. I groaned and muttered quietly to myself, 'Holy crap. What else can possibly go wrong today?'

The police officer was trying to roll onto her side and get up.

I walked to her and helped her get to a sitting position, leaning against the middle post of the carport. 'Are you all right?' I asked.

'I've just been shot; what do you think?' she said indignantly.

I was relieved— her indignation meant she wasn't as badly hurt as I had feared. I replied rather sheepishly, 'I don't know. I don't know how effective those vests are.'

'Well, I'm not dead, so that's a win.' She lifted her chin towards the vomit in the corner. 'More to the point, how are you?'

'Mmmm. Better not talk about it.' I held out my right hand. 'I'm Toby Richmond.'

'Is that the one you just wiped your puke off with?'

'No, I used my T-shirt.'

She took my hand, and together, we hauled her up. 'I'm Senior Constable Golni Gadma.'

She stood, rather unsteadily, leaning against the ute.

We heard a call from the front of the house. *'Stop. Police!'* followed by several shots. A voice called out, *'Golni, coming your way!'*

She said to me urgently, looking over my shoulder, 'Behind you!'

I turned and aimed the gun towards two figures that came spilling over the lawn and ornamental rocks around the corner from the house.

She called, 'Stop! Police!' at the same moment, I flicked on the gun's torch, which was surprisingly bright in the near-total darkness.

The two thugs fired at us, and I returned fire with three or four shots. They were at a disadvantage because they were stumbling over uneven ground and small, ornamental rocks along the flower bed, trying to shoot to their left. I was steady. They died where they dropped, both dead before they hit the ground. My aim must have been improving: moving targets, both hit in the torso, both ripped apart like their mate in the carport. The red spray bursting out from behind them was clearly visible by the light of the torch.

I scanned around the carport for her pistol, found it and gave it to her, and switched off the torch. 'So, Senior Constable Gadma, pleased to meet you at last.'

'Bloody hell, Mr Richmond. What sort of bullets have you got loaded in that Glock?'

'I dunno. I'm just shooting with whatever I can steal from these arseholes. And you can call me Toby.'

'Before we go any further, thank you for saving my life just now. If you hadn't called out and then shot at them, they would have had me cold. I was stuck here.'

'Yeah, I saw them finish off a couple of the opposition bikies over there.' I pointed down the driveway. 'Completely calm—it was appalling, how totally cold-blooded they were.'

Behind Gadma, a movement caught my eye. In the little light from inside the house, I saw two people coming cautiously down the steps on this side of the house beyond the carport about ten or twenty metres away. I put my finger to my lips, quietly said, 'Shhhh,' and pointed at them.

They crept around to the rear of the house and disappeared before we could do anything.

Gadma pulled the microphone near her left shoulder to her mouth and said quietly, 'Two coming out onto the road from the rear!'

A motorcycle started up and roared down the road. Two shots were fired, and then several more from another gun—a slightly different noise. We heard the bike keep going down the hill for a moment, and then there was a screeching, grinding crash as the speeding bike hit the asphalt and the metal slid and tore itself to a halt. Silence again.

'Listen, Officer Gadma—'

'Since you saved my life, I think you can call me Golni,' she interjected.

'Righto, Golni. One of my sons, Ollie, has been taken hostage by the Cannibals bikie gang. They were taking him, they said, to RAAF Base Amberley. My problem is that my chances of getting him back quickly will disappear if I wait here and rely on you and the police. No offence. The police negotiators will want to haggle, and there are all the issues with jurisdiction on a defence establishment and who is in charge of the operation. That all means massive paperwork and time. I will probably be in prison for the duration, waiting for all this to get sorted out. It will take days, possibly weeks. In the meantime, the chances of my son surviving swiftly diminish—he may already be dead. As you have seen, this mob don't take prisoners! The longer we wait, the less chance my son has of surviving this. The quicker I can get to him, the less time he is exposed to the risk of them harming or even killing him. I can't afford the time for the wheels of the police, Department of Defence, and RAAF to grind exceeding slow.'

She just looked at me, not quite sure what to say. I think she agreed. So I continued, 'Furthermore, and I'm sorry to say this about you and your organisation, but I don't trust you or anybody else in the Queensland Police Service. I have already come across at least two crooked cops, or is it three? See, I've already lost track.'

'Well, you can trust me.'

'Oh, yeah, right. Well, you would say that, wouldn't you? One of your mob cut my finger off earlier today.' I lifted my bandaged hand slightly. 'Why should you be any better than him?'

'Because I'm working undercover on an investigation into corruption within the police service related to the drug trade in the Brisbane area. It's fuckers like them that I'm trying to get locked up!'

'Yeah? Excuse my cynicism, but prove it to me.'

She paused a moment as though considering her answer. 'You met a colleague of mine. Does the phrase 'Mick sends his love to Amy' mean anything to you?'

I stayed silent for a long moment and heaved a big sigh of relief.

'Thank fuck for that,' I whispered. 'At last. I was thinking there was nobody left in the world I could trust.'

'I get it,' she said. 'My whole life is like that.'

'How many of you are there that can be trusted?'

Gadma replied, rather sadly, 'Well, there's Mick, AKA Trent in hospital, who you've already met, and who somehow got you involved in all this—I've yet to find out how or why. He's in the operating theatre having some wounds repaired. There's one other undercover, plus my boss, Erik Eriksson. He was running this operation but was killed today at the house you were in at Woolooma trying to make an arrest. Erik's boss might be okay, but maybe Erik, like me, had been embedded undercover as well, and his *real* boss is elsewhere in the organisation. I don't know who it is. So I'm not sure, right now, who I can trust up the line. I think I'll just have to use my initiative for a while.'

'Sounds as though you need all the help you can get. Look, I'm happy to talk to you about the USB memory stick Trent gave me, which has already cost so many lives ... just take a look around the property. Apart from the three just here, you'll find bodies all over the place and at least one inside—your colleague Danal—with his head blown off!'

'What? Is Danal dead now, too? Did you kill him?' She sounded incredulous.

'No, but I admit I did break his arm and tie him up. But then some bikies arrived, and the first thing they did was to kill him. The whole mess out front seemed like two bikie gangs having a turf war and doing a lot of score-settling. Listen, I'm happy to talk to you about all this—'

'Wait, you mentioned a stick. What has that got to do with anything?'

'I had a USB memory stick, which Trent gave me. It had a contacts list off a phone belonging to Alan Smith, a bloke at Amberley—Trent called him a drugs lord. He uses the Cannibals as his muscle. There are heaps of people's details on it, and Trent thought it would be sufficient to bring down the whole operation.'

'Had,' she said. 'What do you mean 'had'? Where is it now?'

'I gave it back to them just now—but don't worry, I still have a copy. Look, I've got to go.'

'Where is your copy?'

I didn't trust her enough yet to tell her about the copy on my website, and I thought her ignorance of its location might keep her interested in keeping me alive for a few more minutes.

I avoided the question. 'As I said, I can tell you my plans to recover my son, but I don't want to be here when your backups arrive because they will just want to lock me up.' I talked as I walked to the ute and got in. Gadma didn't move. 'And I don't want to be locked up until I have my son safely back with me.' I buzzed down the window and started the engine.

'Where are you going to go?' she asked.

'I don't know just yet, but we'll find somewhere safer than here, that's for sure!'

As I reversed out of the carport, I called to her, 'Look, you have my phone number, so call me, and I'll explain how you can access the copy.'

Then I drove off down the driveway and out of the gate, up the road to Marty's. I hoped Gadma had warned her colleague that I was coming—I didn't want to finish up like the two bikies just now. Nobody tried to stop me.

Marty was first, agitated and loud. 'Toby, what the fuck is going on?'

I disregarded him for a moment, collecting my thoughts. Then I said, 'Earlier, there was something of a bikie war at our house—it really was brutal, as I expect Hannah told you. The police are there now. Definitely some of the bikies are gone, and definitely some of them are dead, but there may well be some left holed up in our house. They may try to escape this way, so keep your doors locked. We have to get out of here, maybe for several days. I really have no idea for how long at the moment. We can't take the dog. Mate, please will you look after the dog for us?'

Marty softened. 'That big sook, Merlin? Of course we will. You know he's welcome anytime!'

'Will, please get Merlin's gear out of the ute. Thanks, mate.'

I turned back to Hannah. 'We have to go. If the police get hold of me, they will lock me up until all this has been sorted out, which might be months, or even years! And I want to go after the Cannibals and get Ollie back.'

'But Toby,' countered Hannah. 'We'll never be able to get into Amberley! It's an operational air force base with the latest fighter jets. They must have all sorts of security, fences, cameras, guard dogs, and what have you. And even if we do get inside, it must be huge, and we'd have no idea where to look!'

'Yes, agreed, but we are going to try.'

Will, Hannah, and I left Marty's in the ute. Again, I had misgivings about whether we would be stopped and whether the police reinforcements had arrived. But no. It was all good. We cruised slowly past the house and down Goondiwindi Close, out onto the main road. Once we were safely away from the immediate area and the tension had subsided just a fraction, Hannah broke the silence to ask whether I had a cunning plan.

'Yeah, good question,' I replied.

'And what's a good answer?'

'Not a cunning plan, but the start of a plan. I know where we can stay tonight, somewhere I think they won't find us. And I think I know how we might get into Amberley.'

'That's not a very good answer.'

'Perhaps, but it is the best I can do at the moment, and it's the truth. I'm pretty sure we'll be safe enough, and it will give us a chance to think about what to do next.'

Chapter 27

After Richmond had driven off, Gadma walked to the front of the house. She moved cautiously until Simmo, who was standing in the corner made by the steps up to the front door and the fence shielding the under-floor of the house, quietly called her. 'Are you all right?' he asked.

'Yeah, fine—thank goodness for Kevlar! Where were you when those two came out of the house?'

'I was just 'round there, between the house and the road. I wanted to see if I could see into the house.'

'Let's check this house before we do anything else.'

'Who was in the ute?'

'Richmond.' She didn't elaborate. She also didn't tell him that Telstra was monitoring Richmond's movements using his mobile phone: that information might be better kept to herself for now.

They climbed the steps to the front door. Gadma stood to the right of the door frame, and Simmo stood to the left.

He pushed the door back until it was fully open, pointing his gun down the short corridor. Traditional Queenslander—a corridor from the front door between two bedrooms to the living room beyond. Living room light on. Both bedroom doors open. Not a good place to get caught.

Gadma looked at Simmo and shrugged. He nodded back in reply. Gadma moved quickly down the corridor, slightly crouched, with her gun firmly braced in two hands out in front of her. She hustled into the living room. As she approached the end of the corridor, she panned the gun in increasing arcs left and right. Nobody in the room save for a man with his brains all over the living room floor. Simmo came past her and proceeded cautiously through the door into the kitchen, which was a more recent extension to the traditional house.

Gadma then leap-frogged past him as they worked their way through the house until they were sure there was nobody else there.

She opened the back door and checked around the back veranda.

Gadma's radio earpiece came to life with her callsign. 'Three-fifty-eight, this is Operations, over.'

'Go ahead,' she replied.

'Three-fifty-eight, the phone you wanted monitoring by Telstra? It's on the move. And the ambos are outside your location; they want to know if they can come in.'

'Okay, you can tell them to come to the gate. I'll meet them there. And copied about the phone.'

She then gave Operations a short summary of the situation, making it clear that significant resources would be needed, as there were multiple dead bodies, including a police officer.

She walked out to the front door, tried a couple of switches, and put on the light that illuminated the front door and veranda. Then she found one that floodlit the front lawn.

She reached the driveway as the ambulance pulled in through the gates. As it pulled up next to her, she said to the ambo on her side, 'There's a dead body there,' and she pointed to the lawn where the body could be seen just out of the direct light from the vehicle's headlights. 'Unless you've got some miracle cure in your bag, there's nothing you can do for him. Over there by the carport, two more, ditto. Inside, one more, ditto. So have a quick look 'round and see what you can see. If you don't find anybody that needs your help outside the house, get straight back in your vehicle and leave the crime scene.'

The female ambo in the driver's seat, scanning the area with her torch, said, 'There's at least two more over here on my side. We had a quick look at the two out on the road as we passed, but they were beyond help, too. And the Mobile Forensic Facility van is here behind us.' The ambos climbed out to get on with their work.

Another van pulled just off the road into the driveway. The crime scene forensic team had arrived. She briefed them and left them to their devices.

Gadma walked back up to the house and said to Simmo, 'We had better make a wider sweep of the property. There are still some bikes here, so maybe their owners are as well, if they aren't dead. They may be hiding somewhere, waiting for the heat to die down.'

'Okay. Are you having Richmond's phone tracked?'

'Yeah. I trust him. He's got mixed up in something outside his experience, but he's handling it well so far. He saved my life back there in the carport, so I want to keep tabs on him. If I hear he's got into more trouble, I want to know where he is.'

Over the course of the next hour, more forensic specialists arrived in more vans, and more police officers arrived: senior police officers, plain clothes, uniformed. Mobile floodlights were set up. A major crime scene bus arrived. Hearses arrived. The road outside was full of vehicles.

Gadma gave a detailed briefing to the senior police officer, omitting the part about letting Richmond go, and was told to brief some of the other officers who would pick up the investigation from her and then to get back to the office and start her report. It took quite a while for her to get all the information over to them.

After a mandatory medical check by the ambos for any adverse reaction to the gunshot that hit her in the chest but was stopped by her body armour, she set off to drive slowly back to the office.

Chapter 28

Once we were a few kilometres away from home, I told them about what had happened when I went back to the house: my meeting with Officer Gadma, the shootings, the killings, the undercover operation. We discussed whether we could really trust Gadma. I said I thought we could because she knew the 'safe word' that Mick had given me in hospital. We also pondered how she might help us without bringing the whole of the Queensland Police Service down on our necks. We quickly ran out of conversation and fell silent with our own thoughts.

'Dad,' said Will, rather startling me. 'Do you think we ought to, like, switch our phones off? You know they can be tracked quite accurately from every mast.'

'Yeah, but I'm not sure they can track you from only one or even two masts. I think they need three or more to get a triangulated fix. It's the same principle as the old long-range navigation aids for aircraft like Decca and Loran. And now GPS. But yes, you're right. Let's switch off our phones.' Then I said, 'On second thoughts, I think I have to leave mine on so that Gadma can contact me.'

'And Ollie!' said Hannah.

'Oh, God, yeah. Ollie might be trying to get hold of us! What about if we just sent him a short text? I really want to know how he is, as I'm sure you do. The trouble is, if we text him now, those arseholes who are holding him might hear it chime and realise they have forgotten to take his phone off him. He might really need it later.'

Hannah held up one of the phones we had stolen from either Orlov or Danal and said, 'You gave me one of the phones we took—this one was Danal's, I think. Did you give Will or Ollie the other phone?'

'No, not me,' Will replied.

'Okay, it must have been Ollie. That means he now has one or two phones. Or none.'

I sat and thought about it some more, rolling the permutations around in my head. Assuming they have already done the logical thing and taken his personal phone away from him, if we texted Ollie on Orlov's phone to stay in contact with us on Danal's phone, then we could switch off all our phones, and the police—crooked or not—wouldn't be able to track us. The risk was that they would hear the text arrive and take Orlov's phone away from him—if they hadn't already. Or we could use Danal's phone to text him on Orlov's phone, but he wouldn't recognise the number and might think it was the Cannibals trying to trick him in some way—like paedophiles do on the internet by pretending to be someone they aren't. So, I concluded, no texting Ollie on his own phone or on Orlov's from one of ours or from Danal's phone. I explained my thinking to Will and Hannah.

Will said, 'What if we only text Ollie at the last moment to let him know to be ready?'

Hannah replied, 'I don't think that will help, Will, because—"

'No, it will just tell the bastards what our plan is,' he interrupted.

'Will, please don't interrupt,' admonished his mum. 'And mind your language.'

'I think all we can do is wait for him to contact us, if he is able to, and we can take it from there,' he continued, completely unfazed by his mother's admonishment.

Hannah asked, 'What are we going to say to him if he does contact us?'

We discussed that, and I got Will to write down some questions. It did depend a bit on what he answered to each one, but at least we could get some vital information from him first.

Hannah said, 'Toby, you'll have to leave your phone on for both Gadma and Ollie and hope that the police are slow to track our position.'

'Yeah, let's hope they have to go through some long-winded bureaucratic hoops to get a tracer on it.'

I switched Danal's phone off, too. They might get it traced, anyway. We all sat, engrossed in our own thoughts.

After a while, Will piped up, 'Why do you need three masts, Dad? You said they need three to get, like, a position.'

I didn't really feel like talking, but I thought it might keep our minds off the horrific events of the evening. I replied, 'Okay, I don't know how it works on phones, but the principle is that you can get an idea of how far the phone is from the mast by measuring the time it takes for the phone to reply to an interrogation signal sent from the mast. There may also be a way of sensing the distance from the mast by the strength of the returned signal, but I don't know. So, the mast sends an interrogation pulse to the phone, and the phone replies. Depending on the time taken, that mast can say that you are at a certain distance away, which gives you a circle of possible positions around that mast. Do you follow me?' I looked up at him quickly in the rear-view mirror to confirm he understood. 'All right. If you have two masts that are receiving signals from the phone, the two circles will intersect, but they will intersect at two places on each circle. Still with me?'

He nodded.

'However, when you have three masts, the three circles will intersect to create a small triangle in only one place called a 'cocked hat'—don't ask me why—so you've narrowed it down to a very small area, and the phone will most likely be somewhere in the triangle—that's why it's called triangulation. The more stations that can 'see' the phone, the smaller the margins of error and the more accurate the position.'

'So, Dad, why's it called a cocked hat?'

'I knew you were going to say that—it's called a cocked hat from the hats worn back in the olden days. Yes, even before I was born. They had three corners, in the shape of a triangle.'

'That still doesn't explain why they were called "cocked hats".'

'Yeah, nah, dunno. I did say, "Don't ask".'

We stopped to top up the fuel tank in the ute, and I paid with some of the cash I had taken from the poor lad on our lawn. I didn't want to use a credit card that might indicate the direction in which we were travelling.

About forty minutes later, we arrived at Caboolture Airfield.

Chapter 29

I pushed the appropriate code buttons on the security gate, and we drove to my hangar. I opened the roller door just long enough to allow Hannah to drive the ute inside and switched on the lights. My aircraft, a Cessna 172, sat there just as I had left it, shinily glinting under the fluorescent lights. Cessna built tens of thousands of 172s, and there are thousands still flying. Mine is still going strong and is always ready to go.

I had already decided the first thing I would do was carry out the pre-flight check. I thought there would be enough fuel remaining in the tanks from the last time I flew. I try to leave it with sufficient fuel to fly for a couple of hours, but not so much that if we filled all four seats, it would overload the aircraft.

The reason aviation is so incredibly safe is that current pilots have learned lessons from the hundred-plus years of pilots before us, many of whom died so we could learn from them. Therefore, I went carefully through the checklist from memory—I had flown this aircraft enough that I didn't need to refer to the actual paper checklist. I worked my way steadily and methodically around the aircraft in the time-honoured fashion. Even though I was the last to fly the aircraft, and I knew I had left her in an airworthy condition, I still checked everything—you never know. I'll never forget being at Stephenville Airport in Texas many years ago when a bloke in a ute, what they call a pick-up truck, rolled to a stop next to his aircraft. His truck had a pair of Texas Longhorn cattle horns on the bonnet and a gun-rack mounted with rifles in the rear window of the cab. He climbed out of his truck and into his aircraft, fired her up, taxied out, and took off. No checks, no nothing. I thought at the time, *Now there's a bloke who's in a hurry to get to the scene of his accident.*

I bent slightly to go under the wings to drain a small amount of fuel from both tanks into the transparent, plastic sample tube, examined the colour and sniffed at it to make sure it was, indeed, fuel. I had done this thousands of times and had many times wondered at the value of it. Until on one occasion, after a torrential downpour at Whitted Airport in St Petersburg, Florida, the whole sample was water. I held it to the sky to see that it was blue and, of course, against the blue sky, it *was* blue. Fortunately, I followed my training, sniffing the sample, and it didn't smell of fuel. I had to drain three or four samples from the tank until the liquid showed the correct blue colour and smelled of Avgas. There would have been just enough fuel in the pipe to get airborne when the water arrived at the cylinders, and then the engine would have stopped. Not recommended! That's why we have checklists and follow them assiduously.

Satisfied that all was well, I sat down at the small desk in the corner and calculated how much fuel I would need for the flight I was thinking of taking. There's an old pilots' adage: three things are useless to pilots—fuel in the bowser, runway behind you, and air above you. However, on this occasion, I didn't need to refuel the aircraft—as I suspected, there would be plenty for what I planned to do.

I went online and logged in to the website of the avionics maintenance company that looked after the electronics in my aircraft. I looked up the electrical system for the circuit breaker protecting the ADS-B. Old-school primary radars just provide the position of the aircraft 'return' up to fifteen times per minute. Secondary radars, in addition to position, can provide identity and altitude. ADS-B, Automatic Dependence Surveillance-Broadcast, is the modern 'radar'. It updates twice per second and is programmed with a variety of useful information, including the GPS position, which can be shown on the controller's display. The aircraft tracking apps on smartphones showing the air traffic around the world get nearly all their flight data from ADS-B. I didn't want the controllers at Amberley to see the position of my aircraft flying towards them on their displays, so I went back into the aircraft and pulled the circuit breaker out for the ADS-B; there was then no chance it would give me away unintentionally. The other device for displaying position to air traffic controllers was the transponder—but mine had an On/Off switch on the front that allows me not to turn it on. Too easy.

The others had unloaded the ute and set up a couple of camp beds for Hannah and Will. I could sleep in the rear of the ute with the tailgate down. My phone pinged to tell me a text had arrived. I quickly pulled it out of my pocket and looked at the text, which was from a number unknown to my phone—it came up just as numbers.

'I'm okay. They took my phone off me. What's happening. Where are you. Are the police coming for me. I'm really frightened.'

Hannah and Will gathered around me to read over my shoulder.

'Oh, thank goodness!' said Hannah. 'He's alive and well! Oh, my God, what a relief!'

'He must be using Orlov's phone. Good for you, Ollie, well done!'

'Supposing it's not him, Dad? Supposing it's them trying to suck you in?'

'Good on ya, Will. Smart thinking! What can we ask him that only he will know?'

Will replied, 'That's easy. Ask him his favourite aircraft.'

I typed in, 'Just checking, what's your favourite aircraft?'

'V22 Osprey. Will, what's yours?'

'That's him!' exclaimed Will. 'He must be wondering if it's us too! Tell him Super Hornet.'

I typed 'Super Hornet' and pressed send. Then I sent, 'Can you talk?'

'No, they'll hear me.'

Will pulled out the questions we had prepared.

I gave the phone to Will. 'Here, Will. You do it; you're quicker than me. We don't know how long he will have.'

Will quickly started typing the first question. 'Are you at Amberley? Can you see out of a window? What can you see?'

'Yes, think so. Baggage trucks below my window then fence, road, small building, and water tank. Far right just see big hangar.'

Another message arrived. *'Moon in 1 o'clock over tank.'* He used the direction based on a clock face that is used in aviation, where twelve is directly in front, so one o'clock is just right of centre.

I ran to the roller door and looked through the small window to see if I could see the moon. It was in front of me, halfway to the horizon. He was looking west.

I pulled my MacBook out of the ute, fired it up, and opened Google Earth. The internet never ceases to amaze me. I once found the address of one of my ancestors in a database online. I plugged the address in a tiny village in Dorset into Google Earth, went to Street View, and could look at a photo of the very house my relative lived in 300 years ago. Astonishing. On this occasion, I zoomed in on Amberley and scanned along the line of buildings on the flight line from south to north. *Baggage trucks*, I thought. *They'll be near the apron—no point in having them too far from where the aircraft parked.*

Towards the north end, there was an arrangement of buildings that might fit. A circular object, possibly a water tank. Not only that, there were C17s parked nearby, which would make sense if they were bringing in drugs on those aircraft. They'd be moving them off the aircraft into a building nearby.

'Ask him to text us a picture,' I said.

'Send photo,' wrote Will, and pressed send.

After a few seconds that seemed like an hour, my phone pinged, and Will tapped on the photo. It was not very clear in the darkness, but it was the area we had identified; baggage trucks in a small group in the foreground, a security fence with low-wattage floodlights along it just beyond them. The fence probably divided airside from landside; in other words, the secure area where the aircraft are from the unsecured area where the rest of the base personnel can go. Then there was a narrow road, and beyond that, a small building. The unique feature was the circular concrete tank just visible from the light of distant floodlights on the apron. Got him! He must be in the end room of a building just inside the fence. *That's good,* I thought. *We'll be able to get to him more easily, and the ground personnel will need a pass to get through the gate. That'll give us more time.*

I told Will, 'Tell him we'll send him a text on the other phone, the one Mum has, and to use that number so I can switch my phone off in case they are tracking it. And tell him we'll come for him between three and four a.m. Better write it as zero-three-zero-zero and zero-four-zero-zero.'

Hannah said, 'Tell him we love him.'

Will sent him a text on the other phone, and I switched mine off.

I asked them to sit with me next to the desk where they could see my map and we could discuss what we should do next. 'I have the start of a plan.'

'Cunning, I hope, babe?' asked Hannah.

I outlined my tentative, possible, potential beginnings of a plan. Not so much cunning as brute force and ignorance, but the best I could come up with in the time available. We knocked it around, finding multiple holes in it and trying to think of how we might mitigate the many problems we identified. In the end, tiredness and a lack of further ideas—good, bad, or indifferent—overtook us.

There seemed to be nothing more to be said, but we all seemed to feel that there should be. The sudden end to the frantic activity all day was an anticlimax, and I felt desperately tired—I badly needed to sleep. We each sauntered away to the toilets and settled into our sleeping bags upon return. I was pretty sure nobody would know we were here, but just in case, we slept fully clothed. With no phone to play with, Will went straight to sleep. I was still parched from not having drunk enough water during the day and losing liquid in the form of vomit, twice!

I knocked back four cups of cold water from the ten-litre container I kept at the hangar.

Chapter 30

I sat at the desk and rang Gadma on the phone I had taken from Danal, telling her we were planning to break Ollie out of the building where he was being kept, and woe betide anybody who got in our way. She was sceptical and tried to dissuade me.

When just telling me to leave it to the appropriate authorities didn't work, she tried practicalities. *'But how the hell are you going to get in there past guards and fences and floodlights?'*

'I'll give you two guesses.'

'Wire cutters. Cut a hole in the fence in some remote location.'

'Nup.'

'I have no idea. Crash the gate with a big ute. Tunnel under the fence. Pole vault over it?'

'That's four. Nup, nup, and nup.'

'Okay, I give up.'

'If you wanted to go to, let's say, Perth in a hurry … how would you get there from here?'

'Fly.'

'Yes. To Perth Airport.' I paused. 'We are going to an airport. So, we're going to fly in.'

'Can you fly?'

'Yes. And I own an aircraft.'

'Stuff me drunk. You crafty bugger.'

'What's crafty about flying into an air base? The RAAF do it all day, every day in massively noisy aircraft. So I expect someone has noticed there's an aerodrome there by now. Do you want to come?'

'Bloody oath, mate; try and stop me!' she replied without hesitation.

'Okay, good, thanks. Where are you now?'

'On my way to the office in the CBD. Where are you?'

'I'll pick you up somewhere convenient for both of us. The southwest corner of the cemetery at Archerfield Airport at zero-three-zero-zero. It's nice and quiet and out of the way. I'm not waiting, so if you're not there, I'll go without you.'

'They have a cemetery at Archerfield Airport?'

I chuckled. 'Yes, it's not what you think—it's called "God's Acre" from the old settler days when it was farmland.'

'Okay. I'll be there. But why so early? Wouldn't it be better to wait for daylight?'

'You've worked night shifts. So have I—many years as an air traffic controller. What time of the day are you most tired? When your body is at its lowest ebb? Between three and four in the morning. That's why we're going to hit them then. Catch these bastards fast asleep, I hope.'

'Okay.'

'And look, Golni, I am bringing my son out, come what may,' I said with heavy finality. Through gritted teeth, I continued, 'I've had enough of being beaten, shot at, kicked, and threatened. If these fuckers think they can push my family and me around, they are seriously mistaken. I am not running away anymore. So don't get between me and the people who are holding my son. You can arrest any of them that are still alive when I've finished with them, but don't get in my way. I'm going on the offensive, and I intend it to be very offensive!'

'I understand.'

'Do you? I'm pretty sure you will have no authority or jurisdiction on the base. So you'll be like me—a member of the public breaking into a military establishment. Do you still want to go on those terms?'

'Yes, Toby. I want to get these people. They're responsible for a lot of the death, misery, and crime around here and are making shedloads of money out of it, and they don't give a shit who they hurt in the process. Plus, they beat my friend and colleague 'til they nearly killed him, and they *did* kill my boss. It has to end. I'm going to help you end it.'

'Good on ya. Okay, thanks, Golni.' I paused to collect my thoughts. 'Can you get hold of body armour for three plus yourself? If not, for as many as you can lay your hands on. Oh, and as much firepower as you can muster.'

I put on my spectacles and spent quite a long time planning the three flights that I expected—or, rather, hoped—we would be making: Caboolture to Archerfield, Archerfield to Amberley, and Amberley to Brisbane Airport. My transponder would be off, and I had made sure I would not be transmitting an ADS-B signal, so the only possible way for the air traffic controllers to see me would be using their primary radar. On my flights tonight, I intended to fly so low that, with luck, they wouldn't notice my aircraft's primary radar return in and out of the base of their radar cover as I skirted the Brisbane Airport controlled airspace. And if they did see me, I wanted them to think, *That's not an aircraft; nobody flies that low at night.*

I scoured the aeronautical chart—yes, I'm old-school. Paper maps with hand-drawn lines. I am usually pretty diligent with my flight planning, but on this occasion, I took it to a new level and particularly focused on obstacles. I rarely fly below 1,000 feet—aviation works in feet for elevation and knots for speed. Remember the adage: sky above you is wasted. Navigation is much harder the lower one flies because one's view is more restricted, and things seem to happen more quickly compared to being at a higher altitude. So flying at 500 feet and below at night was going to be a real test of my skills, lookout, and nerve. Not to mention illegal. But, hey, the Civil Aviation Safety Authority would have to get in line to prosecute me!

I looked for a route that would allow me to fly as low as I could and remain outside Brisbane's controlled airspace. I also wanted to avoid all the obstacles, of which there were many—power lines, hills, buildings, TV masts. I didn't want to go too far to the west because there were some significant hills—you could see them from our house. Too far to the east would take me into Brisbane's control zone, where, I was sure, the radar coverage would be down to ground level. I did consider going through Brisbane's controlled airspace without calling them, but an 'airspace bust' would draw attention to me. I wasn't concerned so much about breaking the law—what's one more? Add it to the list. No, I didn't want anybody thinking, *That's odd. I wonder what they are up to. I'll watch them to see what they do next.*

I didn't want anybody remembering the flight. What do they say? 'I'm not paranoid; they really *are* out to get me!' Well, it was true in my case. It was possible at this time of the morning; the controllers may not be paying too much attention, especially if they had no traffic to control. However, paranoia or not, I wanted to reduce the risk that they would spot me, then track me, and then notify the police.

I found a route that would be easy to follow, south from Caboolture along the highway to the interchange at Bald Hills just north of the control zone, slight right turn southwest-bound towards the tall masts at Mount Coot-Tha. Turn slightly left, keeping the masts on my left, and run just east of south to cross the Brisbane River over its big, southern loop. Then, with Archerfield in sight, fly over the aerodrome and a left-hand circuit to land on Runway 28 Right—the longer of the two parallel runways. It was also nearer to where I wanted to park.

I then did the same process for the Archerfield to Amberley leg. The main thing I wanted to check was the length of the apron at Amberley, where the C17s park to be loaded, unloaded, and serviced. I wanted to finish my landing roll as close as possible to the building where we thought Ollie was being kept. So, using the 'ruler' function on Google Earth, the usable concrete measured at about 450 metres. The landing and take-off distances were shown in graphs in the aircraft operator's manual. I estimated the approximate weight of the aircraft on landing at Amberley with the fuel and three people, and the temperature, which would be about twenty Celsius. The data plotted onto the graph left me pleased and relieved there would be plenty of room for the landing and, also, for the take-off with the addition of a fourth person, Ollie.

Examination of Google Earth also showed me that there would be no obstacles in the direction from which I would be coming. The floodlight poles down the side of the apron were thirty metres off the concrete—well away from where we would be landing. Same on the other side for take-off. The wind from the northwest would mean a slight crosswind from the front-right on landing and a slight tail crosswind from the left on take-off. Shouldn't be a problem.

Finally, I planned the Amberley to Brisbane Airport leg. If we survived whatever was to take place at Amberley, I didn't care about hiding. In fact, I wanted Air Traffic Control to know where we would be at all times. So I planned to fly at a safe altitude to avoid obstacles, switch on my transponder and ADS-B so they could identify me on their 'radar' displays, and call them on the tower frequency to let them know I was coming.

I checked the weather forecast, and on the mobile phone, I dialled the AWIS for Amberley and Archerfield. AWIS was an automated weather service that, among other things, gave the wind speed and direction. I looked up all the Air Traffic Control frequencies I might need. I checked the NOTAMs, a contraction of 'Notices to Airmen', relating to the places we would be going by logging into the NAIPS internet briefing system for pilots. There, I read about arcane information like taxiway closures due to maintenance or failed lighting systems. Nothing significant for Caboolture or Archerfield. However, I got a shock when I looked at the NOTAMs for Amberley. The Air Traffic Control would be operating outside its normal hours. That meant they must be night flying—probably an exercise, or they had money left over in their monthly flying budget and the fighter pilots wanted to burn it off. That could be a problem—we would be able to get in okay, but if the controllers were looking out for the few minutes when we landed, they would alert security earlier than I had hoped. Anyway, I thought, *Nothing to be done—committed to the plan now*. I noted everything down on the knee pad I wore when flying. I calculated the headings, ground speeds, and elapsed times for each of the legs and noted them, too.

We discussed who should come with me to Amberley. In the end, we decided it should be Will because he can fly the aircraft. The Cessna is a four-seater, so we had to save one seat for Golni and one, of course, for Ollie. Hannah wanted to come instead of Will, but we discussed it and felt that it was more important that Will come so he could fly in case anything happened to me.

I put my black flight bag in the aircraft and plugged my two nice, new noise-cancelling headsets—one each for Will and me—in the front and my two old spare headsets in the back for Golni and Ollie.

At about half-past midnight, I was completely knackered! It was warm and cosy in the sleeping bag in the back of the ute, even though I was on a thin, foam mattress. Normally, I thought it was a bit too firm and rather uncomfortable, but I was so tired after my day I could have slept on a rope strung between two posts. The stress and adrenaline had drained my body of energy. My mind was numb with tiredness. What a day! I had stabbed one man, shot another, run down a third, smashed the wrist of a fourth, and blown three to smithereens. I'd been threatened with a gun, punched and kicked, and had my finger cut off. And that was as far as my conscious thinking got.

Chapter 31

The man they called Dezza, one of the two wearing a balaclava, bundled Ollie into the car and followed him into the back seat, slamming the door shut behind him. The other man in a balaclava got in the driver's seat and drove out of the Richmonds' driveway onto the road, and accelerated off down the hill. Ollie had never been so frightened. He had once been in a shop when some young thugs had tried to rob it, but they hadn't taken hostages, and it was all over in a flash once they had stolen some cash and fled. This was entirely different. Different. Entirely. This was not going to end quickly, and these guys seemed completely ruthless. He was absolutely petrified. His guts started to churn, and he felt as though he might need the loo any minute.

'I think I need a toilet,' he said.

'Tough shit,' replied Dezza from within the balaclava next to him. 'Hold it in. We're not stopping.' He chuckled and said, 'Hey, did you see what I did there? Tough shit when he's got the runs!'

They drove in silence for a few minutes until they had passed Samford. Then the balaclava driving said, 'We need to get hold of someone from Amberley to help you get this lad into hiding on the base.'

'I'll ring Glebbo,' replied Dezza.

'No, you can't ring him. He's in hospital with gunshot wounds from where this little shit's dad shot him. Try Jiwani.'

'Oh, I don't like talking to him. He's so unpredictable. He always makes me feel as if he's going to jump down my throat for no reason. He's a fucking psychopath.'

'Ring him.'

Dezza rang Jiwani and told him what was happening, asking for help to get Ollie onto the base.

Jiwani gave him instructions on where to pick him up in Ipswich, and they drove on.

They came off the highway and into the suburbs of Ipswich. They meandered through various side streets and pulled into the front driveway of a house. Ollie was told to get out and walk around to the back of the house. Once out of sight of the road, Dezza pulled a strip of duct tape off a roll and stuck it across Ollie's mouth. They made him stand with his legs apart, leaning hard against the wall of the house. Once stuck in that position, they pulled a balaclava over his head with the eyeholes to the back so that he couldn't see.

'Give me your phone,' demanded Dezza.

Ollie handed over a phone, making sure, by feel, that it was his own and not the one his dad had given him.

They pulled him off the wall and tied his hands behind his back with some rope. Then they shepherded him back to the front of the house.

'Make any noise, and we'll kill you, understand?'

Ollie nodded.

They made him climb back into the boot of the car he had just scrambled out of and slammed the lid shut.

Ollie was somewhat relieved. They hadn't hurt him or even threatened to hurt him except if he made a noise, and he didn't intend to do that. He'd seen what these people could do. More importantly, they hadn't searched him, so they hadn't found the other phone. It looked as if he was set to stay in the boot of this car until they were on the base. If that was the case, they wouldn't be making any noise or disturbance when they arrived at their destination for fear of drawing attention to themselves.

The car drove on for a few more minutes. It stopped at one point, and he guessed that was as they passed through the gate to the base. The car slowed again and then stopped. He heard some low, quiet voices but couldn't make out what they were saying. The car waited for a few moments and then drove on very slowly. He could feel it manoeuvre around some tight turns, and then they stopped again. He heard the doors open, and the lid of the boot popped open.

'Sit up.'

He sat up.

'Climb out.'

They helped him climb out. They held him by his arms, one on each side, and guided him into a building and down a short corridor. A door closed behind him.

As one of them started undoing the rope, the other said, 'No noise, okay?'

He nodded.

'The quickest way to stop you making a noise is to shoot you. Understood?'

He nodded.

'Leave the balaclava on until we close the door. Understood?'

He nodded again.

The rope came off his hands. He heard them leave and the door close. The key turned in the lock. There was silence in the room.

He pulled the balaclava off and looked around the room. The light was out, and he looked for the switch but couldn't find it—it must have been outside the door. There was a little light coming in through the window from streetlights and the security floodlights. It was a very small room with the brickwork just painted over in some drab beige colour, one small window quite high up the wall, and some suitcases stacked in a pile in one corner.

In another corner was a pile of half a dozen military-style camouflaged rucksacks. He took a couple of paces to the window but couldn't reach it.

He pulled a couple of suitcases over, stacked them one on top of the other, stepped up onto them, and looked out. Nothing special—some baggage-handling equipment, a fence, a building, a tank. A water tank, not an armoured tank with a cannon. If he pressed his face against the glass, there was nothing more to see to the left, but to the right, there was a big hangar.

He looked at the door and wondered if they would come back any time soon. He stepped down, took a few paces over to the door, and put his ear against it. Nothing. Keeping his ear against the door, he pulled out the phone his dad had given him and, using the code on the back, unlocked it. He turned the volume down—he didn't want them to hear a call come in. He'd been lucky that so far, nobody had rung it.

He shakily opened the texting app and wrote, *'I'm okay. They took my phone off me. What's happening. Where are you. Are the police coming for me. I'm really frightened.'* After a few moments, a reply arrived. *'Just checking, what's your favourite aircraft?'*

He paused, thinking, *Okay, they want to check it's me.* But he wondered if it was his dad. Could they have found out his dad's phone somehow? Or hacked into it? Who knew what was going on and who was doing what? He typed, *'V22 Osprey. Will, what's yours?'*

'Super Hornet' came back. He sighed, relieved. It was Will's ambition to fly Super Hornets. He was so much happier that he had contact with his family. He didn't feel so alone, even though he knew they couldn't do anything for him.

They asked for information and a photo, which he sent. His hopes rose as they texted back and forth. They told him to use the number on the other phone in the future, as his dad was going to switch his off in case the police were tracking it. They told him they were coming for him between 0300 and 0400. He checked the clock on the phone: *2310*.

The phone seemed to be well charged, so he switched on the torch and looked in some bags and suitcases. Maybe there would be something useful he could use as a weapon: tools, knives, scissors, wire, maybe real weapons—it was a military base, after all. Some bags were not locked, and he opened them and dug around inside. Nothing suited his needs, just personal clothing and belongings. He did find a couple of wash bags, but the scissors were tiny—for cutting fingernails or something. The only thing he pocketed was a metal nail file with a nasty-looking pointed end for getting dirt out from under fingernails. Might come in handy. He switched off the phone's torch, set the alarm to ring at 0230—early, but he wanted to be ready—and switched the alarm to vibrate only. Making himself comfortable on the pile of rucksacks, he tried to go to sleep.

Chapter 32

Ollie lay on the bags, wide awake, fretting. He was frightened about what they might do to him. He was anxious about what was going to happen if and when his dad arrived to try to take him. What kind of a fight would they put up for him? He still could see no advantage in holding him now that they were all clear of the house. Why didn't they just drop him by the side of the road somewhere? Would they just ignore him and let him go? His mind continued to jump from one topic to the next in his anxiety. He thought about the aircraft just outside on the apron. His ambition was to be a pilot—not a private pilot like his dad—a commercial pilot or in the RAAF. He didn't mind what he flew, just as long as he flew something. He kind of leaned towards rotary-wing but liked some fixed-wing aircraft, too. That's probably why his favourite aircraft was the V22 Osprey: a cross between a helicopter and an aeroplane.

Moving over to the window, he stood on the stacked cases to look out. It was still dark. The floodlights appeared to be on, to his right, but he couldn't really see—it was just too far to the right, even when he pressed the side of his face to the glass. Nothing different. No cars, no people. As his dad always said when they were flying straight and level, in balance, properly trimmed—he would point to the instruments and say, 'There you go. Nothing moving but the clock.' The moon had set, but it had made no noticeable difference to the light in the room from the floodlights and streetlights.

He wondered how his dad would come to rescue him. Would he turn up at the gate and say to them, 'You have kidnapped my son. I demand you turn him over to me!'? Probably not. He supposed he might come with the police—the police could demand access. He tried to remember what his dad had said earlier; the police weren't allowed on the base without permission; was that right? Or would he come with his bolt-cutters and cut his way through the fence? Surely they have cameras or sensors or something along the fence? Ram the gates? No. Obviously, he could fly in. That seemed the most likely to him. What would he do? Give them a call on the appropriate frequency and ask to land? No. Maybe declare an emergency and just come in and land? No, they'd be waiting for him before he got off the runway.

He sat down again on the pile of rucksacks to wait. Every time he thought of what was to come, he felt a little spike of adrenaline pump into his system. The anxiety and fear returned.

He couldn't just sit and do nothing. He looked at the battery strength in the phone and decided there was enough that he could have a look at the local news websites to see what they were saying. They were full of shootouts and bodies, but the reporters hadn't made it into their house in Samsonvale yet.

Ollie kept browsing the internet for a while, interspersed with going to the window to see if anything was happening. Eventually, he got bored and put the phone in his pocket. He sat back on the rucksacks and closed his eyes, hoping for sleep.

He was startled awake by the sound of footsteps near the door. The thought that this might be his dad jumped into his brain and raised his hopes, which were dashed when the light came on, the door opened, and two men in RAAF uniforms walked in.

One of them said, 'Neil, hold this kid down while I fuck him to a standstill.'

'Do I have to? Can't you do it on your own, Jiwani? I hate watching you shagging boys.'

'Okay, fuck off outside and shut the door, but wait there so you can let me out when I've finished with him.'

Ollie was astonished and petrified, looking and listening to this conversation going on as though he wasn't there. They were talking as though they were having a dispute over who was going to carry the dustbins out. The man called Neil left the room and closed the door.

The man called Jiwani turned to Ollie, now clearly enjoying himself. 'There's an aircraft due with a load on board for me to fetch, but there's enough time for us to enjoy ourselves in the meantime. Then I can go about my business before the boss arrives for the stuff. Now, get your clothes off and lie face down on those bags.' He nodded towards the rucksacks where Ollie had been resting.

'No.'

'Oh, now, look, don't be like that. I'm not like those blokes you see in the prison movies who like a little refusal and resistance and call it "playing hard to get".' He made a couple of air quotes with his two index fingers. 'I would much prefer it if you were willing and, better still, if you were enthusiastic. Any chance of that?'

'None.'

'You do understand that I am not averse to beating the shit out of you until you are unable to refuse, don't you?'

'Go fuck yourself!'

'Very *drôle*. Remember I said we are against the clock? Last chance; get your kit off, young lad.'

'No.'

Even though he was trembling with fear and adrenaline, ready for a fight and expecting violence, the speed with which Jiwani attacked him took him by surprise. In three quick steps, Jiwani crossed the space between them and slapped him with full force on the left side of his face. Ollie sprawled to the floor, putting his left hand to his cheek. He didn't make a sound. He just looked up at the man standing over him and saw him for what he was: a sadistic bully. He thought, *Okay, bring it on. I'll be ready next time.*

Jiwani said, 'Now, don't waste my time. It'll get worse the longer you hold out on me.'

'Yeah? Come on then, you little fuckwit!' Ollie jumped to his feet, pulled the metal nailfile out of his pocket, and clenched it in his fist to use like a knife, crouching, staring at Jiwani in the eyes. Jiwani was a product of what is known as 'The School of Hard Knocks'. He had extensive experience with bar brawls near military camps around the world, the torment of being beaten repeatedly by homophobes and white racists, and learning speed and aggression from many fights, and he was in-built with the basic killer instinct of a sociopath. Ollie just had courage.

Ollie charged, but Jiwani was much too quick for him. He stepped slightly to his right and hit Ollie with a vicious uppercut to his left chin, which broke his jaw and knocked him unconscious. Ollie went headfirst into the suitcases, out cold. Jiwani flexed his knuckles and said gently, 'There you are, young lad. I did warn you.'

Jiwani rolled Ollie on his back, took off his shoes, undid his trousers, and pulled them and his underpants down until he was naked from the waist down. He then rolled Ollie over onto his front, face down among the cases. He stood, looking down at Ollie's backside, smiling as he undid his own trousers and underpants and let them drop to his ankles.

Chapter 33

I was sore. Every time I moved, my ribs or my hand reminded me they were there. I was overtired, both physically and mentally, and my mind would not really rest. It took what seemed like ages to drop off to sleep, and even then, it was disturbed; dreaming, waking, worrying about Ollie, the plan, the risks. It was a simple plan: fly in, use Orlov's pass to get into the building, get Ollie, fly out to Brisbane Airport, surrender to the police. Very straightforward when you say it quickly. What could possibly go wrong?

The alarm clock on my phone rang at 0200. I felt dreadful. My head was groggy, my eyes seemed to be covered with a layer of grit, and my eyelids wanted to slam shut all the time. My tongue seemed two sizes too big for my mouth and covered with dry, hairy foam. I felt really grim.

I forced myself to sit up, still in my sleeping bag, with my legs over the end of the ute's tailgate so I wouldn't fall back to sleep. Just sitting felt sore—I gently felt around my ribcage with my fingers. It was bad. If I moved, breathed deeply, or coughed, my ribs stabbed me in the side. I was pretty sure laughing would be painful, but I didn't think there was much chance of laughing any time soon. And the bandage on my finger was a dirty, bloody mash of material. It needed changing. I rubbed my eyes with the heels of my hands. It didn't help.

In the corner of the hangar, on the end of my desk, was a kettle. I knew it was there, but I couldn't see it in the darkness. I looked in its direction, blinking and thinking, *This is bloody hard yakka.* Rubbing my eyes some more, I slid my bum off the edge of the tailgate, dropped the sleeping bag to the floor, and stepped out of it. In the corner near the door, I flicked on the overhead fluorescent lights. Shit! They were bright!

Standing, blinking, trying to get my eyes fully open in the glare of the lights, I waited for the kettle to boil. In between mouth-stretching yawns, I rubbed my eyes to try to get the grit out of them. I made teas and coffees: tea for Will and me and an instant coffee for Hannah, while they groaned and grumped and got themselves out of their sleeping bags.

I decided to drink a cup of cold water, pondering, as I did so, the consequences of drinking so much with what we faced that morning, but I was still gagging for a drink. I had once set off from Sumburgh in the Shetland Islands to fly non-stop to Aberdeen in another Cessna 172—a distance of about 400 km. I had had some breakfast and two cups of tea early that morning. We hadn't even reached Kirkwall in the Orkneys, about 150 km, when my bladder told me the second cup of tea had been a mistake. I had to land in Kirkwall very briefly—I told them why, but they still charged me a landing fee! As an older bloke, one must always consider the future availability of toilets.

The ache in my ribs and soreness in my finger had increased as the painkillers wore off. I wanted more painkillers. Would the painkillers compromise my flying ability? Or would it be better to take some and be pain-free? I decided I had better not take any. I needed to be sharp, and not just for the flying. Notwithstanding the crap night's sleep I'd had, rolling around worrying about what the next few hours might hold and picking a hundred holes in the plan, I felt a bit better. We had kept out of the way of the police and two motorcycle gangs; we had taken necessary action to protect ourselves when threatened with deadly danger, and we had a plan to go on the offensive. I was fed up with defending myself and running from one dreadful situation to another, hiding from the police and taking fright at every loud noise that could be some thug coming to get us. Now we would take the fight to them, and I felt good about it.

My tummy rumbled, and I remembered I had chucked up my meal a few hours ago. No wonder I felt hungry. I considered breakfast; I would feel better with a Maccas brekkie sandwich inside me. I'm one of those people who can't function without brekkie in the morning. But that wasn't going to happen today—no Maccas where we were going. Then I remembered there were a couple of tinnies of beer in the esky by the desk. I saved them for after I'd been flying and when some of the other aeroplane-nuts come by for a chat and a cold one. But they wouldn't be cold, and I generally didn't drink at two in the morning. I slept. So no beer, either. However, speaking of nuts, I remembered there was a bag of peanuts and a box of biscuits in the desk drawer. I ate a couple of handfuls of nuts and four or five chocolate hobnobs—the world's finest biscuits!

'Good morning,' I said as I kissed Hannah on the cheek and handed the coffee to her. 'How are you both feeling?'

'Like shit,' Hannah replied. She sighed. 'Didn't sleep a wink. Worried sick about Ollie.'

I kissed Will on the top of his head and gave him his tea. He didn't like me kissing him. Tough. I asked, 'You all right, Will?'

'Shit, yeah, Dad!'

'Will!' said his mum.

'Sorry, Mum,' he chirped, obviously not a bit sorry.

I offered Hannah, 'Peanuts, Hobnobs, or both?'

She shook her head. 'Can't face them at this time of night.'

Will took a handful of nuts and all the biscuits that were left.

We collected the guns together on the desk, and I rechecked them all. The Glock with the silencer and the 'exploding' bullets had seven rounds left. The other Glock had fourteen rounds, and the two from the ute were as before: ten in the M&P and sixteen in the PPQ with the laser. The bullets all looked the same calibre, but I wasn't at all sure if they were. I was pretty sure I could use the bullets from the Glocks interchangeably in either Glock, so I popped the magazines out of the

Glocks and reloaded the one with the silencer alternately with 'exploding' and normal bullets until it was full, with one in the chamber—eighteen in all. The remaining three, I left in the second Glock.

So, four guns, one with silencer and light, one with laser, and, in total, forty-seven rounds of ammunition.

I gave the M&P to Will and showed him how to work it and the Glocks. I put the Glock with three rounds in the door pocket on the passenger side of the aircraft. The Glock and the PPQ with lights I put on the back seat, ready for me to take with me when we got to Amberley.

I sat at the desk and checked the weather on my iPad, listening to the AWIS automatic weather report again. I don't know what a perfect night for an illegal landing at Amberley should look like, but the weather seemed okay to me: light winds from the northwest and some scattered cloud at 1,500 feet. I thought the cloud shouldn't be a problem, as I was hoping to stay well below 1,500 feet.

I went to Hannah and hugged her. She hugged me back. I said, 'Hannah, I love you.'

'I love you too,' she replied.

We let go, and I walked around to the front of the aircraft, buzzing the remote to open the hangar door as I went. I picked up the hand-draw bar and pulled the aircraft out of the hangar. Will climbed into the right-hand seat, and I climbed into the left. Before I started the engine, I switched on the power and the radios and tuned them to the frequencies I might need after departure: unnecessary fiddling with the radios while flying at low level at night is not recommended. I had decided I would not make any of the normal calls during the flight on any radio frequencies to alert other traffic to my position and intentions, but I wanted to be able to hear any calls other aircraft might make. To keep as low and unobtrusive as possible—that's what I wanted. To that end, I was also going to switch off my lights as soon as I was airborne, keeping them off until I got to Archerfield. If I heard any traffic on the radio, I might switch on my lights if they were anywhere near me. Otherwise,

I would leave them off until I was overhead Archerfield. Archerfield had pilot-activated lights for night flying, so I wouldn't be able to hide my presence. It's a great system—just click the transmit switch on the radio the required three times, and on come the aerodrome and approach lights for half an hour.

I opened the small half-window in the door next to me, went through the pre-start checks, and automatically had a good look around for pedestrians—who would be walking around at 0220? So I didn't shout, 'Clear!' as I normally would. Hannah had set off in her ute to the far end of the runway because this aerodrome had no lights for night flying. I cranked the engine. It started immediately, and I adjusted the throttle to 800 RPM while I completed the after-start checks. I switched on the radios but not the transponder, released the parking brakes, and we taxied to the runway.

It was only a short taxi to the threshold of Runway 29, which I had selected to use for take-off because it was into what little wind there was. Also, it was conveniently close to the hangars and would reduce the amount of time people might hear my engine. I completed the engine run-up and pre-take-off checks. Hannah had driven out to the northwest side of the aerodrome to the far end of Runway 29 and turned her ute so the headlights pointed directly down the runway towards me. I saw a couple of big eastern grey kangaroos just standing, looking at me as though to say, 'Don't mind us.' But I did mind them. Where there's one, there is often a mob, and kangaroos are the most stupid animals. When they're at the side of the road, they'll stand a look at you as you drive towards them, and as you get to them, instead of bounding away like any sensible animal, they'll leap straight in front of the vehicle. I had to hope the others were not grazing on the grass of the runway I was about to use.

As I taxied onto the runway, I automatically looked up the approach to ensure there was no traffic approaching. *You're nuts,* I thought. *There are no runway lights; why would there be traffic?*

I lined up on the centreline of the runway, pointing directly at Hannah with all my lights on, applied full throttle, and was quickly airborne. I flicked all the lights out and turned right (as required for noise abatement) at about 400 feet onto my planned heading, levelling off at that height. I told Will to keep his eyes looking permanently out of the windscreen for obstacles and that he had my permission to take control of the aircraft to avoid any he saw.

It was a beautiful night, still and smooth, with the lights of Brisbane reflecting a little glow off the few clouds dotted about, making the navigation fractionally easier. We didn't talk. He knew I was concentrating hard on navigating at low level, which is not easy even in daylight.

I followed the M1 motorway as planned—easy enough even with the sparse night-time traffic. Just a few massive B-double trucks pounding along beneath us. After a few minutes, Will pointed out the lights on the Bald Hills masts in front of us. I thanked him. I turned slightly right onto my new heading and noted the time. *Stick to my heading and timing*, I reminded myself. I flew on, and when I saw the lights of the railway station at Ferny Grove, I noted the time again and turned slightly left.

I told Will to watch out for the strobe lights on the TV masts, which should be coming up in our eleven o'clock. We both got a fright when we realised the masts were directly in front of us, most of the masts sticking up above the base of the low cloud and the top lights not visible. I swung slightly right to avoid the high ground and the towers. I rechecked the map—I knew there was more high ground further to the right. I was planning to climb to about 1,000 feet to stay at what I thought was a safe height above the ground that rose up to about 700 feet in front of me. However, I kept at about 800 to 900 feet—just above the ground and just below the base of the cloud. Every now and then, we felt the slight tremor as we clipped the bottom of the cloud and the lights disappeared. I eased the aircraft lower, a few tens of feet. It went against all my training and the training I had given to others when I was a flying instructor, but I had to do it. I didn't want to climb into the cloud because I couldn't be sure how high or far the cloud extended and how low it might go once over the ridge. Equally, I didn't want to go any lower, as I was frightened there might be a power line or mobile phone mast that wasn't marked on my chart.

We scudded along the bottom of the cloud, and the houses and streetlights flashed past just underneath the wheels. I fretted that the ground would continue to rise—I would be really in trouble then. We flew on for a few more seconds—I breathed a quiet sigh of relief as the ground started to drop away from us, and I was able to edge lower out of the broken base of the clouds. I was monitoring the radio frequency that Brisbane Air Traffic Control used in this area. The air traffic controller broke the silence in my world. *'Cas-evac fifty-six, traffic in your ten o'clock, four miles, left to right, non-squawking, so no level information.'*

The casualty evacuation helicopter replied, *'Looking. Cas-evac fifty-six.'* Then, a few seconds later, *'Nothing seen. Request updates.'*

'He appears to be very low level. I lost his primary radar return as he passed behind Mt Coot-Tha. On his present track, he should pass behind you in about two miles. I don't know what he thinks he's doing at such low level at night.'

'Roger. Nothing seen, Cas-evac fifty-six.'

Bugger, I thought. *They've seen me. And I've managed to get myself close enough to another aircraft that ATC had to provide traffic information. I hope this is not an indication of how the rest of the night is going to go. Now she's going to be watching me all the way. Bugger.*

My plan to stay unobtrusive had failed royally. I couldn't let it worry me—just concentrate on the task at hand. I steered my aircraft to the right, behind the helicopter that was lit up brightly, flashing white strobes, red anti-collision lights, and the red navigation light glaring steadily at me to give way. Watching the helicopter pass to my left, I settled on the last heading towards Archerfield, noted the time, and gently climbed to 1,000 feet. No point in trying to hide now.

I had been monitoring the Archerfield frequency on my other radio and pushed the button to toggle from Brisbane's frequency to Archerfield's. I clicked the transmit switch three times, and there, straight in front of us in our twelve o'clock, appeared the lights of the whole aerodrome. Switching on my strobes, navigation, anti-collision and landing lights, I went through the various pre-landing checks. Gently closing the throttle, I started to slow the aircraft down.

The aerodrome slid quickly beneath us, and I flew the left-hand circuit to land on Runway 28 Right. I didn't make any of the required calls on the radio because the frequencies are recorded, and I still didn't want anybody identifying me, if avoidable. I was going to be in heaps of trouble with the police, the Department of Defence, and the Royal Australian Air Force as it was—I wanted to avoid crossing swords with my former employers, the Civil Aviation Safety Authority, if I could.

I decided to practise my short-field landing technique in preparation for the apron at Amberley. Got the speed on the approach okay, stuck the aircraft down pretty firmly near the white line marking the start of the runway, braked, and turned off at the second exit. Okay. Maybe not full marks, but at least a 'pass'. I taxied to the apron and found a place to park. Switched all the lights off and shut down the engine. It was 0300. Let's hope Golni was where I asked her to be.

'Will, you stay here. I'm not expecting to see anybody at this time of night, but if anybody comes, just say you know nothing and wait for me.'

'Okay, Dad.'

I picked my flight briefcase out of the back and jogged across the apron to the gate near the cemetery. I opened the foot-gate and put the briefcase in the gap to stop it closing and locking me out—I didn't know the access code here.

Golni was right there. She said, 'I parked over there. Is that okay?' She pointed to her car.

'Golni, we could all be dead or, at best, in military prison in an hour! If you get a parking ticket, that'll be the least of your worries! Did you bring some armour-plated jackets?'

'No, I only have my own. But I did bring my weapon and my taser.' She was wearing her uniform with the standard utility belt; the gun was in the holster on her right hip, the taser on her left.

'Good on ya. Okay, then, let's get this party started!' I pushed the gate open, picked up the briefcase, and trotted off towards the aircraft.

As we jogged, she said, 'I should have checked my text messages sooner. They told me your phone was stationary at Caboolture Airfield and then switched off. I would have guessed what you had in mind.'

'Okay, well, that's good. Maybe you can tell me because I'm still not sure what I have in mind.'

Chapter 34

I introduced Gadma to Will and got her installed in the right-hand front seat with a headset.

'What's the plan?' she asked.

Will was sitting in the rear right passenger seat where I could see him.

'Will, you tell Golni while I get us going,' I replied.

'Well, it's like this,' he said, smiling. 'Dad says it's simple. I am not convinced!'

'Simple plan,' I interjected. 'Not necessarily simple to execute.'

Will continued, 'We fly into Amberley, land on the apron where the C17s park so that the landing roll finishes next to the building where we think Ollie is being kept. Dad has a security pass, which he stole from a RAAF bloke yesterday and which we're hoping will open the building where Ollie is. We go in, get Ollie, come back to the aircraft, and take off on the apron, but in the opposite direction. Then we fly to Brisbane Airport and hand ourselves over to the police at the Queensland Government Air Wing. Or, if things don't go so well, we'll go to the Royal Flying Doctor Service hangar for medical treatment—there'll be doctors on call there twenty-four-seven.'

'What happens if your father is injured and can't fly?'

'I can fly,' Will replied.

'You can fly, too. 'Course you can,' she said flatly. 'Why the Police Air Wing? Why not the RAAF police?'

'Because we think they are sufficiently removed from the mainstream police that they won't be corrupt. And we don't trust the RAAF police and security because they are on the base and may have been bought as well.'

'How do you know which building your brother is in?'

'We compared his description of what he could see out of the window with what we could see on Google Earth.'

'Are you sure we can land on an apron? Aren't they small areas where aircraft park? It sounds dangerous.'

'Yeah, but this apron is huge—it can take several C17 Globemasters, which are the large freight aircraft used by the RAAF. We measured the apron on Google Earth and checked against the take-off and landing distances we need. The wind is not going to be much of a factor because it's so light tonight. It all looks doable.'

'Okay, Will, but what if there are some of these C17s on the apron?'

'There's still room to land between where they park and the edge of the concrete. They have what's called self-manoeuvring parking. In other words, they don't park nose-in to a building like airliners do at a terminal; they taxi along one edge of the apron, turn ninety degrees, and then stop. So there's an area for them to turn, which will be big enough for us to land on behind where they park. There's a similar area in front of them so that they can taxi straight out without the need for a tug. That's where we will be taking off. So even if they are in the way of the building where Ollie is, we can probably taxi under their wings—these C17s are huge! The main problem will be lining up with the narrow apron edge where we want to land when we are a mile or two out. Especially if the floodlights are off.'

'But don't they have anti-aircraft missiles or something to stop people landing?'

'Don't know. Hope not. Another issue is that it looks as though they will be night flying—maybe training, maybe an exercise in progress, and the Super Hornets are operating. All the lights may be on everywhere, people all over the place. Could make the landing difficult if there are vehicles where we want to land.'

'Bloody hell, this sounds like chaos. What do we do if they are operating?'

'It's very late. With any luck, it's all finished, and they're all tucked up in bed. If there is nothing happening, maybe the air traffic controllers will be too bored to look out and notice us. But if they are still operating, maybe they will be too busy to notice us. I mean, how often do light aircraft land at night without lights, unannounced, on their aprons? Never happens. However, lastly, and worstly, the apron where we are going to land may be active if they are dispatching or receiving a C17 flight.'

'What's your plan, then?'

'Wing it!'

'Ha, ha,' Gadma said sarcastically.

'No, really, that is the plan—we'll play it by ear. Have a look. If the apron is blocked, then there's always the runway, but it means a longer taxi after landing—not optimal. Then, see how close we can get with a little judicious gun-waving. If we are in and out quickly enough, they may not be able to get security fast enough to stop us.'

I turned in my seat slightly so I could look at both of them. 'Righto, the flight to Amberley will take about twenty minutes. Golni, have you ever flown in a light aircraft before?'

She shook her head.

I gave her a briefing on how to undo her seatbelt and open the doors. I continued, 'After we've landed, I'll taxi as close to the building where Ollie is as I can. I plan to shut down the engine some distance away and coast to a halt so that the noise of our engine is less likely to alert them. Golni, you and I get out of the aircraft as fast as we can. Will, you get into the left seat of the aircraft and make sure it is ready for departure as soon as we get back on board. If the door to the building isn't open and the pass won't open it, I'll be open to suggestions as to how to open it. Golni, can we shoot the lock out—is that a possibility? Or is it just a Hollywoodism?'

'Yeah, of course you can shoot at the lock, but you have to hit the lock. You can't just blast away—especially as we are limited on ammunition. The other risk is ricochets. So maybe I do the lock-shooting, as I have the body armour.'

I said, 'Okay. If all goes well, we put Ollie and Golni in the back seat, and I'll fly from the right seat. Are we all clear? Any questions?'

There were no questions.

I started the engine and taxied out to the holding position near the end of the runway on which I landed and from which I was going to take off: Runway 28 Right. I ran through the checks, and the aircraft was ready. I taxied onto the runway and, in one smooth movement, turned the aircraft to point down the length of the runway, applied full power, and we were rolling. Once airborne and beyond the end of the runway, I switched off the navigation and anti-collision lights. I climbed straight ahead to 300 feet and, having crossed the M7 motorway, turned the aircraft slightly left so I could keep it in sight on my left-hand side.

We flew along the motorway towards Ipswich, and when the railway joined alongside the road, I switched my attention to following the railway lines. The few cars and trucks on the road going in the opposite direction flashed beneath us, and the ones going our way slowly slipped behind us. The sensation of speed was so much greater at low level. It seemed as though we were ten times the speed we normally cruised at, and I was deliberately flying the aircraft at a slower speed than normal because I knew navigating at low level would be tricky, having never done it before.

I had the map orientated so the direction in which we were flying, towards Amberley, was at the top. I kept checking our progress on the ground and, every few seconds, moving my finger up the map.

As the centre of the town and the main rail station zipped beneath us, I started slowing the aircraft and ran through the various pre-landing checks. Having studied Google Earth earlier, I knew there was a huge railway marshalling yard directly at the point where I needed to turn towards Amberley to make my final approach to the apron. I spotted the rail yards up ahead and kept following the railway tracks to them. I looked out to my left, where I expected to see Amberley, and I was a bit shocked to see how brightly it was lit up—like day! The runway lights and all the floodlights were on. There were several C17 freighters on the apron where we would be landing, and I could see some vehicles with flashing orange lights on their roofs moving near them. *So the C17s must be just arriving or soon to depart,* I thought. I turned the aircraft towards the point on the apron I was going to use as my aiming point for the landing. The floodlights were actually a help in lining up on the edge of the taxiway. I lowered the flaps and adjusted the power, attitude, and elevator trim to slow the aircraft to the correct approach speed.

Will said, 'Dad, do you think we ought to go back to Archerfield and, like, think about this again?'

'No, we're committed. Anybody comes close, you get out and persuade them to stay away. But don't shoot anybody. You give up before you have to shoot someone.'

'Dad, I don't like this.'

'It'll be fine, Will. Just behave as if you own the place. Tell them we have permission from the Base Commander and Air Traffic Control—it'll take 'em a little while to prove that wrong. With luck, it will take several minutes to get security there. Be calm but forceful. Now be quiet, and let me try to land this thing without taking out a hundred-million-dollar C17.'

I made small adjustments to the power and the attitude of the aircraft to control the speed and flight path. I stole quick glances both ways up the approaches to the main runway a few seconds before crossing it. No traffic seen—lucky. I was committed. I was getting a bit low and slow, so I gave the throttle a burst of power, which was just enough to avoid landing short of the concrete on the bare dirt. I was disappointed and concerned that the burst of power would be heard by those standing around on the apron. Nothing to be done about it now, and perhaps the noise of my engine had been masked by the noise from the jets, the auxiliary power units, and service vehicles.

The Cessna planted itself firmly on the taxiway that marked the beginning of the apron, and I braked hard to slow down to a fast taxi speed, keeping my eyes peeled for pedestrians near the C17s parked in a line on my left. I switched on the navigation lights and anti-collision lights. If they hadn't seen us land, they might think we had just taxied onto the apron from the runway.

I taxied quickly down the apron following the taxiway centreline. I noticed that the last two parking bays—nearest to the big hangar—were occupied by C17s. The giant hangar doors were open with people coming and going. *Damn*, I thought. I wanted to swing across directly in front of the hangars so I would be pointing in the right direction for take-off. I couldn't risk going at speed among all those people, so at the empty third bay from the end, I swung to the left between two of the C17s. With the enormous aircraft one on either side, dwarfing my Cessna, we crossed to the taxiway on the other side and then swung right. I was taxiing against the one-way direction indicated by the markings on the ground, but whatever.

At the end of the apron, there was plenty of room for a little aircraft like mine to swing around 180 degrees and point in the opposite direction. I would have to use a burst of power to get around, which might alert the arseheads holding Ollie. I gave the engine a short blast to help bring the tail around and brought the aircraft to a halt with the nose aiming down the centreline of the taxiway where I hoped, pretty soon, we would be taking off. I shut the engine down and quickly started undoing my seat belt to get out.

Out to my right, I noticed the first light was starting to creep over the low hills for the new day. It was nearly the longest day of the year, and it would soon be Christmas.

Immediately after the propellor stopped turning, Golni jumped out of the right-hand door. Will followed her, handing me the two guns with lights as he went. People around the C17s stood looking at us, but just standing and looking for the moment. I didn't expect that to last long. In fact, as I got my door opened and scrambled out, I could see a man walking quickly and with great purpose towards us.

'He's all yours, Will,' I called as I stuffed the Walther PPQ with the laser awkwardly into my trouser belt. I set off at a run, Glock in hand, and pulled my wallet from my back pocket.

We ran straight past all the baggage- and freight-handling vehicles to the door of the building, the layout of which I had etched into my brain. On the wall to the side of the doorknob was a pass reader. I placed Orlov's pass against it. A green LED on the box blinked, and I heard the lock unlatch in the door. Success! I put the pass in my pocket in case I needed it quickly again and put my wallet back in my hip pocket. I thought my heart would jump out of my chest; it was pounding so hard. Fight, flight, or freeze. I would have dearly chosen flight or freeze at this point, but I was resolved to get Ollie back. I looked at Golni. She nodded. I switched on the torch on the Glock, pushed the door sharply open, and we piled in.

Chapter 35

I held the Glock with its torch shining brightly out in front of me. I didn't need it, as the lights were on, but it would dazzle anybody I shone it at. In a second, I scanned the room—some side cupboards along one wall with a sink, a kettle, and some mugs, and a desk against another wall. I pointed the Glock at the bloke sitting behind the desk, who was staring at me, mouth gaping.

'Say nothing,' I commanded.

He nodded, jaw slack, bouncing with his nods.

I said to Golni, 'Did you bring handcuffs, cable ties, or duct tape?'

'No.'

'You watch him.'

To my left, there was an open door leading to a short corridor. There was another door, closed, mirroring it on the opposite wall. My heart rate felt as if it was up around a thousand. I thought about the orientation of the building and where Ollie might be. I moved to the closed door to my right. I started turning the handle slowly, but it squeaked, letting anyone on the other side know the door was opening. So I swung it sharply open towards me and stepped into the short corridor. The light was on, but it was a dim, low-wattage bulb. The torch was brighter, and standing in its beam, at the end of the corridor, was a bloke in uniform leaning against the wall.

He pushed himself off the wall, putting his hands up to try to shade them from the glare of the torch, and said, 'What the fuck? Put that light out, arsehole.'

Behind me, there was an urgent hammering at the main door to the outside. I heard Will shouting, 'Dad! Dad! Let me in!' *Well, there goes the element of surprise,* I thought.

Golni said to the bloke in the office behind me, 'Don't move.'

I stood motionless, not daring to take my eyes off the man in front of me down the corridor. I heard her move to the door and open it. Will came in quickly, and they closed it immediately behind him.

He said, 'Sorry, Dad. That guy outside wouldn't take 'No' for an answer, and you said not to shoot anyone!'

I said to the man in the corridor, 'Come into this room.'

I backed into the office, keeping the torch and my eyes on him.

He walked slowly and came past me to stand in front of the desk.

'Where's my son?' I asked.

'Fuck you, mate! You're too late. That nutter has probably already killed him.'

'What do you mean?'

'He some sort of psycho sex freak. Once he gets started, he can't stop. He sometimes beats kids to death; he gets so wound up.'

'Where's Ollie?'

He prevaricated, 'I don't dare. He'll kill me if I tell you.'

'I'll kill you if you don't. Now, last time, where's my son?'

He prevaricated a second too long, so I shot him in the leg. The sound of the bullet was muffled by the silencer, and the bullet, not the 'exploding' variety, smashed through his knee, almost cutting the lower part of his leg off. His shin and foot flapped around as his upper leg spun him backwards and upwards, and he crumpled onto the floor, silent except for short gasps, in shock.

I turned to the bloke behind the desk, pointing the Glock at his stomach, and said quietly, 'Where are you keeping my son?'

'He's in the back room! Down there.' He pointed to where the other man had just come from.

I took a couple of steps to shine my torch down the corridor. 'Who else is there with him? How many?'

He didn't reply.

I turned my gun on him, and he said quickly, 'Yes, yes, one guy! Just Jiwani—the nutter he told you about.'

'Okay, you help your mate—find a tourniquet. I've already discovered today that a belt works well.' I looked at Will. 'Will, you stay here and guard them. You can shoot them if they give you the slightest sign of trouble. Golni, let's get Ollie.'

I turned back to the corridor, gun raised, torch trained on the door. As I approached, I took my left hand off the gun to take the pass out of my pocket. I listened at the door, turning my head to get my ear close to the timber. Faintly, I could hear some rhythmical grunting. I placed the pass against the reader, and the door lock buzzed. I turned the handle with my left hand and crashed into the door. The light was on, and I looked at the two people in the corner on the pile of rucksacks. Ollie was on his back, his face bloody where it had been bashed, his knees bent up tight. He looked vacant, unseeing, staring at the ceiling. Between his legs was another man, his bare buttocks thrusting him against Ollie. The man, Jiwani, turned and smiled up at me, serene. His face was bloody. His shoes, trousers, and underpants were strewn on the floor. He looked completely overpowered by what he was doing, unable to pay any attention to what was happening around him. He was subjugated by it and couldn't stop.

I walked towards him. 'Stop!' I said. Then again, increasingly angry, 'Stop … stop!' I pointed the gun at his head. 'Stop, or I'll fucking blow your head off!'

Golni pushed around me and hit him so hard with the butt of her pistol that he collapsed where he was. We dragged him, groaning, off Ollie and dropped him on the floor. Ollie's legs fell limply onto the rucksacks. I went to my son.

'Ollie, Ollie, Ollie, oh my God, Ollie.'

I put my gun down beside him, slid my arm under his head, and cradled him in my arms. His eyes were wandering in random patterns; they wavered to one side and then the other, unfocused. His jaw was skewed off to one side. He looked at me, but there was no recognition. I said quietly, 'Ollie, it's me … Dad.'

Gradually, I could see his eyes coming into focus, and they fixed on my face. 'Dad?'

'Yes, mate. It's all over.'

With his mouth clenched tight, he said, 'My jaw's broken.'

'Yes, mate, I can see that. You don't have to say anything. Just lie there quietly.'

Jiwani tried to get himself upright into a sitting position.

'Stay where you are,' I said.

He continued to push himself up, climbing the walls with his hands as he got his legs underneath himself. I pulled the PPQ from my belt, switched on the laser, and pointed it at him so the little green dot was in the middle of his chest. 'Don't come any closer.'

He looked me in the eye. 'How the fuck did you get in here?' he asked. 'How did you get past the security, the police, the two fences?'

'We flew in.'

'You old, rich, white fuckers. So fucking clever, all of you.' He looked down at Ollie and smiled. 'Did you like what I did to your little boy?' he mocked. 'He was great. Young, innocent, firm, tight, and so strong!' He wouldn't stop. 'Oh, yes, he was wonderful. Best I've had for months. He was—what can I say, what words can—'

'Shut up!' I shouted.

'—describe his smooth softness? Was it after the third or the fourth time—'

'Shut up!'

'—I realised I would have to kill him to make it sublime, perfect? Lucky for him, you came. Another five minutes …'

He was in ecstasy, entranced as he relived the experience. I pointed the dot of the laser at his groin. He stopped talking and looked down to where I was aiming the green dot steadily on his semi-erect, blood-smeared penis. He must have guessed what was about to happen. I fired at the same instant he jumped forward towards me. The sound of the shot in that confined space was shatteringly loud. Jiwani collapsed, bright red, almost crimson blood pulsing from the wound in his upper right leg. I had missed his penis but hit his femoral artery. It would kill him in seconds; at most, he had a few minutes. But he would definitely die. His strength in those moments, though, was unbelievable. He climbed up the wall again, leaning his weight on the wall, propping himself up, and steadying himself with his arms and hands. He slid backwards up the wall with his blood-smeared shirt stuck to his chest and the blood pulsing from the wound at the top of his thigh running down his leg to the floor.

As I looked at him, his face lit up with the light from the torch on the Glock. Before I could say anything, a hole had appeared where his left eye had been. The bullet fired by Ollie had blinded him, and the back of his head exploded. It just vanished in a rain of lumps of skull and brain and a haze of red spray across the wall behind him. Some of the blood and tissue splashed off the wall and came back over us. His head flicked as the bullet passed through it, then his face, now unsupported by a spine, flopped forwards onto his chest. He stood for a split second before collapsing for the second time, this time forever.

I turned to Ollie, who still had the gun pointing at Jiwani. 'Oh, Ollie, no, you didn't have to do that. He was going to die from the wound where I shot him.'

'I wanted to,' was all he said.

I kneeled next to him and tried to comfort him by adjusting some bags under him and stroking his hair off his forehead.

Golni left the room and came back a few seconds later. She handed me a mug with some cold water, and I supported Ollie's lower jaw while we tried to pour some between his lips so he could drink.

He flinched with the pain and said, 'No good, Dad. When are the police coming?'

I took the Glock out of his hand and tucked it carefully in my belt as I gently replied, 'We have to go to them. We don't know who we can trust on the base.' I gestured at Jiwani. 'As you can see. So we must get out of here. How do you feel about getting up?'

'Give it a go,' he replied.

I tucked the PPQ in my belt in the small of my back. Bloody uncomfortable, but not as bad as the Glock with the silencer and light!

Golni and I reached down and lifted him under his armpits, and he struggled to a crouching, standing position. 'Oh, Christ, my arse hurts!'

'Yeah, I'm not surprised.'

He rested his hand on my shoulder as I bent down to put his underpants where he could put his feet into them, just as I did when he was a small boy on the beach, and we pulled them up. Then the same with his trousers. He was a little taller than me, so he was easily able to rest his arm across my shoulder as we walked out of his cell down the corridor.

'We'll get you sorted out when we get to Brisbane Airport. This is Golni Gadma. She's the only police officer we can trust just now.'

Will said gently, 'Hello, bruv, howyagoin'?' That's what they called each other: 'bruv', short for 'bruvver', like a pair of East London cockneys.

'Not so good, bruv.' Ollie was still looking dazed. 'Where's Mum?'

Will replied, 'Not here; she's at home. We didn't have room for all of us.'

'Oh, yeah.'

I said, 'I'll ring her when we are on our way and ask her to meet us at Brisbane Airport. That's where we're going to try to go next. But listen, Ollie, we have to get out of here first, and that may not be at all straightforward. You up for it?'

'Yeah, Dad.' He pointed to the desk. 'Can I have some of that duct tape to put 'round my jaw?'

Will leapt forward to pick it up and wrap two or three loops around Ollie's face, under his chin and over his scalp.

The front door had no window in it, so we had no clue what, or who, was on the other side. We were stuck. The only window in the room looked out the back—in the opposite direction to that which we wanted to see. Going out of that window would put us outside the fence that protected the operational area of the base, called airside, from the rest of the secure area, called landside. If we went that way, we would have to go around to a gate and try to get past security and back airside. Risky.

I trotted as fast as my aching ribs would let me to the room in which Ollie was being held and climbed on the same bags he must have used to look out of the window. I could see the security gate to airside to the right and a couple of vehicles with orange flashing lights on their roofs, passing through the formalities. If we could get out here, we would still be airside. I tried the window catch, but it was stuck with old paint. If we broke the glass, we might alert the guard. Also risky.

I trotted back through the building to the room at the other end to look out of the window there. I pulled a table over to the window and climbed, gingerly, up onto it.

Activity on the apron. Vehicles, all with their orange lights flashing on their roofs, collecting near the parking bay we taxied across. Baggage trolleys pulled by small tractors, freight loaders, what looked like a toilet truck, and an SUV in military paint, presumably for the flight deck crew. There must be a C17 nearby, inbound. All very interesting, but I still couldn't see the front of our building. And this window opened to the landside of the airside security fence like the back window.

I tried to open the aluminium window with the handle. It wouldn't budge—same problem as the other one. No good. However, just as I was about to turn away, I saw the flashing strobe lights of a C17 taxiing slowly along the taxiway towards the entrance of the apron. With it came a lot of noise and a lot of distraction. No time to lose.

I hurried back to the office, thinking as fast as I could as I went.

I nodded towards the room where Ollie was kept. 'I'll climb out of the window at that end and see what's happening in front. If it is all clear, I'll come and knock on the front door, and we'll all go to the aircraft and get out of here. No time to lose.'

Will said, 'And what if there is the whole of the RAAF police force outside the front, locked and loaded like the Bolivian Army at the end of *Butch Cassidy and the Sundance Kid*?'

'Yeah, thanks, Will! I dunno. Think positive!'

I ran down the corridor again and hefted a few of the cases. I found one that was quite small but quite heavy and had a hard, plastic, shell-like case. I picked it up by its handle and hurled it like a shot-putter at the window. With a huge crash, it went straight through. I picked up another and knocked out the remaining shards from the bottom edge of the window. I climbed up and slithered through the hole headfirst. As I overbalanced outside the frame, I swung my feet down, but I was too slow, and my arms couldn't hold me; I fell onto the conveyor belt of a baggage loader beneath me. At least it was not the full distance, but it really knifed my ribs into me. I sat and tried not to gasp for a moment, thinking, *If anybody heard that, they would be here by now.* I checked the guard. There were two of them in the box. One had come out of his box and was looking in my direction. Not distracted by the C17—he'd seen plenty of those before around here. He turned and went back into his box and picked up the phone. The other left the box and strode towards me.

I slid off the loader and walked quietly to the corner. I looked around with my left eye. There was one young lad standing looking nervously towards me and then towards the gate guard. I walked around the corner with my hands out, palms up in a defensive gesture, and said to him, 'We don't want to hurt anyone. Just stay out of our way for a few minutes more.'

The young lad said, 'The Flight Sergeant said I had to keep you here.'

Keeping him firmly in sight, I knocked on the door. 'Okay, let's go!'

The door opened, and they all came out, Will supporting Ollie and Golni carrying her gun.

'Well, look, we can't wait to discuss it. You'll have to explain that we were in too much of a hurry.' We hustled past him.

Rather plaintively, he called to our receding backs, 'But, sir, you have to wait. I have my orders!'

Chapter 36

The shortest route to the aircraft took us precariously close to the guard hut, and the purposeful man intercepted us. He was tall and well-built, with broad shoulders and a rigid, straight back. He stopped, legs astride, hands on hips, and looked at us as we hobbled and limped past him, bloodied and bruised. We must have looked like a really sad, rag-tag group.

In a loud voice, easily heard over the sound of the C17's engines, he said, 'Excuse me, sir. Is that your fucking little-piece-of-shit aircraft parked over there, making a bloody mess of my air base?'

'Yes,' I replied, putting my left hand up towards him, 'and please don't try to stop us getting to it.'

Golni added, 'Queensland Police Service, on official business!'

'You have no jurisdiction here, you know,' he said as he walked parallel with us but a few metres away.

Golni waved her gun at him. 'This gives me jurisdiction. But I don't want to exercise my jurisdiction on you. So stay back.'

We reached the Cessna, where Will helped Ollie into the rear seat and climbed into the left front seat. I walked to the right-hand door looking at the aircraft as I went, checking for dents, bumps, anything out of the ordinary. I couldn't help myself—habits of a lifetime.

In the distance, I noticed the ululating wail of police sirens.

The purposeful man said loudly, 'Sir, my name is Flight Sergeant Fletcher. I order you to stay where you are!'

'Sorry, Flight Sergeant, we have to go.' I was holding the right-side door open for Golni to get into the back seat, but she paused as a small tractor for pulling convoys of baggage trolleys came bustling out from under the wing of the nearest C17 and shuddered to a halt in front of us. The driver jumped off and hustled towards the right wingtip.

I said quietly to Will, 'Get it ready to start, and let me have your gun.'

The M&P didn't have a light or silencer on it, so it was more manoeuvrable in the tight space where I was standing under the wing and behind the open door.

He pulled it out from his belt, racked the slide, and handed it to me across the front seats. 'Safety's off,' he said quietly.

'Thanks,' I replied, keeping my eyes on the driver and the gun below the level of the window but pointing at the driver.

'No worries, Dad.'

The door—in fact, the whole aircraft skin—is made of very thin aluminium alloy, so a bullet will go straight through. Flight Sergeant Fletcher said something to the driver, who ignored him and kept walking. He was close enough to me now to see his name tag on his tunic breast, 'Smith', and the corporal chevrons on his sleeves. The penny dropped. I thought, *Aha, so this is Alan Smith, the drugs baron. He is going to be severely pissed off with me!*

As Smith circled the flight sergeant to my side of the aircraft, Golni was circling the tail towards the tug.

Fletcher stepped into Smith's path and said, 'Corporal Smith! This is none of your business. I can handle these civvies. Now get back to your work. That C17 has to be turned 'round quick smart—it's going back to Minhad today!'

'Oh, fuck off, Fletcher,' Smith sneered at him, pulling a small pistol from under the loose front of his tunic.

'Smith! What the fuck are you doing? Don't you fucking threaten me with a firearm, you mongrel!'

Smith stood still and looked Fletcher in the eye. 'Stay away, Fletcher, you fuckwit.'

'Don't you talk to me like that, you grubby little arse-wipe. I'll have you up on charges!'

Smith raised his gun to point directly at Fletcher's head. 'Fuck you, Fletcher! Now, keep away from me, or I *will* shoot you!'

I could see Fletcher thinking about it, but he stood his ground, watching Smith closely.

Smith turned to me and pointed his pistol at me. 'Get out from behind that door. I'm gonna fucking kill you, and I want you to see it coming.' Smith looked back as he noticed Golni climbing onto the tractor. 'Get off that tractor!' he screamed.

I tried to distract him. 'So you're Alan Smith, are you? You run this operation?'

His head swung back towards me.

'Nice to meet you at last,' I said, trying to keep my voice even.

I stayed stock still, trembling with nervous energy and anger at the pain and grief he had caused my family and me.

His head swung back to Golni, who was crunching the gearbox, trying to get the tug in gear. 'Get off that fucking tractor, I said! Now, come over here!'

She put her hands up and started to move as though she was getting off.

Fletcher could see what we could see; Smith was losing it. Fletcher played along, saying, 'What operation does this civvy think you run, Corporal Smith, you snivelling snotgobbler?'

Smith's head swung back to Fletcher.

As soon as Smith turned his head away from Golni, she went back to pumping the clutch and trying to find a gear in the old vehicle's gearbox. She got the tug in gear and revved the engine, bouncing the tug forwards. Smith's head snapped back towards her. He stepped to his right one pace, raised his gun, and fired twice at her, past Fletcher's shoulder.

Fletcher was too fast for him and must have anticipated what he was about to do. He blocked Smith's view but stepped into the path of the bullets. They caught him in his left arm and shoulder, and he spun to the left, grabbing at his arm with his right hand. As he fell, I saw my chance.

'Smith!' I screamed at the top of my voice. I was ready for him now. I wanted to kill him. I wanted to vent all my rage and pain and frustration and fear from the last few hours on him. I didn't feel nervous or anxious; I didn't register terror. I didn't want to run away, and I wasn't frozen with fear. I didn't feel incandescent with anger, although I had every right to be. I was strangely calm. I knew my hands were shaking, but I could control them. I could feel I was clenching my jaw, but I could still talk. It was as though I was almost in a trance. The world had slowed almost to a stop. I was so totally focused. On Smith. Hoping he would turn around and try to shoot me.

I watched his head swing back towards me, and I knew it would be the last time he would turn his head. In slow motion, he raised his gun towards me and fired. I knew it would be the last time he would squeeze the trigger. I knew it would be the last conscious action he would ever take. Unlike his RAAF comrade, Orlov, he didn't miss. I watched him pointing his gun at my head. I saw the muzzle blast flash, and I leaned my head fractionally to the left. The bullet went through the Cessna's door window, spraying my face with shards of Plexiglass. A few made pinpricks across my face and drew blood. The bullet's flight continued; it creased the side of my face and clipped my ear before fizzing off into the cavernous hangar behind me. I wasn't in pain—I hardly registered it. He didn't miss, but he missed by just enough.

Before he could even register that he hadn't killed me and pull the trigger again, I shot him through the door, once. He started to fall as I stepped out from behind the door over the undercarriage wheel, and I walked slowly towards him, pulling the trigger in time with my steps. With each step and with each bullet from the gun, my emotions flamed out of me. My powerlessness to prevent the suffering of my son, the anguish of my family, my frustration, my pain, my fear. The deafening cracks as I fired the bullets from the gun were silent to me, such was my concentration.

By the time I was standing over him, I was six paces closer, I had shot him six more times, and he was dead. I stood over him with my gun pointed at his head, looking down at his body sprawled in that lifeless way that transmits 'death' without even needing to check for life signs. Blood from the wound across my face and ear dripped from my cheek down onto his uniform. I saw them falling, but it still hadn't occurred to me that it was my blood. But my few drops of blood were nothing compared to the small lake of blood that haemorrhaged from the wounds in his head and body, expanding from underneath him. Where it crept and pooled across the concrete, up against the edge of the painted centreline marking of the taxiway, in those few seconds, it formed into a small rivulet draining towards the dirt. There was no need to try to see if there was anything we could do to save him, because one bullet had lifted a chunk of his scalp off his head.

Fletcher was sitting on the concrete a few metres away, holding his shoulder—blood oozing out between his fingers and running down into his sleeve.

Golni trotted to him. 'You have to move, Flight Sergeant. Please. These people want to get this fucking little-piece-of-shit-aircraft out of here. You are in the way and making, literally, a bloody mess of your air base.'

She started to try to help him up, but he wasn't having any of it and shook her hand off.

'I'm staying here. You people must wait for security. You're not allowed on this base, and I am telling you, you're not allowed to leave. You have to face the consequences.'

I walked the few paces to him and urged him, 'Flight Sergeant, we are leaving … Now … Get out of the way!' I was becoming increasingly concerned that he would succeed in delaying us until his security people arrived.

Golni said, 'Flight Sergeant Fletcher, thank you for taking that bullet for me and saving my life. Please let me help you with your wounds. I have first-aid training.'

Fletcher sat upright, holding his shoulder and looking around for someone other than us to help him.

Golni came to me. 'Can you get the aircraft 'round him?'

'Yes, easy.'

'You go; I'll hold on to him so he doesn't get himself in the way.'

'What about being out of your jurisdiction and all that?'

'No worries. We can shut down the operation with the information you have. You do still have the contacts list, don't you?'

I nodded.

'We can make it a joint civil/military sting—give them some credit. The senior management and pollies'll love it.'

The light of the new day was pushing inexorably above the horizon behind her. The sun would be up in forty minutes or so.

'Okay.' I turned, calling to Will, 'Will! Crank up that little hummer!'

I turned back to face Golni. 'Thank you so much for your help, Golni.'

'Look, you push on. I'll get in touch very soon. I know where to find you!'

'Yeah, I'll be in one of your squalid jails on remand while your mates try to sort out the mess I've made!'

The Cessna's engine started and drowned out any further chance of conversation. I gave Golni a short wave and ducked under the right wing. The propellor wash buffeted the door as I climbed in.

'Go 'round them!'

Before I had lifted my right leg in and slammed the door shut, Will released the brakes. He opened the throttle to get the aircraft moving, pushed hard with the left rudder pedal and toe brake, and the aircraft swung in a very tight turn to the left. Once he was clear of Fletcher and

Golni, who had a smother tackle on him, he straightened the aircraft to aim down the taxiway and opened the throttle to full power. I put the M&P in between my legs, having first checked the safety was 'on'. I struggled against the acceleration to pull my seat forward so my feet were on the rudder pedals. The PPQ was uncomfortably sticking in my lower back.

Glancing back, I saw Fletcher push Golni off, haul himself to his feet, and stagger to the police cars, their blue and red lights flashing urgently, that were coming at high speed through the security gates. He was gesticulating to them and pointing at us. Golni's body language indicated she was putting forward a counterargument.

I fished my spectacles out of my top pocket and put them on my nose so I could see over the top of the frames for longer distances. *That's better,* I thought; a bit sore where the stem went near the gash in my ear, but at least I could see the instruments now! I switched on the navigation lights, anti-collision and landing lights, white flashing strobes, the circuit breaker for the ADS-B, and all the radios, including the transponder, which I noted Will had pre-set to 7700—the emergency code. *Good thinking, Will,* I thought.

The old Cessna was gathering pace, but it was heavily loaded, and I was fearful that the police cars would get in front of us now they had a straight run down the taxiway next to us.

I tried putting on my headset, but it was awkward to keep my specs straight and not clip the right earpiece over my cut face and ear. After a short struggle, I got the left earpiece on snugly by clipping the right earpiece around the back of my head onto my neck, and I swung the mic down in front of my mouth. We rolled, gathering speed, down the taxiway, passing the C17s on our left.

Through clenched teeth, Ollie said, 'Dad! Police cars catching us on the right!'

I put my hands lightly on the control wheel and throttle and my feet on the rudder pedals and said to Will, 'I have control.'

'You have control,' he replied and took his hands and feet off the controls.

Police cars came into my peripheral vision on both sides—the red and blue light from the flashes of the police lights reflecting off the propellor and freezing it for a split second. The aircraft approached take-off speed.

Will shouted, 'Shit, Dad, they're gonna shoot at us!'

I pulled gently on the control wheel to coax the old Cessna into the air, focused on the end of the apron. I heard a bullet clunk into the aircraft somewhere in front of me—*Fuck! They're shooting at the engine!* Another *clunk* somewhere in front. The Cessna became light on its wheels as the wings started to generate enough lift to fly. *Let's see you do this,* I thought. They dropped away and braked when they realised they could no longer stop us. We were airborne well before the end of the concrete—plenty of room, even with the slight tailwind. Dunno why I worried!

I climbed the aircraft at maximum rate. Not over yet. *What did the shots hit?* I wondered.

Chapter 37

I checked the engine temperatures and pressures: okay. The needle on the suction dial was at zero. *That's not right,* I thought. Suction was used to power some of the flight instruments, but nothing I couldn't live without this morning. The engine seemed to be running a little less smoothly than usual. I quickly went across the dashboard, touching the controls as I went: mixture—rich; throttle—full power; carburettor heat—hot for a second, then back to cold; and all circuit breakers—in. I switched the key from 'both' magnetos to left magneto only—okay. I switched from left magneto to right magneto, and the engine coughed and nearly stopped. I immediately switched back to the left mag, and the engine picked again. Okay, so they hit the right magneto. We would be okay on one magneto. That was why we had two! I fed the flaps back up in stages until the aircraft was 'clean', which necessitated a slight tweak to the trim wheel to take the load off the control wheel, and we climbed into the lightening dawn sky. I could feel the draft coming through the holes in the door and its window, and the noise-cancelling headset did a good job of suppressing the wind noise in my left ear, but it was damned noisy in my right ear.

The radio was already tuned to the frequency for Amberley Control Tower. I was just about to press the transmit switch to call the controller in the tower when I heard over the radio, *'Rhino three-six, traffic, eleven o'clock low, has departed the Great Northern Apron.'* The slight but deliberate urgency in the controller's voice told the pilot we were close.

'*Visual, Rhino three-six,*' said the pilot very calmly. She'd probably been watching us for several seconds with the police cars flashing alongside during our take-off roll. I looked right and saw the Super Hornet rocketing towards us a couple of hundred feet above, landing lights blazing, strobes blindingly bright on its wingtips. I pushed the control wheel slightly to arrest the climb for a moment to ensure we passed underneath the fighter aircraft as it flashed overhead. Then I didn't hesitate further; I took a deep breath, pressed the transmit button on the control wheel and said, 'Mayday, mayday, mayday. Amberley Tower, this is two kilo eight, a Cessna one-seven-two, sick passenger on board, just departed your northern apron, turning left towards Brisbane Airport, climbing to one thousand feet.'

I had, once or twice in my life, wondered if I would ever need to declare a mayday and what it would be like. Now I knew. Mayday means I am experiencing an emergency and need immediate assistance— it comes from the French *'m'aidez'*, meaning, literally, 'help me'. It may not have been entirely appropriate, as we were flying okay and wanting to go to Brisbane, not back to Amberley. But I wanted to get the controller's full attention, and declaring an emergency was the quickest way to do that. And I thought, how often am I going to get the chance to say 'mayday'? I hoped never again!

'*Two kilo eight, Amberley, roger mayday. I see your seven-seven-zero-zero squawk; you are identified passing one-five-zero feet.*'

We passed over the main runway as I turned left onto the heading that I had written on my pad what seemed like days ago, towards Brisbane Airport. I had lifted off right under one of the Super Hornets running at right angles to me, flying at high speed along the main runway, making a circuit of the air base getting ready to land.

I transmitted, 'Two kilo eight clear of traffic.'

'*Two kilo eight, all our runways are available. Nearest is two-two on your right, and we can have an ambulance waiting for you when you land. Request your intentions.*'

'Roger, I intend to fly directly to Brisbane and go to the Royal Flying Doctors' apron. Request you cancel my mayday.' I thought I'd made my point with the mayday. No need to push it.

'Two kilo eight, roger, mayday cancelled, and I'll give Brisbane a call and let them know you're coming.'

The mayday code being transmitted, known as 'squawking', would automatically cause my position to be displayed to all the air traffic controllers in the local area, probably with some red flashing lights and a buzzer or something to draw their attention to it.

The controller at Amberley came back to me. 'Two kilo eight, Brisbane have you identified. Squawk two-two-four-two, contact Brisbane Tower on one-one-eight decimal zero.'

'Squawk two-two-four-two, Brisbane Tower, one-one-eight decimal zero, Two kilo eight. Thanks.'

I levelled at 1,000 feet but didn't reduce the power to normal cruise speed. With the throttle at full power, I pushed the nose down and wound the trim wheel to relieve the load on the control wheel. We were going as fast as the old thing could carry us.

I rotated the little knobs on the transponder to squawk the new code of 2242. With that code, the controllers would have programmed their display system to show my callsign instead of the emergency code—they knew who I was and what I needed.

We flew towards the rising sun, which was now just below the horizon over the Pacific.

I turned to look at Ollie. 'You okay, mate?' I asked gently.

He nodded.

'Not long now, Ollie, and it'll be over.'

He looked at me unsmilingly and nodded. He put his hands on either side of the seat to lift himself gingerly to shift position.

'Hurry up, Dad.'

'We're going flat-chat, Ollie. One hundred and twenty knots. Sorry, not as fast as that Super Hornet.'

I selected the frequency 118.0 on my second radio and flicked the switch to that radio. I called Brisbane Tower. I told Brisbane I needed to get a passenger to a doctor as soon as possible. She replied that they had already pre-warned the Flying Doctors, who were ready for us at their apron but wanted to know the nature of the illness. I asked them for a telephone number, and Will called them on his mobile phone to explain what we needed. Next, we got a number for the Queensland Police Air Wing at the airport, and he called them and told them we wanted to hand ourselves over to their custody and protection. He asked them to come to the Flying Doctors' apron to meet us, which they agreed to do.

I pulled out my phone and dialled Hannah.

'How are you?' was the first thing she said when she answered.

'We're fine, except Ollie is not so good. One of his captors abused him.' I was unsure how to say it. 'He's been sexually abused, Hannah. Raped.'

'Oh my God, no!' I could almost touch the anguish in her voice. *'Those bastards! I will fucking kill them all!'*

'You're too late, Hannah. We already killed the one who did it.'

'Good. How is Ollie?'

'Look, he's obviously in pain, but he walked to the aircraft. Sorry, Hannah, just a moment.'

I put the phone down and called the tower. 'Two kilo eight, field in sight. Request visual approach, straight in Runway zero-one right.'

The runway and approach lights at Brisbane twinkled in the distance.

'Two kilo eight, cleared straight in, and you're cleared to land Runway zero-one right,' replied the controller. *'Surface wind is calm.'*

I read back the clearance.

I turned the aircraft fractionally right to intercept the final approach track for the runway.

I picked up the phone. 'Sorry, Hannah, I have to fly this thing. Here, I'll put Will on.'

I handed the phone to Will to give directions to the apron where we would be parked. I went through the pre-landing checklists to make sure the aircraft was configured correctly to land.

Will said, 'Mum's already been in the car for fifteen minutes coming down the highway, so she shouldn't be long. She said she couldn't just sit still and wait.'

At max cruise speed, the trip took less than fifteen minutes, and I eased the throttle back a fraction and started a gentle but fast descent towards the runway. From an altitude of 1,000 feet—say, 300 metres—I only needed to start the descent about three miles from the runway.

I had been cleared to land on Runway 01 Right, the right-hand of the two parallel runways. It's a very long runway, and I wanted to turn off at the far end to go to the General Aviation apron, so to save time, I flew at a much higher speed than usual over the threshold, along the runway, gradually reducing the power, the speed gradually decaying and slowly lowering the flaps. Once I passed halfway, I closed the throttle and landed. I braked firmly, taxied off the runway, switched off the white strobe lights on the wingtips, and made my way to the Royal Flying Doctor Service apron, where we were greeted by a person in a fluorescent yellow, hi-vis jacket, and marshaller's 'wands'—like miniature lightsabers in the half-light. I followed his directions to the parking area in front of the Flying Doctor's hangar and parked when he brought the wands to make an 'X' above his head.

We climbed out of the aircraft and helped Ollie out of the back seat. I gave Will the M&P and the Glock from the door pocket, both of which he tucked into his belt like some Mexican bandit in a western. There was a gaggle of people gathering around but standing a short distance back from us—mostly staff from the Flying Doctors—but also two police officers in one-piece flight suits with police insignia.

Ollie could walk—stiffly. In obvious discomfort, he walked slowly, with a doctor on one side and me on the other, towards the rear of the hangar. The doctor, also dressed in a flight suit, asked Ollie if he would prefer to lie on a stretcher. He nodded. The doctor waved forward a gurney, and he and a nurse helped Ollie lie flat on it. They wheeled him into the hangar and through double doors into the two-storey office area, which was at the rear of the hangar but on the street side of the building complex. There was a brightly lit medical centre within the building, and the Flying Doctor staff ushered everyone out except the doctor, two nurses, Ollie, and me.

According to the name badge on the left breast of her flight suit, the doctor was a woman named 'Thomas'. I assumed that was her surname because, where I come from, Thomas is a boy's name if it is a first name.

'My name is Georgie Thomas. I'm a doctor,' she introduced herself and asked Ollie, 'What's your name?'

'Ollie Richmond.'

A nurse started writing on an iPad. Looking down at him on the gurney, Thomas asked concernedly, 'What has happened to you, Ollie? They told me your dad had to declare a mayday to get some help?'

Ollie smiled wanly and turned to me. 'Erm, Dad, can you do it, please?'

I said, 'Georgie, Ollie was kidnapped by a gang of drug runners and taken to RAAF Base Amberley. At least one of them bashed him, as you can see, around the head and face.' I looked at Ollie. 'Did they hit you anywhere else, Ollie?'

'Yeah, in the stomach and around here,' he indicated his kidneys.

'Then he was raped.' Again I looked at Ollie. 'Was it just that bloke I killed who raped you, Ollie?'

Thomas's head snapped up to look at me, but she said nothing. I held up my hand and nodded slightly as though to say, 'Just go along with me for a moment.'

'Yes, but he did it several times. I can't remember now how many. And he bit me on the neck as well, here and here.' He pointed at red weals below his ears. The tears welled in his eyes, and his shoulders jerked as he turned his head towards me.

I leaned down and hugged him as best I could without hurting him.

He sobbed. His body was racked with juddering, moaning sobs from one to the next.

I cried, too, the tears rolling down my cheeks. 'Oh, Ollie. Oh, mate.' I hugged him as tightly as I could.

He groaned, 'Dad, careful. That hurts.'

I relaxed my grip. 'Sorry, Ollie. Listen, mate, we'll get you sorted out. Georgie and her team will get on it straight away and make you feel a bit more comfortable.'

'Okay, Ollie. Anything else you want to tell me about?' asked Thomas.

He shook his head.

Thomas looked at me and offered her hand. I looked at my hand, which was bloody from the wound to the side of my head, and said, 'Sorry, Doctor, I'm in a bit of a mess. I'm Ollie's father, Toby Richmond.'

'What happened to you?' she asked, nodding towards my ear.

'My cheek? Yeah, it's a bullet wound. I'd be grateful for anything you can do to staunch this bleeding.'

'Yep, and your left hand looks a mess?'

'Had my little finger cut off a few hours ago.' I looked at the grimy, bloody, soggy bandaged hand.

'And your shirt? That blood looks old.'

'Oh, yeah, that's all other peoples'.'

The doc said, 'Okay, Toby, are you right to wait for a couple of minutes?'

I nodded.

'Look, before we start, we have to get some information from you about your son's medical history.' She nodded to the nurse with the iPad. 'This is Mary Grace Dimakulangan, but we call her Maz. She'll get your details, and I'll be back in a moment.' And she left the room.

Maz asked me questions about Ollie's date of birth, home address, allergies, whether he'd had any antibiotics in the past, and so on. She jotted the replies down on the tablet. Before she had finished, Thomas returned carrying some equipment. She said to me, 'We're all good here, Toby. Ollie might like some privacy now.'

'Is that what you want, Ollie?' I asked him.

Ollie craned his head around but couldn't see me, so I walked into his field of view. 'Is that okay, Dad?'

'Yes, of course, Ollie. I'll be outside. I'm sure your mum will be along in a few minutes.'

'Can you bring her in as soon as she gets here, please?'

'Yeah, no worries, mate.' I turned and left.

Thomas called as I left, 'We'll get your face sorted out in a moment.'

'No dramas.'

In the corridor outside were a group of people, including Will and the two aviation police officers. I walked straight past them to the toilet. That tea had finally caught up with me!

Back in the corridor, I said to the two police officers, 'I place my family and myself in your protective custody.'

One of them pushed open a nearby door. 'We have been given this room. Please come in here, sir, and explain what you want.'

I walked towards the door, and Will followed. I said to one of the medical team, 'My wife will be arriving in a few minutes. Please, will you bring her here?'

Another medic said, 'Sir, you need to get that wound seen to before you do anything else—it'll get infected if you keep putting your hand on it.'

'Have you got a room, maybe another treatment room, where I can talk with the police, and you can sort my face out? Also, I need a new dressing for my finger.' I held up my hand with the dirty bandage oozing blood. 'And some painkillers for my cracked ribs, please.'

'Yes, this room will do—it has a sink. I'll go and get the doctor to prescribe some painkillers.'

Once in the room with the door closed, I knocked back a glass of water. She started working on my face and ear, cleaning, swabbing, patching. I think it was more painful than the bullet.

I said to the officers, 'I am Tobias Richmond; this is my son William Richmond; through in the other room is my other son, Oliver Richmond.' I continued, 'I have been abducted, I've had my ribs broken, I've been tortured, I've had my finger cut off, and I've been shot at. I've been responsible for shooting and injuring a person—no, two people,' I thought back. 'No, make that three people. I stabbed a person. No, wait, I stabbed two people. I knocked over another person with a car, and I shot dead a man at Amberley just before we came here. Oh, and I blew three bikies apart who were on my property with this you-beaut Glock 17.' I pulled the Glock with the silencer and light out of my belt, popped the magazine out, and racked the slide a couple of times. I caught the bullet ejected from the breach as though I was an old pro and laid the gun, the magazine, and the single bullet, standing on its end, on the table. They made solid, satisfying clunks on the wood.

I deliberately didn't hand over the PPQ tucked in the belt at my back. Just in case. We still hadn't verified the honest credentials of these two police officers.

Will seemed to be waiting, probably wondering if I was going to give up both pistols. He was taking his cue from me, so I nodded to him. 'Will,' I said.

'I was threatened with a gun by having the barrel placed against my cheek. I was at the house when the other killings took place during a war between two bikie gangs.'

He stepped forward to the table. He pulled the two guns from his belt with their barrels pointing to the ceiling, held them up for the officers to see, and then, one after the other, made them safe and placed them on the table. He said, 'Another Glock 17 and a Smith & Wesson M&P.' More solid clunks.

I continued, 'None of these weapons is ours—we took them from people who were trying to kill us, and we used them only in self-defence. There were other casualties; a young man named Brown was killed at our house by that Glock with the silencer. As Will said, several other murders took place at our property, including that of a police officer named Danal. Also, the police may have shot and killed other bikies on our property, but I didn't see those—I only heard them. Furthermore, my son Ollie, in the other room, has been kidnapped, bashed, and raped.'

The two police officers and the nurse stared at each of us in turn and down at the array of weapons on the table, silent, stunned.

The spell was broken by a knock on the door, and Hannah came in with a medic. We fell into one another's arms and hugged each other tightly. I groaned as my ribs complained.

She eased and stepped back. 'Sorry, darling,' she said. She held me at arm's length and looked at me. 'God, Toby, you look dreadful! Grey-faced, bags and black rings under your eyes. Are you all right?'

'Mmmm, thank you, sweetie, you're too kind. No, not feeling all that flash, really. But nothing a month's sleep and a truckload of painkillers won't fix.'

'They told me that someone will come and get us when they have finished Ollie's initial treatment. They're making him a bit more comfortable. Should only be a couple more minutes, and we can go in and see him.'

The sun was streaming through the window and reflecting off the table into the medic's eyes. He shaded his eyes and handed me a packet of tablets. 'Painkillers. Two now and then two every four hours.'

While the nurse swabbed my cheek with some disinfectant, I spoke again to the officers. 'Now, what you need to know is that there are police officers in the Queensland Police Service and people employed by the Royal Australian Air Force who are involved in a sophisticated drug operation. They are bringing drugs from the Middle East to Amberley, from where they are distributed within Queensland by local bikie gangs. I have a contacts list that came into my possession from an undercover police officer. On it are the names and contact details of those involved in the drugs operation. It is obviously very incriminating because all the death and destruction that we have been subjected to was to recover that list. I will happily turn it over to the police when I have some assurance about the bona fides of the officers requesting it. Trust me, this won't be as simple as it sounds—the corruption could be widespread within your force.' I flinched as the nurse applied a dressing to my cheek. 'Not unnaturally, I am concerned for the safety of my family and me because we don't know who we can trust within any of the security agencies. I have come to you on the basis that your unit here at the airport is sufficiently removed from the mainstream that you won't have been tainted by the corruption. However, if either of you shows any sign of proving me wrong, I won't hesitate to deal with you appropriately.'

The nurse pulled the bandage off my finger and started to wash the stump.

One of them offered, 'What do you mean by "appropriately"? Is that a euphemism for something violent? Are you threatening us? Because we won't tolerate—'

I interrupted him, 'You can take that as a euphemism for whatever you like. And it's not a threat—I'm just telling you what will happen.' I pulled my hand away from the nurse and held it up at them. 'One of your colleagues in the police service assisted in the amputation of my finger, so the police are definitely off my Christmas card list at the moment. Let me put it this way: I'm an old guy, and I don't like being up past nine at night. Apart from a not-very-restful few minutes in hospital and a few more in the back of a ute, I have been awake for the best part of twenty-four hours, and I've had a very bad day, so I'm a bit cranky! Just sayin'.'

Chapter 38

Over the next hour or so, we explained in more detail. I had caught them at sufficiently short notice, and they had no recording equipment with them except their phones. I refused them permission to record our conversation on their phones or take notes—at this stage, I wanted them to know what we were up against. I also wanted a lawyer with me when I made a formal statement.

Hannah and I took a short break when we were called in to see Ollie. He was feeling a little better physically, but I feared there was a very long journey ahead of him before he would feel better mentally about his ordeal. We advised him not to say anything to the police until he had spoken to specialists in dealing with such crimes—psychologists or psychiatrists; I wasn't sure of the correct nomenclature. Then he should not talk to the police without a lawyer, his mum, or me being present.

It turned out we had chosen wisely—or luckily—to hand ourselves in to the Police Air Wing officers. They were great. They mounted an armed guard on the Royal Flying Doctor Service offices and called in their mates from the mainstream force whom they could trust to assist. I gave three of them the password for the page on my website with the contacts list.

Golni called to check on us. She had been held for a while, but once she had proved who she was, they let her go while the investigation by the RAAF police went on. She had said previously that she didn't know who her undercover boss's boss was. I suggested she go to the hospital and talk to Trent Kipek, her fellow undercover operative—maybe he knew who to trust in the hierarchy higher up the undercover chain. I texted her the password for the website page, too.

Eventually, we were allowed to leave, and police officers drove us to a hotel.

Ollie was made very welcome by the RFDS and stayed in a bed there. Hannah stayed with him. Will was offered a separate room at the hotel but chose to sleep in my room—it had two large beds. We showered and crashed into bed, but I couldn't sleep. My head was whirling with thoughts and flashbacks. I would drop off to sleep and then wake a few seconds later from a nightmare, my heart pounding, my body sweating, trying to grip the bed as though it was rocking.

Later that day, we were allowed to go to a local shopping mall to buy some clothes. I guessed our home was a hive of forensic activity.

Time passed, and it became apparent that there was more order in the police organisation. More, different police officers came to protect us—people we didn't know but who, we assumed, had passed some integrity test. They were all very pleasant. Eventually, some senior people came and explained what would happen to us.

I had spent a few minutes on the internet researching the 'ten best criminal lawyers in Brisbane' and found someone who was willing and available to represent us. She met us at the main police offices in the CBD, and we spent some time explaining what had happened. She guided us through what would likely happen to us. Which is what did happen to us.

We were all interviewed at length, separately. I handed over the PPQ and downloaded the contacts list off the hidden page of my website. Hannah and I had agreed that I would take responsibility for the shooting of the lad, Brown.

Epilogue

Months have passed, and I am still appearing in court occasionally. My lawyer is confident that when the police have got a real handle on the investigation into the drugs ring, and they have dug out as many of the corrupt cops as they can find, I will be exonerated. Until then, I am on bail—'don't leave town', as they say.

Golni keeps in touch. She told me they had discovered how the drugs are brought from the Middle East. They are packed in plastic bags and stashed on the aircraft at the air force base, Minhad, near Dubai. The bags are hidden in places that only the engineers are likely to know and would want, or know how, to look in. They would use the space behind an inspection panel on the pylon that holds the engine onto the wing or in a space in front of the engine accessory drive gearbox, which can be accessed quite easily through another access panel. These places are, apparently, too high off the ground for the sniffer dogs, and the smell is also disguised to an extent by the hydraulic oil and fuel fumes. Another place sometimes used is hanging from a hook specially installed for the purpose under the non-return flap in the toilet bowl—tricky and smelly to recover—make sure you're wearing your rubber gloves! Another is attached with duct tape to the back of the cap covering the toilet-waste outflow pipe. The service vehicle moves in close; the operative unscrews the cap and retrieves the package. All done during normal post-flight service/inspections.

None of the sites was large, but there are plenty of them on a C17 Globemaster if you know where to look. The drugs were moved off base in personal vehicles. Too easy.

Smiggins was arrested and was refused bail. Probably for the best because I wouldn't have wanted to be in his shoes if Hannah could have got anywhere near him! So, he is on remand somewhere awaiting trial, charged with drugs offences and the murder of Danal. A couple of the Rabid Dogs are willing to testify against him in the hope of not being prosecuted for murder and thus receiving lighter sentences. Smiggins' goose is well and truly cooked—he'll be very old when he gets out.

The law looks to be on my side. The Criminal Code Act of 1899, states, 'If the nature of the assault is such as to cause reasonable apprehension of death or grievous bodily harm, and the person using force by way of defence believes, on reasonable grounds, that the person cannot otherwise preserve the person defended from death or grievous bodily harm, it is lawful for the person to use any such force to the assailant as is necessary for defence, even though such force may cause death or grievous bodily harm.' In other words, if I thought they were gonna kill me, I could kill them. Which is exactly what happened.

Ollie's jaw has healed well, but his mental wounds might take a while. He goes to see a psychologist every couple of weeks and talks to a counsellor occasionally when he needs to. Actually, all things considered, he is doing very well. As for shooting Jiwani, the argument my legal team is putting forward is that the shot I fired into his leg was fatal; there was an independent, trusted witness—Golni—to say I needed to defend us. Ollie's shot was superfluous. That's the gist of it.

Will says he has bad nightmares related to house break-ins, but they are gradually getting less frequent. Uni is keeping him and his brother busy.

Hannah frets about the lads, but there is only so much she can do. She has a good friend who works for a local charity as a counsellor for teenage boys at risk of self-harm or suicide, so she gives Hannah plenty of support both in relation to her concerns for the lads and to Hannah's own mental health. I think the fact that killing that lad, Brown, was an instantaneous decision to protect me and that there was no doubt he would have killed me seconds later has allowed her to come to terms with the horror of taking his life. She has reconciled that there was absolutely no alternative and just set it aside.

Among the family, we all support and talk to one another frequently. It's good to have the boys at home so we can keep a gentle eye on them.

I have wondered whether I should buy a gun. I mean, I lived sixty-eight years without ever touching one. Do I really need one now? What are the chances of something like that happening again? I do still keep the junior baseball bat by my bed. Just in case. And I'm more careful to lock the house up as I go to bed now.

I have paid my psychologist a couple of visits but, counter-intuitively, I am able to rationalise my part in the terrible events of that day reasonably well so far and have had little in the way of nightmares and flashbacks. The only thing that really devastates me is that I was unable to save Ollie from his awful, brutal experience. That will forever haunt me.

Quite honestly, I did the best I could. I take some solace in the fact that my family and I survived against significant odds.

If, during the investigation, the prosecutions are not dropped, and I am not exonerated, any one of the multiple crimes for which I will be tried—if it does eventually come to that—could mean life in prison. Needless to say, I am anxious about that. However, I have confidence in my legal team, and they are confident the cops will drop all the charges. My solicitor and barrister must have contacts within the police service and the prosecution service—maybe they have been given a quiet nod that all will be well. Either way, I try to remain phlegmatic about it and not let it worry me. I tell myself there is nothing I can do; it's a long and difficult process, which I will just have to endure.

I am back at home most of the time, so you know what that means … reading, dog walking, and nap taking. No. It means work, and lots of it—I'm always as busy as. The grass still needs cutting, the fences still need fixing, the weeds still need spraying, and all the household chores still need choring. I appreciate much more what I have in life these days and make more time for my family and for myself. Okay, I admit, there may be some reading, dog walking, and nap taking. And I'll admit to the occasional visit to a Samford café to sit in the warm Queensland sun and read the papers. Shopping? Yes, of course, but now I always check around the car before I drive off.

And, yes, I know I should organise that first-aid course that Hannah keeps reminding me about, but there are so many things for a retired bloke like me to do.

Look, I really will arrange it tomorrow.

Or maybe the day after …

About the Author

Peter Cromarty spent his paid working life in aviation, first as an air traffic controller and pilot and later as an Air Traffic Control safety regulation specialist and manager. He finished his aviation career with nine years as an executive manager at the Australian Civil Aviation Safety Authority.

Peter, when not sitting in a café in Samford, is now a consultant, homemaker, aircraft builder, and writer.

www.thecrom.com

linkedin.com/in/peter-cromarty